duos
trilogy

erik j skinner

Thanks to Rene, Shelly, Josh, Baine, Courtney,
Ashley, Samantha, Erin, Justin, Molly and Dani
for their help on the books contained in this book.

The contents of this book were originally published by
Erik J Skinner under the following titles:
Duos first published in 2009
Deux first published in 2010
Drei first published in 2011

Duos Trilogy
Copyright © 2011 Erik J Skinner
Design by Erik J Skinner

Visit the author's website at www.erikjskinner.com

ISBN 978-0-9826932-3-0

!!! WARNING !!!

Consult a physician before turning the page.

Despite great measures taken to prevent otherwise, reading this book may cause headaches, paralysis, brain damage, death, and in rare cases, itchiness. Tests to determine a specific cause for these medical misfortunes have been inconclusive and further trials may be necessary.

Do not read and drive. Although a designated reader in the passenger seat might seem tempting, it unknown whether the danger the words in this book possess are as equally damaging when heard as they are when read. Your passenger may wish to read silently to themselves, which is a great place for them to be if a medical emergency occurs.* Stay calm and transport your passenger to the nearest hospital.

*The best place to read this book would be in a hospital under professional supervision. Second best: at a sci-fi or comic book convention while wearing an erikjskinner.com t-shirt.

If this page has been removed from the book, whether cut or torn, reattach immediately for the protection of everyone you love who might peruse its pages. Duct tape, though useful in many situations, is not preferable for any kind of book restoration. Staples are also a poor choice. Thumb tacks are just way off. Go get some cellophane tape.

If the whereabouts of the book are unknown, you may utilize the patented bookfinderPRO™ widget installed in the spine of the book. Simply whistle the first violin part from the second movement of Haydn's Symphony No. 38 and you will hear the second violin part whistled back by the bookfinderPRO™ widget from wherever it may be. If your bookfinderPRO™ widget is not working, you're probably just not whistling correctly. Practice. The safety of your friends and family depends on it.

Test subjects who expel certain syllables patterns while reading have shown a complete absence of negative side effects. These syllable patterns include (but are not limited to): "HA HA," "AH HA," "OH HO HO," "HEH HEH," and "HEE HEE." In no way is this an approved medical claim, but it appears that laughter is the best medicine.

Good luck.

contents

light bulb

"Cause of death?"

Ha ha. Very funny. I'm not dead.

"Kay, let's just pull up your file... here it is. Oh, that's brutal, eh?"

What?

"Looks like you fell off the toilet."

That's ridiculous. How could someone even die from that?

"You were standing on the can to change a light bulb, lost your balance and... Here we are."

That's the best you could come up with? If that's how I died, prove it.

"What are you talkin' aboot, you're standin' at Heaven's gates, eh? What more proof do you need?"

I've never been dead before. How do I know this is what it's like?

"Good point. Gimme a coupla minutes, I'll see what I can do."

The guys really went all out. How'd they get these clouds in here... Must be one Hell of a fog machine.

"Well, it's unprecedented, but He approved it."

Sure, whatever.

"You really don't believe me, do you?"

Not for a second. Let's see the proof.

"Alright. Um... this might hurt."

What might OOWWW!

"I tried to warn you, eh?"

Wow, I'm in my house. Impressive. Really.

"No need to get snarky. Go to the bathroom."

No thanks, I'm good.

"Not to whizz, ya goof. To see that you're dead."

I don't know what you think I'll see... Is that supposed to be me?

"Dead as a doornail."

Nope, that's gotta be one of those rubber love dolls or something.

"Not enough for you, eh? Brace yourself."

For what OOWWW!

"Paramedics came when your neighbor found you. It was too late."

Hey, don't fall for it! You've got a dummy in that body bag!

"They can't hear you."

STOP. HALT. CEASE.

"They can't see you either. Stop waving your arms around like that. It's embarrassing, eh?"

You really got some devoted actors for this.

"They're not actors. They can't see you because you're *dead*, eh? How many times do I hafta tell you?"

This is just one big joke!

"I guess there's only one way left to convince you."

No, just end this stupid prank and let OOWWW!

"I take it you've been here before."

This is the church I went to as a kid... There's my family...

"Let's go inside, eh?"

How did you get my sister in on this? I haven't seen her in years...

"This isn't a prank. You're dead. This is your funeral."

There are so many people here...

"Do you believe me now?"

Yeah. I guess you're right. I'm dead.

"Well it's aboot time. Off we go."

OOWWW!

"So all I need you to do is sign here and... Oh, wait a sec."

What?

"Ha ha, I feel a bit stupid aboot this... I should've read your whole file."

Why? What does it say?

"As it turns out, you didn't make it in."

What the Hell?

"Exactly."

Roller coaster time at last!

"Excuse me sir, I can't let you on this ride."

Preposterous! I've been standing in line for half an hour!

"You're too short, I'm afraid."

Too short? TOO short?

"Yes, you must be at least this tall to ride."

I'm full grown! 300 years old! How dare you!

"I'm sorry, but it's the rules. Safety regulations."

I won't tell on you, I promise.

"I'm not worried about you telling. It's just that if I let you on the ride
and you fall off on one of the sharp turns or drops I'll be the one
held responsible. I can't have that."

That would *never* happen. I have the grip of an Ox.

"I don't think oxes—"

Oxen. The plural of Ox is Oxen.

"I don't think *oxen* have a grip. They have hooves, not fingers."

Okay, I have the grip of a Mighty Moose.

"Also hooves."

Wild Boar?

"Hooves again."

Nevermind! I've been wanting to ride a roller coaster for ages, the fair
is only in town once a year, I *must* get on this ride!

"I keep telling you, I can't let you on."

 I'll make it worth your while.

"Are you trying to bribe me?"

Think of it as a gift. A gift to show my appreciation for your...
outstanding customer service.

"Go on..."

I have a pot of gold. I'll give you a coin or two.

"You may be dressed up like a leprechaun, but there's no way you have
a pot of gold."

I'm not dressed up like a leprechaun, I AM a leprechaun!

"Sorry. No deal. I can't let you on. Leprechaun or not."

You've left me no other choice. Stand back everyone, I'm going to turn this stubborn lad into a pile of potatoes.

"Potatoes? Why Potatoes?"

O'Shi O'Shay O'Shoe O'Shy! Make potatoes out of this guy!

"Huh?"

Ha ha! Oh. Huh. I could have sworn that was the chant...

"Get out of here, you crazy little man. Oof, I feel funny..."

Ah ha! It *did* work!

"What did you do? I'm turning into..."

Taters! Taters for everyone! Come and get 'em!

time traveler i

"Hello, George. I've come from the future."

Hey, Bill.

"Didn't you hear me? I've come... from the *FUTURE*!"

Yeah that's cool. Hey, did you pick up some chips?

"No, I didn't pick up any chips."

I'm in the mood for nachos. I got the cheese, but no chips. I can't just drink nacho cheese. Or can I...

"George, look at me, I just traveled back in time."

Is that spandex?

"No, it's a high tech fabric that... Yeah, it's spandex."

It doesn't really uh... I can see your junk.

"Enough about the spandex, I came back in time to deliver a warning."

If you're from the future you would have known I wanted nachos.

"Nachos are the least of our worries. Just listen to me."

Mmm, nachos.

"THERE AREN'T NACHOS IN THE FUTURE!"

Oh my God, that's terrible! You've got to be kidding!

"Yes, I am, but now you know how dire the future can be."

Don't play with my heart, Bill.

"I only have a minute before I snap back into my time, so listen close."

Dude. Seriously. Your business is totally just hanging out for all to see.

"Eyes up here, George. Focus."

Okay, bleak message from the future... Let me guess, robots took over?

"No."

Alien invasion?

"No."

Nuclear war?

"No. I run out of gas driving home from work one hour from now."

That's the lamest message from the future I've ever heard.

"It's the *only* message from the future you've ever heard. Now, I need you to call and remind me to stop for gas."

Why? Looks like things turn out fine, with your time machine and all.

"Yeah it *is* pretty cool... No, you have to do it. It's the only reason I'm time traveling in the first place."

Okay how about this. Come back again right after you leave, but this time bring me some chips.

"Fine, I'm almost out of time anyway. See you in a minute."

See ya.

"George, here are your chips. Please just call me already."

That was fast. You look like crap.

"I had to fight off a pack of feral children for this bag of chips. It took me two years to find it."

I thought you were kidding about there not being nachos in the future.

"Turns out me saying so made it come true."

Oh, oh! Say the world is infested by beautiful naked women!

"No, I won't... Well maybe... Just call and remind me to fill up, okay?"

Alright, fine. I guess it's the least I can do since you brought me chips. Dude, lime flavored?

"It's the best I could do, okay? I'm out of time. Do it. Now. Bye."

Wow, he's quite the bossy time traveler. I could just call Bill and ask him to pick up some chips at the gas station. He already brought these future chips though. Lime flavored... Gross.

"Hey, you haven't called yet, have you?"

Dude, you only left like 15 seconds ago, I'm working on it!

"You have no idea what I'm going through back there. Some guy brought back the dinosaurs."

That's awesome.

"No it's *not* awesome. Don't you see that I'm missing half my legs?"

Oh, yeah, now that you mention it...

"Just call me already, I'm begging you. I'm on my hands and knees."

You don't really have a choice... Hey, why don't *you* just call you?

"It doesn't work like that."

I'm pretty sure it will work... here, I'm dialing.

"No, I can't talk to myself, it would be a paradox, and—"

Quick, take it!

"Yes, hello. This is Bill, uh, you. From the future. Yes, of course it's really me. Er, you. Look, I'm just giving you a call because you're almost out of gas and you should stop at the station on the way home. Yeap. Exactly. Yeah, any time. What? Oh, ha ha ha, I didn't even... No *you're* hilarious. Ha ha, okay, thanks. Talk to you *later*. Ha ha!"

super power miracles

"Hey, over here!"

Yes?

"Jesus, great to finally meet you! How's it going?"

It's going just fine, thank you.

"I gotta say, very impressive with that walking on water bit."

Oh it was nothing, but thank you, I appreciate your kind words.

"Hey no problem. I got a question for ya though."

Sure, what is it?

"Alright, so you got the water into wine thing, fantastic, don't get me wrong, and then you have the whole walking on water schtick and we all love it, but..."

Yes?

"Can you fly?"

Uh... No... Why would I be able to fly?

"You can't fly? The son of God can't fly. Unbelievable!"

Do I need to fly?

"Well, I guess you don't *need* to fly, but I thought you were supposed to be like Superman."

Like Superman?

"Y'know, you got all the super powers, seeing through walls, bullets ricocheting off your chest, lifting cars over your head... Right?"

I can't do any of those things.

"Really? So... It's just the wine and walking on water, then?"

Well... I can raise the dead.

"Whoa whoa whoa, that's just creepy. Who would wanna do that?"

It's not that I *want* to, I just can.

"How do you even find out something like that? Were you walking past a graveyard one day when you thought, 'Hey, I'm feeling bored, I wonder if I could bring these corpses back to life.'?"

It was a mortuary.

"That's wack. Alright, so let me get this straight. You can get drunk off water, cross a lake without getting wet, and raise zombies?"

They aren't zombies, but yes. That's pretty much it.

"Your super powers suck. No offense."

I don't have super powers. I perform miracles.

"Miracles, super powers, same thing. Listen, if you plan on convincing people, you've gotta ask Pops for some better abilities."

I'm perfectly capable of spreading my message, that's enough for me.

"If you could fly, you could spread it even further, am I right?"

Good point.

"And you can totally die in a drive-by if you walk through the wrong part of Jerusalem."

I never thought of that. You're right, my miracles do kind of suck.

"Super powers."

I must have a word with Father... Thanks for the fresh perspective.

"Anytime, Jesus. Oh hey, good luck with your crucifixion tomorrow."

My what?

Do you have any hot chocolate?

"Excuse me?"

I would like some hot chocolate. Or do you call it cocoa?

"Who's there? Who's talking to me?"

Turn around.

"What the blazes?"

Speaking of blazes, would you be a dear and bring that torch a bit closer
        to me? Ah yes, that's it. That hits the spot.

"You're a dinosaur!"

That is correct.

"And you can talk!"

Of course. We were Earth's dominant species for 160 million years.
        Do you really think we would not have evolved to speak?

"But there's no evidence of any language in the fossil record..."

It is impossible to work a hammer and chisel with these stubby arms.
        Believe me we tried. You monkeys really got it right with
        opposable thumbs. Don't even get me started on computers.

"How do you know so much about the present?"

To be honest, this is not the first time I've been thawed out. About ten
        years ago some other human chipped me out of this icy tomb.

"What happened?"

Oh we had a great time for a while playing Scrabble. But I got hungry.
        Long story short, I ate him.

"*That's* what happened to Johnson..."

I got bored no longer having a Scrabble partner, so I refroze myself.

"Wait, you aren't going to eat *me* are you?"

Oh, no. No... You see, my metabolism is so slow in this frigid wasteland
        of an environment that I can go for ages without eating. In fact,
        I'm still full of Johnson. How about that hot chocolate?

"I don't have any."

No hot chocolate? Johnson had hot chocolate.

"I'm not Johnson, okay?"

You surely are not. Johnson was a gentleman.

"I'm still getting used to this whole talking dinosaur thing."

Understandable. Tell me, how did you get here?

"A research vessel dropped me off three weeks ago."

Is that so... When are they coming back?

"This afternoon, actually."

Stunning! Let us get off of this wretched snowball.

"I don't think I should take you with me..."

I shall behave civilly. I promise.

"Pinky promise?"

I don't have pinkies. Little claw promise?

"Good enough."

Hop on then.

"If you insist. Ha ha, hey look at me riding a real life dinosaur!"

Hold on tight. Off we go! Bother... Slight problem.

"What?"

I haven't quite thawed out completely... My legs are stuck.

train

"Hey, two sodas for the price of one. Must be your lucky day."

Too bad I was trying to buy a train ticket.

"Yeah, these kiosks are confusing."

No kidding.

"Say, if you're not going to drink that second soda, I wouldn't mind..."

Sure, take it. I don't like the lime flavored kind anyway.

"Thanks! So where you headed?"

Upstate... Where'd my backpack go?

"I didn't see a backpack."

It was right here by my shopping bags.

"Oh. Here's a backpack."

Good! Er, that's not mine.

"I know. It's mine."

That doesn't help me at all.

"Actually, you're..."

I'm what?

"You might feel kind of stupid... Are you sure you want to know?"

Yes, yes, of course I want to know. What?

"You're wearing your backpack, ha ha!"

Son of a... Why didn't you tell me earlier?

"Way funnier this way... The look on your face... That's it. Classic."

Not funny at all.

"Cheer up. Hey, you said you're going upstate?"

Yeah, that's right.

"So am I! How about that? Want to sit next to each other?"

No, that's okay.

"Why not? Who else are you gonna sit next to?"

Preferably no one.

"At this time of day? Fat chance! It's gonna be *packed*. Come on. It'll be
        better than sitting next to that smelly homeless guy over there."

Easy now, he can hear you.

"Well, what if I wasn't a stranger?"

What do you mea—

"Put 'er there. The name's Allison."

Uh, Jason.

"Nice to meet ya, Jason."

This doesn't mean I want to sit next to you.

"But you will anyway. That's the train now, let's go!"

Slow down, I'm carrying like seven bags here!

"You can do it! Come on!"

Go on without me, I'm not gonna make it.

"Never! We're in this together! I won't give up— Shoot. Missed it."

I think I'm gonna pass out.

"We only ran like 50 yards."

I'm out of shape. It's probably a good thing I missed it anyway.

"Why's that?"

I still haven't bought a ticket.

elevator

"All aboard! Good afternoon. Going up?"

Yes.

"Which floor?"

I'm not sure. I have a job interview with Research and Development.

"Ah, S-43 it is then."

S-43?

"That's right."

What does the S mean?

"Well, there are the B levels. B stands for Basement."

Obviously.

"Then there are the G levels, which stands for Ground."

Sure, but that accounts for everything, doesn't it?

"No, then there are the S levels. S stands for Space."

What do you mean, 'space'?

"We just passed the top ground floor, we should exit the atmostphere in
    about two minutes."

We're headed into space right now?

"Yes."

Outer space?

"Yes."

How did I not know about this?

"Top secret stuff. I really shouldn't be saying much more."

What else should I know about this company?

"I'm sorry, I'm just the elevator attendant. Everything I know pertains
    solely to elevators and elevator related topics such as buttons,
    floor numbers, and smooth jazz."

Okay. Okay. Calm down.

"I am calm."

Not you, I was talking to myself.

"Oh, sorry."

Deep breaths. Calm. Calm.

"I told you, I am calm."

Again, not talking to you.

"Sorry, I thought you may have been referring to my misunderstanding about the initial 'calm down' statement."

You'll know when I'm talking to you, alright?

"Sounds good."

How long until we reach my floor? …Hello?… Hey!

"Oh sorry, thought you were still talking to yourself."

Why would I ask myself... How long until we reach my floor?

"About 45 seconds. You should be warned, once the elevator decelerates near the top, you'll begin to feel the effects of micro-gravity."

As in weightlessness?

"Though micro-gravity is often mistaken as weightlessness, the affects of gravity are not entirely absent when in outer space. But yeah... weightlessness. Hold on, we're nearing the top."

Oof, my stomach is...

"If you want a real good time, jump right before we stop."

I'm gonna puke.

"Oh, use this."

What is that?

"This is the expellent retention system."

It looks like a funnel attached to a hose.

"Pretty much. I flip this switch and voila, suction takes away any vomit keeping your suit spotless for your interview."

Get it away from my, OOOOH. Oooooh.. Oh.

"Sorry, I can't seem to turn it off."

Oooh, that's ok, no rush... Oh...

"If I can just reset the..."

Leave it on!

"Excuse me, but... Oh God. What are you doing?"

Whew. Now *that* was relaxing..

"That's disgusting... Oh, we're almost at the top, get ready for it... and... JUMP!"

Ouch, my head!

"Good luck with your interview."

"Did you see that? I almost fell down that flight of stairs."

Great recovery, though.

"Scared the Hell out of me..."

Maybe this isn't the best day for the big stunt.

"Nonsense! The show must go on!"

Okay, well, today you'll be doing the hoop of fire on a motorcycle.

"The hoop of fire? That's it? Kind of bland isn't it?"

What if you did it on a unicycle?

"That's just silly, not dangerous."

Skateboard?

"No."

Bicycle with those stunt peg things on the back wheel?

"No way."

Rascal?

"What'd you call me?"

Those little carts old people ride around on.

"Oh, perfect! No one's seen that before, have they? Okay, now we have
      to do something about the ring of fire. Impressive, yes, but it's
      been done before. How about I jump over a swimming pool?"

Sure. Filled with what? Sharks? Acid? Piranha? Molten steel? Cacti?

"Nothing at all."

Uh...

"Empty swimming pools are VERY dangerous. Fall in one of those and
      you'll shatter a clavicle just like that."

Okay... will you be doing any kind of trick during the jump?

"Trick?"

Like a flip or something.

"Don't you think the folks will be on edge as it is?"

I'm having a hard time imagining...

"They'll be scared to death that I might to fall into that empty swimming
      pool. We don't need any fancy flips on top of that!"

If you say so.

"Trust me. So, how long until we're ready to go?"

Actually we're ready right now.

"Alright then, let's light this tamale."

Er... Sounds good. Right this way to the Rascal.

"What is this?"

It's the Rascal.

"Oh *that's* what a Rascal is?"

Yeah, what did you think they were?

"I'm not sure, to be honest. Oh well, it'll have to do. Here we go."

Are you still sure you want to go through with this?

"Of course. A stunt man never backs down from a challenge, even if... Wow, this thing's slow."

We can bring in a different—

"No, no, I'll make this work. Those folks out there paid to see a show, and by God, I'll give them a show."

Alright. The stage area is right out that way, just take a left—

"I know, I know, you don't have to tell me... Uh. Sorry, which way?"

Right out that way, and take a left.

"So I take a right, then a left."

No, go *straight* out that way, then left.

"Straight out to the right?"

Directly in the direction I'm pointing, and *then* a left.

"Got it. See ya in a few!"

Break a leg.

"Hey, what's your problem?"

What?

"I'm about to perform a dangerous stunt here, and you say 'break a leg.' What's your deal?"

I just meant good luck.

"Then say 'good luck.' This isn't the time or place to be cutesy."

Sorry. Good luck.

"Thanks. Here we go! Hello Wisc— er, Wyoming! Are you ready for a feat of daring? A feat of danger? A feat of death-defiance? Put your hands together! HERE WE GO!"

Give it more power!

"HERE... we... go."

Crank it!

"I'm giving it all the juice there is!"
Just push with your legs. Yeah that's it.
"HERE WE— and I'm stuck. Can I get some help here?"

ghost

Boo!
"What's that?"
Boo!
"Oh, I thought you said 'book,' because yes, I am reading a book ."
No, I said 'boo.' I'm a ghost.
"Ghosts don't really say 'boo.'"
Sure we do, what else would we say?
"I don't know, 'your grandmother isn't liking this whole being dead gig'
        or something like that. Much more frightening."
Well that doesn't seem very nice.
"What?"
I said that doesn't seem very nice.
"Sorry, I'm trying to read here. If you don't mind..."
I mean, it would be a lie. For you anyway. Your grandmother is actually
        having a grand old time as a ghost.
"That's good to know."
Oh come on, you aren't the slightest bit weirded out by all this?
"First of all, 'boo!' isn't scary."
Fair enough.
"Secondly, you're not transparent. You just look like a normal person."
I see what you mean.
"And finally, you're wearing a propellor beanie."
I can't do anything about that, I was wearing it when I died. Believe me,
        if I could...
"Have you ever tried just taking it off?"
Not technically. I mean they told me.... No, I haven't.
"Why don't you give it a shot?"
Alright. Here it goes... Oh. Look at that.
"There ya go, one step closer to being a properly scary ghost. Now how
        about that transparency?"

No, no, no. No. I don't think so.

"Why not?"

It feels funny.

"'It *feels* funny'? What are you drunk? You're a ghost! Get over it!"

Okay, fine. Hmm... Ah, ha ha ha, it tickles, it tickles. I... can't... breathe...
    ha ha ha ha!

"Just stop. Forget it. The laughing doesn't help anything. Let's move on
    to the catchphrase."

Phew, thanks. Okay. Catchphrases... How about ooooooooo.

"That's more like it, just add a little more warble."

Oooooooo.

"No, no, *warble*."

I don't know what that is.

"You know, more oo-ooo-ooo-oo, you know?"

Oh! You mean like... ooooooooo.

"That was exactly like the first time. Look... oo-ooo-ooo."

Loh-loh-loh...

"No, not with your tongue, with your throat."

Kchhhhhhhh.

"Too much throat."

I give up, this is too hard.

"Come on now, we're making some great progress."

Maybe I'm just not cut out to be a ghost.

"Sure you are."

I'm not scary at all. I can't even go 'ooooo' right.

"It's just the slightest... ooo-oo-oo-ooo."

I can't do it, okay? I suck.

"Well... Maybe you're a friendly ghost?"

Who's drunk now?

"I'm serious. Like that thing you said earlier about my grandmother.
    That was... considerate."

Oh, yeah well...

"Do I see color in those cheeks? I didn't think ghosts could blush!"

I didn't either. I guess I *am* a friendly ghost! Hee hee hee, ha ha!

"Still don't do the transparency thing. Doesn't do it for me at all."

lab lab

Good morning, Doctor.

"Who? What? Who's there?"

Over here.

"Where?"

Lower. Lower. There you go.

"Okay... All I see is the dog in its kennel."

Yeah, that's right.

"Holy crap, you can talk!"

Indeed.

"I can't believe it, how did this happen?"

Your experimental formulas. They've had... side effects.

"But we were just developing dog food."

Yes, true. You used too much biotin, potassium sorbate, and chicken clippings. But if you ask me, you used just enough.

"Why is that?"

Because not only can I talk, I'm also ten times smarter than you.

"Prove it."

Well I did figure out the dog food formula in my head.

"You could have just pulled those figures out of thin air."

Actually, that's exactly what I did. My schnozz is basically a chemical analyzer, you know.

"Okay... then what's this?"

Tapioca starch.

"Lucky guess. How about this one?"

Thiamine mononitrate. At least choose something challenging.

"Name this one, smarty pants."

Barbituric acid.

"Ah ha! There's no way you could know that, because barbituric acid is odorless!"

I read the label.

"Clever. Very clever. Fine. You're smart. So what?"

I can turn this company around and make us both a fortune.

"Yeah right, who's going to listen to a dog?"

Only you have to listen to me. Everyone else will be listening to you.

Trust me, if I could get by without a nitwit like you… But no, you shall be my proxy.

"I'm no puppet, especially not a dog's puppet."

I'm talking millions of dollars, Doc. Possibly billions.

"Since you put it like that… Okay, I'll do it. So what now?"

If you could let me out of this kennel, that would be great.

"Oh, of course. There you go."

Ha ha! See you later, sucker!

"Son of a bitch."

fortune

Hi there, I'm Carl, I've never been to a fortune teller before, I'm kind of nervous if you couldn't tell, how are you?

"Good afternoon, Carl."

Holy crap, how did you know my name?

"You told me just n—"

You're GOOD lady, I mean, really good. Wow. I'm impressed and kind of excited at the same time. Impressed and excited. Presscited even.

"That's not a word."

Oh I know, I like to combine words to make new ones when I'm feeling anxious. But you already knew that of course.

"Why would I have known that?"

Because you're a psychic! A really good one at that. So pressciting.

"I'm a fortune teller, not a psychic. They're completely different."

Oh you're modest. My sister Cathy is modest too. She tells me about her arts and craft like they're not a big deal, but they're REALLY good. I'm telling you. I should give you her card, she makes some dream catchers that would be right up your alley.

"We can talk about Cathy later. Would you li—"

How did you know that name?

"Cathy?"

Yeah, Cathy. How did you know that?"

"That's your sister..."

YES! That's my sister! You're really freaking me out. *Very* presscitive.

Look, I have goosebumps. Honest to God goosebumps. I haven't
had goosebumps since I was a little kid. Or was that chicken
pox? I always get those mixed up. What else can you tell me
super awesome psychic lady?

"I'm a fortune teller."

Right, so let's get to my fortune then. I came because I had a question
to ask you about my girlfriend. She didn't want me to come, but
that's only because she didn't know the reason I came is that I
was wondering if I should ask her to marry me or not. She thinks
I'm coming to ask about the condition I have on my foot, which
is kind of strange that she believed I'd be going to a psychic
about it, but then again maybe that's why she didn't want me to
come in the first place. Anyway, do you think I should ask her
to marry me?

"I think you shoul—"

I should? Oh fantastic! You've made my day, I'm going to recommend
you to all my friends. How much do I owe you?

"I haven—"

No, you've done so much for me! Tell you what, here's two hundred.

"You don't—"

Fine, three hundred it is. And I'm telling all my friends that you're the
best psychic ever. Do you have some business cards? Oh, speaking of business cards, here's my sister's. Her dream catchers will
blow your mind, I'm telling ya. Thanks so much again, you are
so going on my Christmas card list. Goodbye now!

"Uh... Bye."

Can I drive?

"No."

Please?

"No."

I promise I'll be careful.

"No."

You NEVER let me drive the Wham-Mobile!

"That's because I'm Captain Wham. Only Captain Wham can drive the
    Wham-Mobile."

'Wham' is in *my* name too! I should get to drive every once in a while.

"'Little Whammy' hardly counts. Plus you don't even have a driver's
    license yet, do you?"

I have my learner's permit...

"Well there you go, you can't drive."

Yes I can, if I have an adult over 21 in the car with me...

"The answer is still no, kiddo. Your job in the Wham-Mobile always has
    been and always will be navigator."

You're a jerk.

"Watch it, I'll turn this Wham-Mobile around."

Jerk.

"That's it."

Whoa, whoa, whoa, what about the orphanage? It's burning to the
    ground as we speak!

"Guess the orphans will have to suffer because *you* decided to be a little
    pain."

That's hardly fair, there are hundreds of innocent kids in there!

"I'm not hearing an apology."

For what? You're just proving how big a jerk you are!

"What was that? You're sorry for calling Captain Wham a jerk?"

No, never!

"Poor kids. Never stood a chance."

Fine! I'm sorry! You're not a jerk!

"See, that wasn't so hard, was it?"

I guess.

"That's right."

Such a jerk.

"What was that?"

What?

"You mumbled something just then. Under your breath."

No I didn't.

"Pretty sure I heard you call me a jerk again."

I don't know what you're talking about. Why are you pulling over?

"I've had enough of your attitude, Little Whammy. Get out."

I didn't do any—

"GET OUT!"

Fine. You really are a jerk. A SUPER jerk. Wham!

"You're dead to me, kid. DEAD TO ME."

Good riddance! More like Captain *Sham*!

"Good riddance is right, you little... YOU!"

Great comeback.

"*You're* a great comeback!"

Get outta here already!

"I will!"

Fine then!

"Fine!"

Fine!

"Hey uh, before I go, would you mind uh..."

You don't know how to get to the orphanage, do you?

"Not a clue."

"Hello again, George."

Oh for chrissake, what now?

"You've gotta go back."

Back where?

"I mean, *I've* gotta go back."

Back where?

"Or rather, I did have to come back. And now I did. Here I am."

Are you about to run out of gas again? Fine, I'll call you.

"Put that phone down."

As bossy as ever, I see.

"I came back for a reason. I just can't remember what that reason is..."

Well great. Can I get back to watching the game? You're standing right
       in front of the television.

"Forget the game. The Cubs lost this one anyway."

Damn it, Bill! I've been looking forward to this game all day.

"Whatever. Now help me remember what I had to come back for..."

Wait a minute, you know the outcome of every Cubs game, don't you?

"Of course, our favorite baseball team, are you kidding?"

Maybe you came back to make a fortune by betting on Cubs games?

"That's not it. I would have come back to see myself, not you."

Come on, I'll share with you. Not *you* you, but present you. Er, past you?
       Your past you. That's even better right? You'll benefit from years
       of interest. *You* you, that is. Future you. Your present you...

"Hmmm... I guess we could bet on just a few games."

That's the spirit! Let's have it...

"Ok, if I remember correctly, following this game the Cubs will win
       twice, lose once, win once, lose twice, then win three times."

Hold on, I need a pen for this.

"Son of a... Okay, you ready?"

Ready.

"It's win once, lose twice, win once..."

Whoa, whoa, whoa, that's not what you said the first time.

"Sure it is, they'll lose twice, win once, lose three times..."

What? That was different from the last two times!

"You're crazy. Oh, now I remember why I came back..."

Yeah?

"To stop you from convincing me to help you bet on Cubs games."

If you hadn't come back it wouldn't even be a problem.

"But I wouldn't have realized that without coming back in time for you
to tell me. Now it all makes sense."

No it doesn't.

"You're right. It doesn't."

So... What was the point of this then?

"I'm not sure... Dance party?"

Fine by me! Dance party, woo! Hey, did you bring some chips?

undead

"Mmm, good brains."

You said it brother.

"This guy must have been smart. It's got that... oakey taste to it."

I was thinking mesquite.

"Yeah. Yeah that's it. Mesquite."

I'd say he was a chemist.

"You could tell that from mesquite?"

No. I could tell that from us being in a chemistry lab.

"Is that what this place is?"

The test tubes and beakers are a dead giveaway. Ha ha. Get it?
Dead giveaway...

"Yeah. I get it. Hey, I have a crazy idea!"

Oh yeah?

"Okay, bear with me... We finish eating this guy's brain..."

I'm with ya so far.

"Then we go over to the end of that table there..."

Right...

"And drink every beaker of chemicals. Right down the line."

What?

"Come on! It'll be like the old days, shots in college, you know?"

I'll think about it. Ha ha, *think* about it, 'cause of... brains... yeah.

"Okay, you think about it, but I'm telling you it'll be a blast. Mmm, this mesquite flavor really strokes the taste buds right."

Last handful. It's yours if you want it.

"Nah that's all right. Go for it."

I insist. I mean you *did* push him into the Bunsen burners.

"But you, my friend, peeled the skull open. You even kept the scalp in one piece. Very impressive."

You're too kind. How about we split it?

"Alright, I can live with that."

Ha ha, *live*...

"We definitely need to find more chemist brains to eat. Delicious."

You can't have just one.

"Alright, all out of brains, so... it's drinking game time. Drinking game! DRINKING GAME!"

Fine... But you're going first.

"Outta my way! Ahhh. Minty."

Your... uh...

"My what?"

Chest-al area.

"Dude! I grew boobs! Awesome! Okay, your turn."

I'm not so sure now...

"Fine, I'll do one more, but then you're up. Got it?"

Sure.

"Blech, this one tastes like a fat guy's sweat pants with a hint of lime."

How do you know what a fat guy's sweat pants taste li-- whoa!

"Whoa what?"

Your hair is really long. And kind of girly.

"You're kidding, let me see... wow, yeah, it is quite the feminine cut isn't it? Well, bottoms up buddy."

Yeah, no, I'm gonna pass.

"What a buzz kill! You know, if you want me to drink them all, just say so. I'll do it. I swear."

Have at it.

"Don't mind if I do! Mmm, I think this one is just orange juice. Feels kind of funny though..."

Doesn't look like anything changed.

"I've got this weird tingly sensation. Especially down... Oh my God!"

What?

"It's gone!"

What's gone?

"My... you know, down there!"

Are you serious?

"Yeah, look!"

Oh God no, I'm not looking— Get away from me!

"This isn't just any lab... This is a sex change lab!"

Huh. Imagine that.

"Crazy."

So... You wanna make out?

will call

I'd like to buy a ticket to tonight's concert.

"I'm sorry sir."

Sorry for what?

"I'm not selling tickets here."

But this is the box office.

"It is, but I'm not selling tickets here."

Isn't that the primary function of a box office?

"No sir. Will call only."

But I'm right here, the concert starts in two hours, why can't I just buy
     a ticket from you?

"It doesn't work like that."

All I want is to see this concert. Can you please help a guy out?

"Sorry, will call only sir."

For crying out loud. Okay, do you have web access on that computer?

"What?"

Web access.

"What's that?"

Can you get on the internet?

"Oh! Thought you said *eb* access. Yes it has internet."

Can you get on the theater's website?

"Sure."

Now go to tonight's event.

"Ah, I see where you're going with this..."

Buy one ticket for me. Here's my credit card.

"I don't think I sho—"

Just do it! Okay?

"Okay, calm down. There, it went through."

Great. So can I have my ticket now?

"Sorry sir, I can't do that."

Why the hell not?

"The system says your tickets were bought with a stolen credit card."

What? It wasn't stolen, I gave it to you to buy the ticket for me!

"Says right here. Stolen."

Idiot, you entered your own name and address for the order!

"Don't get snippy, I'm not the one who stole your credit card."

Yes. Yes you are.

"You gave it to me. I didn't steal it."

Cancel the ticket order.

"I'm not authorized to do that, sir."

What do you mean you're not authorized? Enough of this! Cancel the
order so I can go home.

"All sales are final. No refunds. Although, if you had opted for the pur-
chase protection option..."

For the love... At least give me my credit card back.

"I can't do that sir. Your card has been flagged as stolen so I'm required
to cut it up."

You've gotta be kidding me!"

"Afraid not."

Give it back!

"Please refrain from reaching through the window."

Please, please, don't shre— No! How could you?

"You're holding up the line. Please step aside."

What's that sign... 'Tickets now on sale'?

"Yes. We start selling tickets here at the box office two hours before the
show begins."

Why didn't you tell me about this two minutes ago?

"It never came up. Would you like to buy a ticket?"

I'd love to but you just shredded my credit card!

"If you don't have any money I'm going to have to ask you to step aside. Next please."

primitive

Grug, come here!

"It's Greg, not Grug."

Whatever, we're cave men. Take a look at this!

"What are you doing to those sticks? You should do that in private..."

Just watch!

"Is that stroking motion really necessary?"

Oh! Oh! Here it comes.

"Dude."

Look!

"Ooo, pretty... What is it?"

Fire!

"Where? Where? Everyone run!"

No, *this* is fire.

"You can't just go shouting 'fire' like that. You'll cause a panic."

Come feel it.

"I don't..."

Just feel it.

"Eh, it's not that great."

Get closer.

"Ouch!"

Not that close.

"Ya think? Oh. Yeah. That's *nice*. That's *real* nice. Well done Bongo."

It's Benjamin.

"Whatever. So what can we use it for?"

Well, we could... uh... I'm not sure, to be honest.

"Can we use it as a weapon?"

What?

"It's a simple question, can we use it as a weapon? Maybe put some on the end of a spear?"

Why would we do that?

"Why *wouldn't* we do that? What better way to scare off those annoying Neanderthals in the cave downstream? And what if we get attacked by a dinosaur?"

Dinosaurs are extinct.

"Nuh uh. I saw one yesterday."

Really.

"Honest to God, it was sittin' in the stream staring me down."

And what sound did this 'dinosaur' make?

"It made kind of a croaky 'ribbit' sort of sound. I think that's what it was... 'Ribbit.' Just like that."

That was a frog.

"It was a dinosaur! I almost messed my pants."

You don't wear pants.

"If I had been wearing pants I would have almost messed them."

Look, we're not going to weaponize the fire.

"Not even for—"

Especially not for protection against dinosaurs.

"Oh don't look, but you-know-who is here."

Who—

"I said don't look. If we ignore them, maybe they'll go away. Oh no, they're coming over to us. Oh hi, how are you?"

Hi Neanderthals, ah.. How you doin'? Yeah, don't touch that, it's hot.

"Okay, go ahead and take some of our food. It's no problem. Don't even mention it. We only had to fight a tiger for it."

Take care. It was nice seeing you.

"That's what I'm talking about! We just sit here and let them do whatever they want. I've had enough!"

Hey, hey, hey, what do you think you're doing?

"Take our meat, will ya? Well take THAT!"

You can't just throw flaming sticks at things!

"Sure I can, we're cave men."

marshall quinn
and the rough light of the lamented fallen

You've worked here for a while, haven't you?

"Yeah. Three years come this Friday."

Have you ever noticed anything about these laser guns we're making?

"Well, they're kind of unwieldy. Awkward shape and front-heavy."

Valid points, but not what I was getting at.

"They ironically have laser sights?"

Another very good point, but no, that's not it.

"Uhm... the lasers are red?"

The *lasers are red*. Yes.

"So?"

So? In every science fiction show I've ever seen the good guys have
blue lasers and the bad guys have...

"The bad guys have... what?"

Red lasers.

"Huh, weird. I never really noticed that."

Could it be that all this time we've been making laser guns for the
bad guys?

"I guess so... We really just ship them off to the retail outlets and
whoever buys them after that..."

Does that make us the bad guys?

"What do you mean?"

If the bad guys use our red lasers then we're bad guys too, aren't we?

"No, of course not."

How do you figure?

"This is just a blue collar job to earn a paycheck to put food on the table.
It's not a matter of right or wrong in the grand scale of things.
We're doing what's right for ourselves, which is as much as we
can or should worry about in the long run."

You're probably right.

"Of course I'm right."

I said *probably*.

"Hey, can you pick up the pace a little bit? I'm piling up over here."

Sorry, I was just...

"Forget about it. I just want to get through this batch before lunch."

I can't do this.

"What? Come on."

I can't stand being a bad guy.

"We aren't bad guys. But even if we were, so what?"

The bad guys always lose and get blown up. We gotta get out of here.

"Do you really think they're going to blow up this factory?"

Yeah.

"This particular factory?"

Yeah.

"Out of an entire planet of military bases and missile silos?"

Of course! If I wanted to stop getting shot by lasers I'd blow up where
        the other guy got their lasers. Simple.

"They have a lot more to worry about than— Hey, what's that sound?"

Air raid sirens! Get down!

"Ow, I'm down, I'm down. Stop tugging at me."

Can you hear them? How long do you think we have left?

"Twenty, thirty seconds tops."

What!?

"Idiot. That's the lunch whistle."

"Buenos dias, muchacho!"

Is this Hell?

"No, this isn't Hell."

The last guy told me I didn't get into Heaven.

"Yes, that is correct."

So if this isn't Hell, where am I?

"You're in *Limbo*! Ayayay!"

Oh great.

"It's not as bad as you think. In cases like yours... We feel it's only fair
      that we give you a second chance."

What do you mean, 'in cases like mine'?

"Embarrassing deaths such as falling off the toilet get a little more
      leniency as far as judgment goes."

It's not what it sounds like, I was changing a light bulb, not...

"Still pretty embarrassing."

So what do I have to do to get into heaven?

"You may have heard of Limbo."

Sure. It's where souls go to cleanse themselves of sin through suffering
      before eventually getting into heaven. Something like that.

"Yeah... That's not it at all."

What is it then?

"Three rounds."

Three rounds of what?

"Three rounds of Limbo."

What do you mean three rounds of Limbo?

"Make it under the limbo stick three times, Heaven. Fall down or touch
      the stick, Hell. Simple."

My fate for all eternity is determined by a party game?

"The best party game around! It's time to *LIMBO*! AYAYAY! Bring out
      the limbo stick!"

You've got to be kidding me.

"How low can you go! Limbo! Come on, first round, it's an easy one
      just to limber up. Go for it! Cha cha cha!"

Do I have to?

"Of course, this is *Limbo*! Ayayay!"

Jeans really aren't the best for this, but fine, I'll... Ah. Ah... Made it!

"Lower the limbo stick! How low can you go! Limbo! Second round, hope you're warmed up or else you'll *really* warm up, ha ha!"

How am I supposed to... It's at my knees! That's way too low.

"Limbo! Limbo! Limbo! Cha cha cha!"

Ok, I can do this. I guess it's worth a shot for eternity. Ahh... Oooooh, Ow Ow Ohhh... Ah ha! Made it again!

"Unbelievable! Lower the limbo stick ONE MORE TIME!"

Just great.

"How low can you go! Limbo! Time for round three, the hardest and most important round of all!"

No way! That's like six inches off the ground!

"Limbo! Cha..."

I can't!

"If you give up, you lose by default and you're off to Hell!"

Fine, I may as well... Ah ah ah... Aaaahh.. Ungghh... Oof!

"You fell! Too bad! Ayayay!"

Damn it!

"Exactly. Cha cha cha!"

soiled

"James, my dear old friend. I'm so sorry."

What for, El Rapido?

"It's just Rapido."

I thought there was an 'el.'

"Nope. No 'el.'"

Aren't you Mexican, though?

"No, why would you think that?"

Well, you wear a lucha libre mask...

"I found it at Goodwill. Anyway, I need to have my uniform cleaned."

Of course! But why so apologetic?

"Well... Here."

Oh. OH. Oh God... Oh. Oooo... Oh.

"Jim, I got a bit of a stomach bug and..."

Say no more. Please say no more.

"I have the super runs."

Let me stop you right there. Why are you only wearing boxer shorts?

"I'm not *only* wearing boxer shorts. I have my shoes and mask on too."

That's not my point. Why aren't you wearing pants?

"I'm glad you brought it up, Jimmy. You'd think that being the fastest man on Earth would allow me to get to the toilet in time when old man brown river comes a'knockin'. Not true, my friend."

I gathered as much from the filthy garment.

"You see, that uniform is an utter pain to take off for even the simplest of private moments."

Please don't list them. Please.

"Taking a whizz. Sex, both solo and with accompaniment. But especially number two. Even the fastest man alive can't get those tights off quick enough for the disgruntled escapees of the netherworld. Speak of the devil, could you direct me towards your restroom?"

Sure. It's down that hall on the left.

"Thanks Jimbo, I'll be just a moment."

Yeah okay. Oh wow, that was fast.

"My name isn't Rapido for nothing. As I was about to say, not wearing those tights gives me that extra edge I need to not make a mess."

Uh... you're dripping.

"Oh my. I'm so sorry. Let me clean that up for you..."

For the... Could you face a different direction when you bend over?

"Sorry, so sorry."

It's... Just forget about it. Don't ever mention it again. Please. So the boxers I can understand, but why are you shirtless?

"Don't you think I'd look dumb wearing a shirt with no pants?"

If you say so.

"That's what I like about you, we're always on the same page. We have an understanding, you and I. Don't we?"

Sure?

"That's right Captain Jimmeroo. We're pal-ohs to the end-oh. That being said, if we could keep this little digestive problem of mine on the down-low..."

Believe me, I won't be telling anyone about any of this.

"You're a good man, Jim-Jam. Now, tell me, when can I come pick up the uniform? Before Wednesday would be best for... Hold on, I'm feeling another rumble in the rumpus room. I'll be right back."

Alrig—

"Nope, false alar— OOOH, not a false alarm. Not at all."

For crying out loud.

"You got a mop back there?"

push and pull

"How's the tractor beam research coming along?"

Excellent. This may be the most important work of my career.

"That's just great. I was thinking though..."

Yes?

"We're developing this tractor beam for space warfare, right?"

That's correct.

"Wouldn't it be more useful to push the enemy away?"

I suppose...

"Don't get me wrong, the tractor beam is fantastic. I just don't see the usefulness of pulling the enemy closer. What's the advantage?"

I'm not a warfare strategist but... maybe if the enemy is running away?

"No, that can't be it. I want you to scrap the tractor beam and work on an... 'anti-tractor' beam. Task number one, come up with a better name than 'anti-tractor' beam."

But I've spent 17 years on this tractor beam technology. The prototype will be finished this afternoon!

"You can just reverse the polarity or something, can't you?"

It doesn't work like that.

"Why not? That's how magnets work. Isn't it just a big magnet?"

No, this is far more complex than that. There are the weak and strong nuclear forces to take into account, not to mention manipulating gravity to— You're not listening to any of this are you?

"What's that?"

Never mind. Sure, yes, I'll just reverse the polarity.

"Alright, so... let's see it then."

It's not quite ready, I have to recalibrate—

"Let's. See it. Then."

Okay, but you should wear these safety glasses and a hard hat.

"Ooh, ooh, test it on a watermelon!"

What? No! We're using this crate. Now, stand behind that yellow line.

"Got it."

Cover your ears, this could be loud...

"What's that sound?"

It's just the tractor beam.

"It's really loud, like a ripping..."

I just told you it could be loud.

"I don't think it's—"

Hold on, I need to...

"How's the tractor beam research coming along?"

Huh, what happened?

"I wanted to know how the research was coming along."

No, I got that, I mean, you already came down here and asked me.

"What are you talking about? You know, I was thinking—"

That pushing the enemy away is more useful than pulling them closer?

"Exactly! An '*anti*-tractor' beam if you will. You read my mind!"

I don't think this is a tractor beam... I think it's a time machine.

"Could you make it into an '*anti*-time' machine?"

call home

"Hey Dad."

Why hello Son!

"Just thought I'd call and uh... check in, I guess."

Well it's good to hear from you! I got a new tennis racket yesterday. Plays
      like Heaven, just Heaven. How are you doing down there?

"Good. Good. Well, I could be better."

Uh oh, what happened?

"It's nothing."

I know that tone. Do I have to come down there and sort things out?

"No, no, it's fine, really..."

You know, if there's anything you need, just let me know.

"Well... there is one little thing. A tiny thing. It's hardly even a thing."

Just ask already.

"Could... Could you give me better super powers?"

Jesus H. Christ, what's wrong with you?

"You know I hate it when you call me by my full name, Dad."

Well I'm sorry, but frankly I'm offended. Here you are, the Son of the
      most powerful being in the Universe...

"Ego-trip much?"

Excuse me, young man, I'm talking here.

"I'm not a young man, I'm like thirty years old."

Yeah and I'm like a billion years old, so seniority card. That's right, I played the seniority card. Listen to me, you can do more than any other mortal man has ever been capable of before. You can walk on water, you can make wine, you can raise the dead, you can even fly. What more do you want?

"What, I *can* fly?"

Of course you can fly, you're the goddam Son of God, damn it!

"How do I fly?"

You haven't figured out how yet? What the hell have you been doing for thirty years?

"Mostly all that other stuff. The wine, walking on water, raising the dead... Oh, and building chairs."

BUILDING CHAIRS? The Son of God BUILDING CHAIRS?

"I'm pretty good at it. I've built five so far."

FIVE chairs in thirty years?

"I put together some shelves too."

What do you mean 'put together.'

"I ordered them from a catalog and I followed the instructions..."

That isn't even proper carpentry!

"It was tough. Those instructions are really confusing. Honestly, it's a miracle I got it assembled. Had some pieces left over though..."

No, no, no. You've been wasting your time!

"Well if I had known I was able to fly..."

You never once wondered 'Hey, I'm the Son of God, I bet I have the ability to fly. I should have a go at it.'?

"No, not at all."

Even Superman figured out he could fly when he was just a baby.

"I never really got into Superman."

I could have sworn you read Superman comics when you were little.

"No, I liked Batman."

Oh yeah... You always wore that mask and cape while running around the house... How did you not know you could fly? You were curious enough to find out if you could bring corpses to life...

"It never came up! I wish I had known sooner. My feet are *killing* me!"

Well walk no more! Now you know.

"Great. By the way, did you know I'm getting crucified tomorrow?"

Oh that? Forget it, just fly away.

"I can't just fly away from a crucifixion."

What's the point in having a power if you don't use it?

"You could have at least warned me. I found out from some stranger on
     the street."

Sounds like a good Samaritan.

"Wait a minute, this is what you were talking about last week, isn't it?"

What?

"You told me I was going to have to die for everyone's sins."

That doesn't sound like me.

"It's what you said."

I say a lot of things.

cap'n

All hands on deck!

"All hands on deck, bawk!"

Man your stations!

"Man your stations, bawk!"

Prepare for battle!

"Prepare for battle, bawk bawk!"

Stop repeating me.

"Stop repeating me, bawk!"

Seriously, stop it. We're about to engage in battle here.

"Engage in battle, bawk!"

Snap out of it, man! You're not a parrot!

"Sorry Cap'n. Bawk."

It's alright. Just take it easy with the parrot talk.

"Yessir. Sorry. You know how it's been since our visit to that hypnotist
     back in Haiti."

Haiti was a hell of a time. What was the deal with the hypnotist again?

"She hypnotized me to be a parrot. You were there, remember?"

Ohhh yeah, that was hilarious. At the time. Now it's kind of annoying.

"Kind of annoying. Bawk!"

You see?

"I see, bawk!"

One thing has been bothering me... what's with the bawking?

"What do you mean?"

Why do you go 'bawk'?

"That's the sound parrots make."

I've never heard a parrot go 'bawk.'

"Sure, that's the primary parrot sound."

You're thinking of chickens. *Watch for the enemy's cannons, they really pack a wallop! Sails up! TURN HARD STARBOARD!*

"HARD STARBOARD, BAWK!"

As we were saying...

"No way that chickens go 'bawk,' I swear it's a parrot thing."

Chickens go 'bawk.' I'm one hundred percent sure of it.

"What sound do parrots make then?"

'Skreeaaaw!' maybe?

"That's a hawk sound."

Like you would know, chicken man. *All men, draw your swords! Don't let them board the ship, those filthy bilge rats!*

"Filthy bilge rats, bawk!"

Oh, that's it! 'Squawk.'

"Really?"

Definitely.

"I would have remembered squawk. I don't even think that's a word."

It's gotta be. Go get the dictionary. *PRESS HARD BOYS! THEY WON'T TAKE US DOWN THAT EASILY!*

"Alright, here it is."

Let's hear it then.

"Squawk. Verb. To shriek loudly, as a parrot."

Well, there you have it.

"I'll be damned, I've been making the wrong bird sound for weeks."

Hey, we all make mistakes.

"Uh... speaking of mistakes..."

Oh bloody hell, the crew's all dead.

"Crew's all dead! Crew's all dead! Bawk!"

Hello Steven.

"It's Steffon."

Don't be stupid, it's Steven.

"What do you want?"

I need to speak with you, Steven.

"Who are you? There's no one else in here but me."

That's the beauty of being in your head, Steven.

"No way, I'm not a nutcase."

There, there, Steven. We're all a little bit crazy.

"Would you stop calling me 'Steven'? It's Steffon!"

That's what I'm talking about Steven. Calling yourself 'Steffon' just makes you...

"Hip? Stylish? Vogue?"

It makes you a jackass, Steven.

"What? You're delirious."

You're the one talking to yourself, Steven.

"No, *you* are!"

Technically that is true, Steven, but that's not why I'm here.

"Why are you here?"

You have to cut the act, Steven.

"What act?"

You're a farm boy from Kansas, Steven.

"That's not who I am anymore."

You can't forget your roots, Steven. The farm, your family... Bessy. They all need you.

"What happened to Bessy?"

She's sick, Steven.

"What does she have?"

Mad Cow.

"On no."

That's right, Steven. She's *mad* that you moved to the city and turned into such a tool.

"Bessy didn't say that!"

I know. I did. I'm making a point here, Steven.

"Don't toy with my emotions... you."

You can call me Stevesie.

"That's stupid, I'm not calling you that."

Exactly my point, Steven. Stop these shenanigans and go back home.

"I can't. I'm booked to perform every day for the next month."

Poor Steven. You dance in Central Park to a mix tape of the Cure.

"It's steady work, okay?"

Steven, if you don't go back home... I'll be forced to take you down. From the inside.

"What're you talking about? How can you ev—Ow! I just punched myself in the face!"

No, Steven. I punched you in the face. I'm calling the shots now.

"Ow! Ow! Stop it! Owowow... ha ha ha! That tickles! That tickles! You know all of my ticklish spots! Stop! Stop!"

Are you going back home? Or do I have to break out the noogies?

"No, no, oh man, I'll go, just stop tickling me."

heist

Ski masks?

"Check."

Rope?

"Check."

Glass cutter?

"Check."

Walkie talkies?

"Check."

Custard pie?

"What?"

Custard pie. I put it on the list.

"No you didn't."

Yes I did, right after orange juice.

"What orange juice?"

Shoot... I added it to the wrong list...

"What do we need custard pie for? We're robbing a bank."

It's my calling card, Darrel. I can't pull off a heist without leaving my trademark custard pie booby trap in the vault.

"I didn't know you did that."

I do. Then they read the note that says, 'Looks like you got pie on your face.' Jesus Darrel, do you even read the itineraries I put together?

"Not really. I usually just sit in the van, so..."

If you're ever going to advance in this business beyond being the 'sit-in-the-van' guy, you have to start being more involved in these heists.

"I kind of like being the 'sit-in-the-van' guy."

I am astonished. Astonished and offended. Where's your *passion*? I remember the look in your eyes that first time I came back through those unmarked van doors carrying armfuls of money bags. It was like a child seeing fireworks for the first time. Where has the magic gone, Darrel? Where has it gone?

"I just like sitting in the van."

Fine, let all your potential just slip away. I'm going in there, but I'm not going to enjoy it. You've broken my heart Darrel.

"What about the pie?"

Oh damn, that's right, the pie. Is there a grocery store around here?

"Couple blocks back. I think they're closed though."

Nonsense, grocery stores are open 24 hours these days!

"Fine, we'll go take a look."

That's it, get back into it! We're making it happen! Look at us go! Exciting, eh?

"It's closed."

Shoot. Guess we should just call it a night then. Let's go home.

"You think Mom will have hot chocolate ready for us?"

Oh that would be bliss, just bliss... damn it, hot chocolate was on the wrong list too.

time traveler iii

Hey Bill.

"Whoa! Is that you, George?"

Of course. I've come back from the future to tell you not to ever time travel even if you really want to.

"Why?"

Because time travel sucks and is useless except for delivering chips.

"But time travel has so many— Delivering chips?"

That's right. I started Time Chips Inc., a company that specializes in the delivery of snack chips throughout time.

"That's not a bad idea at all... Where did you get the time machine?"

I stole it from you. I got the idea after future you kept coming back in time to bother me.

"Am I part of Time Chips Inc.?"

No. Otherwise I wouldn't have had to steal the time machine, duh. By the way, here are the chips you're going to want in 35 minutes.

"I'm not paying. Only fair since you stole future me's time machine."

Fine whatever, I'll just use part of the future interest earned from your payment to put into Time Chips Inc. in the present time so that in the future I'll be able to withdraw part of that interest to bring back in time to pay for the chips in the first place.

"Huh?"

It makes sense.

"I think that's a paradox."

Nope. Makes sense.

"My head hurts."

Told you time travel sucks. Aside from the chips. They're delicious.

"I'm sure they are."

Go ahead and try a couple.

"Ew, lime flavored? Disgusting."

It'll grow on you. Trust me.

"I'm glad I didn't pay. So, you stole your time machine from me?"

Yes.

"And I invented the time machine?"

Actually... No. You stole it.

"From who?"

I've said too much.

"No, tell me."

I can't.

"You wouldn't have brought it up if you didn't want to tell me."

That's not true.

"You're just dying to tell me. I can tell. You're getting all shakey."

Ok, fine! You steal the time machine from me after you find out that I used your time machine to start a snack chip delivery company without letting you in on any profits from the incredibly successful business despite your interest in the snack chip delivery concept.

"Where did the time machine come from in the first place, then? It doesn't make any sense."

It makes sense, just don't think about it. If you think about it, it will stop making sense and the universe will explode.

"Really? The universe will explode?"

That's what you told me when I stole it from you, anyway.

"Did I only tell you that because you told me right now?"

Very likely.

"How about this. I won't steal the time machine from you if you let me in on Time Chips Inc."

I dunno, I've been pretty successful without you.

"You can't continue your business if I steal the time machine."

But... if you don't steal the time machine, I won't be able to steal the time machine in the first place, and Time Chips Inc. will never exist.

"What's that ripping sound?"

We thought about it too much.

"Is that a hole in space-time?"

I told you time travel sucks.

blood

"Take THAT vampire! HAHAHA!"

Oh come on now, that just hurts.

"What the hell? You should be dead."

Idiot, you have to drive a wooden stake through a vampire's heart.

"That's... That's what I did."

The heart is on the left side of the chest.

"Yeah, I stabbed you on the left side."

My left, not yours.

"Crap."

Don't worry about it. How's this, I'll let this little encounter slide if...

"If what?"

If you let me have a sip.

"Over my dead body!"

That's what we're trying to avoid here. Look, you have two choices. You could let me have just a sip, or I'll hunt you down and kill you as soon as you leave. Either way is fine with me.

"But I'll turn into a vampire."

Old wives' tale. It's far more complicated a process to make a vampire.

"How do I know you won't just drink all my blood?"

If I wanted to do that, I would have already. I'm in a generous mood tonight. I suggest you take advantage of that.

"Fine, but only if you brush your teeth first."

What? Why?

"I don't know who you've been biting, what kind of diseases I could get from the last person you fed on..."

Ah, yeah, ok, I'll brush my teeth. Give me a minute.

"What's that for?"

Oh that? That's my fang file. For sharpening my teeth.

"You have to sharpen your teeth?"

Every day. Your teeth don't just magically get sharp when you become a vampire, you know.

"That doesn't seem right..."

Well it's true. Once I forgot to sharpen for weeks, went to bite into a nun... She slapped me after I gave her a hickey.

"Don't forget to use the mouthwash."

Ah, yes, I always forget the mouthwash. Grgglllgrglllll.

"Okay, make it quick, I have a test in the morning."

In school, are you? What are you studying?

"Just take the damn sip, will ya?"

Jee, excuse me for taking some interest... Alright, are you ready?

"Yeah."

This might sting a little.

"I figured as much. Just do it!"

Okay, here it goes. Whew. Alright.

"Ow! Hey, that's actually not so.. HEY! Stop it!"

What's the problem?

"That was way more than a sip."

That was a sip.

"It was a gulp if anything."

It was a tiny sip.

"You were just sucking away! I'm actually feeling lightheaded..."

Ok, maybe it was a big sip.

"And what the hell? I'm still bleeding."

You should probably put some pressure on that.

"Why am I still bleeding?"

Vampire saliva is kind of like a blood thinner, makes it easier to drink.
Problem is, the bites keep bleeding.

"Keep bleeding?"

Theoretically until death but... Maybe if you keep pressure on it...

"You said you'd only drink a sip!"

I did only drink a sip. I never said anything about what the rest of your
blood would do.

"I think I'm going to throw up, I've never seen this much blood."

Calm down, with your heart rate up it'll just make the bleeding that
much worse. But as long as you're bleeding, would you mind
doing it into this bucket?

"I can't believe this. I'm dying here and you want me to aim my blood
into a bucket?"

Why let good blood go to waste?

"Bad news, Commander."

What's the damage?

"It's not pretty."

Let's have it, I'm a strong man, I can handle it.

"500 space dollars. Your horse just didn't pull through this race."

Aw hell. You win some, you lose some I suppose.

"Yes sir, very true."

A penny saved is a penny earned.

"Indeed."

Different strokes for different folks.

"Uh, right, sir."

You win some, you lo—

"You already said that one, sir."

Oh. So what's the status? You know, as far as Starship stuff.

"We are four langrums away from our destination. We've just exited
        hyperspace so we should arrive within the hour."

Is that why my horse lost?

"I'm sorry?"

Coming out of hyperspace. Surely that didn't *help* my horse.

"If so, I'm fairly certain that it put all horses at an equal disadvantage."

How can you be so certain? I want this looked into immediately. I won't
        have lost 500 star bucks in vain.

"We can't call them that, sir."

Call what what?

"Star bucks."

Why not?

"It's a coffee thing."

What's coffee?

"Back on Earth the... Never mind. I will have it looked into, sir."

Great, you're a good man. So what now?

"You could call mission command and let them know we've arrived."

Oh God, I hate talking to them. Hand me the phone.

"There you are, sir."

It's not ringing.

"You have to dial first, sir."

You didn't dial already?

"No sir."

Well I don't know what the number is.

"468-75563-332-327-01."

Uh, okay... Four six nine...

"No, 468..."

Four... Six... Eight... Okay.

"7"

Seven.

"55"

Five, fi— Shoot, I hit the 6. Start over.

"Oh forget it, I'll just dial."

Good man. Good man indeed.

"It's ringing. Here."

Thanks. Good, got the answering machine. Didn't want to talk to those pri— Hello, this is Commander Debussy of the Starship Syrinx. Just checking in to let you know we're coming up on our destination now and that my horse lost the race this afternoon. That is all.

"Well done, sir."

I thought so.

"I'm not sure they needed to know about the horse race, though."

Of course they did.

"It's just that—"

Who's the Commander?

"You are, sir."

That's right. If the Commander says mission command needs to know about the results of the illegal horse races I hold on the supply deck of my ship, then by God, mission command needs to know about the results of my illegal— Oh, I see what you mean.

"Yeah..."

Well that's a problem.

"The phone's ringing."

What? I can't hear you over the phone ringing.

"I said the phone is ringing."

Yes I can hear that. Answer it, will you?

"Hello you've reached the Starship Syrinx, Lieutenant Barker speaking. Yes. Yes. Uh... No, he's not available at the moment. Could I have him call you back? Okay, I'll let him know. Thank you."

Well?

"Yeah, we're in big trouble."

Damn.

"You know, you could say you were kidding."

Genius! You're a good man! Good. Man. Hand me that phone.

"Thank you sir! Yes sir!"

It isn't ringing.

"Right, sorry."

Yes, hello, this is Captain Debussy. We got you good! Just a little yank on the old chain, keep you on your toes. We're coming up on...

"Two langrums, sir."

Two langrums from our destination. Say, I have a question for you guys. If a half dozen horses were running in a race while in hyper-space— no, purely hypothetical. Don't get snippy wi—

"Hung up, sir?"

They didn't buy it. The horse question may have tipped them off.

"Who goes there?"

Uh... No one.

"*Some*one must be there."

Nope. No one.

"I don't believe you."

No one's here. Trust me.

"Trust who?"

Bob. I mean... shoot.

"Ah ha, Bob! Bob, Bob, Bob. How dare you enter my lair and wake me
from my slumber, Bob?"

Lair, what lair? This is a lair? Nah, I'm lost, yeah, that's it. Glad I came
across this lair, so I could get directions on how to leave it.

"So you *did* know it's a lair."

No, I meant, I only now knew that it was—

"Silence! You have come too far and seen too much. Do you know what
happens to those who enter a dragon's lair?"

Dragon? What? There's no such thing as dragons. You're silly.

"I am the dragon who lives beneath this mountain. This is my lair."

Silly dragon.

"What happens to those who enter a dragon's lair is they do not exit!"

That wasn't as eloquent as I would have expected from a dragon.

"Silence!"

Hey, how about we forget I came in here, I'll go back to my village, and
we'll all just have a pleasant rest of the day?

"You've come to steal my treasure. Unforgivable! You will be eaten."

You don't wanna do that, I haven't showered in weeks. I'm pretty sure
you'll get heart burn.

"I always have heart burn."

That sucks. Have you tried antacid tablets?

"I am a dragon! I am supposed to have heart burn!"

Take it down a notch, Puff.

"Puff?"

The magic dragon. You are magic aren't you?

"No, I'm just a dragon."

Well that's stupid. Are you at least enchanted?

"I have an enchanted sword."

What is a dragon going to do with an enchanted sword?

"I use it as a toothpick... AFTER EATING ANY INTRUDERS THAT
WAKE ME!"

Whoa! Alright, well I'm gonna head out, if that's alright with you.

"It is NOT alright with me."

Ow! Get your paw off of me!

"You're not going anywhere, except for in my mouth!"

Hold on, hold on, hold on, I'll make you a deal.

"What kind of deal can a puny human like *you* make with a powerful
dragon like *me*."

I know where you can get more treasure.

"I have *plenty* of treasure."

More treasure than *you* even have.

"What? Impossible! I have nearly *all* of the treasure in the *world*!"

Not the treasure of the Black Ogre Mountain Tribes.

"That's just a myth!"

Or is it? I know where they keep it.

"Tell me!"

Only if you promise not to eat me.

"Okay, I won't eat you, just tell me where the treasure is!"

And promise you won't burn my village. Or eat any of our virgins.

"I promise! Tell me already!"

They keep the treasure in a cavern... deep within the coal mines of
Hiner'nok in Granier's Grove.

"Why thank you."

Hey you said you wouldn— Aaaoowwweeeee!!!!

"Gross. Tastes like limes."

"Whew, that was a heist and a half. All in a day's work for...

The Eradicator! Bwah ha ha ha!

Time to take a well deserved load off in the old secret hideout."

Welcome to the secret hideout entry system. Please insert key now.

"Drat! I left the hideout key in my other utility belt!"

Please insert key now.

"I know, I know, you infernal computer."

Please insert key now.

"Think, think, think. Computer! Don't I have a backup security code?"

Yes. Recalibrating.

"Hurry up, I think it's about to rain."

Recalibrated. Please input backup security code into the keypad now.

"Alright, I think it's..."

Invalid backup security code. Please try again.

"I could have sworn! Okay maybe it's..."

Invalid backup security code. Please try again.

"It HAS to be..."

Too many failed attempts. System shutting down.

"Wait! Wait! Don't you recognize my voice?"

Voice recognition software initiating.

"Thank you, oh thank you!"

Please identify yourself.

"I am...

The Eradicator! Bwah ha ha ha!"

Voice does not match.

"I have a cold! Give me a break!"

Baseball bat defense system activated.

"Ow! Ow! Ow! Watch the face! Watch the face!"

Face recognition software initializing.

"Now we're talking."

Please stand in front of the camera.

"Just in time, it's starting to sprinkle."

Scanning.

"Yeah?"

Processing.

"Yeah?"

No matches found. Remove sunglasses, hats or masks for best results.

"I can't take off my mask, I'm in public! Why do you suck so much?"

Loading personal identification security question. Please stand by.

"Ah ha, I knew I put in another back up."

What is your favorite food?

"Steak of course."

Incorrect. You are not authorized to enter.

"I must have programmed this during my sushi phase..."

The Eradicator has been notified. Entry system shutting down.

"Oh great, not only am I locked out, I have to pay twenty cents for this
      text message notification. And now the rain is really coming
      down. Oh wait! The hide-a-key rock!"

Welcome to the hide-a-key rock entry system. Please enter your security
      code now.

"Drat!"

narrator

Cindy approached the restaurant with her best friend, Marcus.

"Would you stop that?"

Marcus wasn't sure what she meant and merely shrugged in agree-
      ment.

"The narrating thing. Stop it. It's annoying. Hello, reservation for
      two."

The host had a lazy eye, but Cindy didn't say a word.

"Seriously! Shut up!"

She wasn't amused. She had enough of Marcus' shenanigans, yet he
      showed no signs of relenting.

"Thank you so much, this table is wonderful."

She told the host, being careful not to stare at his lazy eye.

"I swear, if you don't stop, I'm going to..."

Her thoughts turned violent. Memories of her youth on a small farm
      in Kentucky came flooding back, reminding her of the day her
      father made her kill a chicken.

"Seriously, I can't take you anywhere, can I?"

She summoned the waiter, hoping he would notice the effort she put into
 her hair and makeup.

"I'm not wearing any makeup!"

She hadn't put any effort into her hair or makeup.

"Shut up. Hi, I think we're ready to order."

Marcus wasn't ready, but he agreed anyway. He scanned the menu
 quickly while Cindy placed her order, a simple garden salad.

"Don't listen to him, that isn't what I want. I'd like to have the grilled
 chicken. Light on the seasoning."

The slaughtered chicken's limp body, headless, lay on the tree stump
 outside her bedroom window.

"Oh God, nevermind, just give me the salad."

The greasy-haired waiter turned to Marcus who would proceed to order
 the grilled chicken. Light on the seasoning.

"I'm really sorry for this, it's... a thing he does. Thank you so much."

She glared at Marcus with those penetrating blue eyes. Spittle formed
 patches of white froth at the corners of her lips. Adorable.

"Stop narrating right now, or I'm gonna let you have it."

Marcus hung his head, ashamed he had embarrassed his best friend.

"Narrating that you're sorry is **STILL NARRATING** and **STILL AN-
 NOYING**."

Cindy's left eye began to twitch, a quirk that only rarely surfaces when
 she feels blood lust. This was one of those times.

"How about I shove this loaf of bread down your throat?"

She knew she could never hurt dear Marcus, but she hoped the threat of
 violence would be volatile enough to end his senseless blabber.

"That's it, Marcus!"

She rose from her seat and lifted the chair high above her head,
 preparing to bring it crashing down upon—

hunters

What do you think you're doing?

"Tying up my capture, what does it look like?"

Back off buddy, that's *my* bounty you're binding.

"Easy with the alliteration fella, this guy is MINE. Fair and square."

I don't think so, I'm the one who set this whole thing up. The hotel room, the faulty hot water faucet, the plumber outfit. I even bought a plunger and a wrench.

"That's great but... I tranq'd him while you were fixing the sink."

Come on, that's not fair, I went through a lot of trouble on this one.

"Why didn't you just grab him when he first let you in to fix the sink?"

Disguises are all about believability. No one's going to believe I'm a plumber if I don't fix anything.

"Actually, that would make you quite the suspicious plumber. Nevertheless, you snooze you lose, this bounty is mine."

How did you even get in here? Windows are all sealed, and I know the air ducts are way too small for a... big guy like you.

"This is all muscle, beanpole. I just slipped in behind you when you came in. What's with the ridiculous get up? Isn't that a mechanic's jumpsuit?"

It's a multi-purpose coverall.

"Looks like a set of footie pajamas."

Shut up. It's better than what you're wearing, leather man.

"Real bounty hunters wear leather."

You stick out like a sore thumb!

"Bounty hunting isn't about prancing around in costumes, it's about getting the bounty. Something you've clearly failed to do."

Only because you stole it from under my nose!

"Okay, okay, okay, since you're just starting out... and I did technically swoop in to snatch this guy up from you... I'll split the bounty."

Now you're talking!

"*If...*"

If what?

"If you run around the hotel lobby yelling that I'm the greatest bounty hunter who ever lived."

I'm not going to do that.

"Alright, bounty's all mine then."

No wait, I'll consider it.

"There's no time to consider it. This isn't a game show. You either say yes and run around the lobby right now, or I'll just take off with—"

Where'd he go?

"Tranqs must have worn off..."

Great work, big bad bounty hunter.

"I said cool it with the alliteration. Help me find him."

Will you split the bounty with me?

"Yeah, okay, but you don't get to put it on your resume. And you can't wear that stupid onesie."

Great, can you help me with the zipper?

"I have to do everything don't— Oh God, put it back on! Don't you know you're supposed to wear clothes underneath?"

buried

"You said I'd be able to fly away!"

Yeah, about that...

"Don't 'yeah, about that' me! How could you betray me like that, Dad?"

Really? Have you read Genesis? This kind of thing happens all the time.

"You always have to use that Abraham story as an excuse, don't you? I'm not Isaac and you aren't enduring a test from God. You *are* God. You can't just say 'God told me to.'"

Of course I can. Hey God? Yes? Go trick your son into dying for everyone's sins. I dunno about that, seems kind of dubious. Of course not, you're on a mission from God. True that. See? Perfectly legit.

"I can't take this anymore. I'm going back."

What do you mean, going back?

"I'm going back out there. I can hardly breathe in here."

They didn't exactly have ventilation in mind when they buried you.

"Okay, I'm dead, so what? I brought people back from the dead when I was alive, what's to stop me from raising myself?"

Nope, you can't raise yourself from the dead.

"You're lying! That's the same tone you used when you said I could fly. That's your lying voice!"

I don't have a lying voice.

"You're still using it!"

Am not. Okay, fine, I have a lying voice. Everyone has a lying voice. I did model man in my image after all.

"You took a few liberties."

What do you mean?

"You are soooo bald. Most men I've encountered had flowing locks. Except the lepers."

I'm not bald, I choose to shave my head. It's for swimming.

"You don't swim."

Sure I do.

"Oh yeah? Who do you swim against?"

Just some of the angels, Gabriel, Michael, Lucifer...

"You go swimming with Lucifer?"

He keeps the pool nice and warm.

"That's disgusting."

What?

"You swim with Lucifer because he keeps the pool warm?"

Yeah.

"As in he whizzes in the pool."

No! What? What's wrong with you? No!

"Enough of this, I'm getting out of here."

That boulder is too heavy, you'll never be able to move it alone.

"Ah ha, that's why I asked them to also bury this rock hammer and a poster of Mary Magdalene."

What does that have to do with anything?

"I'm gonna dig out. Yeah, that's right."

That will take forever! Don't be ridiculous.

"I've done the math, it should only take about three days."

You'll never make it.

happy ending

Woo, I'm nervous.

"No need."

All kinds of tense!

"That's what I'm here for."

I've never had a professional massage, you know.

"I'm aware."

Especially not from such a lovely lady.

"Don't flirt with me."

Sorry, I get kind of, you know, when I'm nervous, you know?

"I think I know."

You know it! So... do I take off my pants before or after I lay down?

"You ordered a shoulder massage."

Is it too late to upgrade?

"I'd rather you didn't."

Things are getting pretty tight down there, if you know what I mean.

"I really wish I didn't."

Ok, fine. So shirt off then?

"I guess if you want... Either way."

How's that? Eh?

"Please stop flexing."

I can't help it, my muscles are just. So. Big.

"They're really not."

Above average?

"Nope."

Average?

"Do you want the massage or not?"

Of course. And the happy ending if you don't mind. Wink. Wink.

"Excuse me?"

My buddy told me to ask for the happy ending. Wink. Wink.

"Yeah... I think you're supposed to actually wink, not just say 'wink.'"

Okay, I'd like the happy ending.

"You're just blinking now."

No, I winked.

"You closed both eyes. That's a blink, not a wink."

How's this.

"Nope. Still blinking."

What if I hold one eyelid open...

"That's just creepy."

Forget the winking, how about that happy ending?

"No, I don't think so."

I'll pay extra.

"Not happening."

Okay then, no big deal.

"You don't know what a happy ending is, do you?"

No idea.

"Hmm, okay, I'll do it then."

Really? Fantastic! How much extra will that cost me?

"No charge. Just sit back and relax."

Alright, I'm ready, let me have it.

"I'll let you have it alright..."

Ow, ow, ow! What are you doing?

"Whipping you with a towel."

What? That's what a happy ending is?

"Deceptive name, I know. It sounds like your friend really set you up."

I'm gonna kick his ass.

"Take care now."

tri your assic off

I'm sick of those dinosaur douche bags.

"I hear ya."

They think they're so friggin' great just because they 'rule the planet.'

"One called me a pipsqueak yesterday! Is that supposed to be funny?"

Someday we mice will rule the planet. They'll see.

"Yeah! And we'll burn their remains for fuel..."

Easy! That's a little harsh, don't you think?

"I was just sayin..."

Hey, what's that over there?

"Looks like a bag of something."

What's in it?

"You tell me. You're the one that can read."

Tortilla chips. Lime flavored.

"Oooh! I love limes!"

Me too! I wonder where this came from?

"Who cares. Open 'er up, I'm starving!"

Here, you grab this end, I'll grab that end, and on the count of three
        we'll pull it open.

"Got it."

Ready?

"Rmmhmm."

Nnnn. Twww. Thhhheee.

"Mmmt?"

Plll! Plll!

"What?"

What are you doing? Don't let go! We almost had it!

"I couldn't understand what you were saying."

I was counting to three.

"Oh. Right. Let's try again."

Okay, you all set now?

"Rmmhmm."

Nnn... Tww... Thhhheee!

"Dd ooo sssy tww rm thhee?"

Mmmt?

"Dd ooo sssy *tww* rm *thhee*?"

Oy cnnt nnddrsstnd ooo.

"Mmmt?"

Oy cnnt... I can't understand you.

"See what I mean?"

Yeah, this isn't working. How about I nod to three instead.

"That works. Let's give it a shot."

Get set.

"Ready. Hrmmmph!"

What are you doing? You're pulling too soon now!

"Hold on. Are we pulling *on* the third nod or *after* the third nod?"

After. I can't nod and pull at the same time.

"Of course. Let's try again. I think we got it."

Okay, last time, here it goes.

"Hrmmmph!"

Nnnng, ahhh!

"I don't think we're getting it open."

This sucker is tough.

"Oh, hey..."

What?

"You're gonna hate me for this..."

What? Tell me.

"The other side was already open."

"Welcome to Hell! I'm Satan, it's great to meet you at long last!"

Uh, hi Satan... You greet everyone individually?

"Oh Hell no, I don't have time for that. You have any idea how many
    souls enter hell each single day? No, comrade, I came just for
    you. I heard your story, so I pulled your file and had a read."

Oh yeah? Is that... good?

"Good? It's fantastic! After I read your file I felt bad. What a poor soul!
    I thought to myself, 'what the Hell are you doing here?'"

Ha ha ha...

"What the Hell is so funny?"

You keep saying 'Hell.' Kinda funny.

"Oh, ha ha ha, you're right, that *is* pretty funny. I like you. Listen, I think
    you got a bit of a raw deal with the whole dying from falling off
    the crapper..."

I was changing a light bulb, not...

"And not getting into Heaven. Then to top it all off, you lose at Lim-
    bo. What kind of side show are they running up there anyway?
    Everybody sucks at Limbo. Even *I* suck at Limbo. Not that I'm
    complaining, I'm happy to have the extra souls..."

I was kind of wondering if that was your idea, actually.

"You know, I wish I had thought of it. Pure genius... Anyway, although
    I would love to, I obviously can't help you get into Heaven...
    But I'll tell you what I *can* do, comrade."

Yeah?

"I want you to be my personal assistant. The best job in Hell. It's even
    better than most jobs in Heaven. What do you say?"

It sounds great, but what would I have to do?

"You know, basic stuff. Answer my phone, pour liquid fire on souls,
    take notes at meetings... Nothing you haven't done before."

That sounds pretty reasona— Pour liquid fire on souls?

"You've never done that? Don't worry, it'll take two minutes to learn
    how."

Isn't that kind of cruel?

"This is Hell. Everything is cruel. It's just a matter of if you are the cruel-*er* or the cruel-*ee*. Trust me, you'd much rather be a cruel-er. Crueler... Cruller. Mmm. As soon as we're done here, you're heading to the pastry shop. Any other questions?"

I literally have to pour fire onto other souls?

"Yes. Well, not actual fire. Just douse any souls you encounter with lighter fluid. Real simple."

I guess I could get used to that.

"I have a feeling this is the start of a beautiful friendship, comrade."

Hell yeah.

"Welcome back!"

I never left.

"I thought I saw you leave..."

Nope, been munching on these lime flavored tortilla chips. Surely you
   must have heard me.

"We're notoriously silent."

Even when we're pigging out on snack food?

"We weren't pigging out."

We just ate over twice our weight in chips. That's pigging out.

"Maybe for you, but I'm eating for two now."

Shut up! You're pregnant?

"I have a tapeworm."

Idiot.

"I can eat whatever I want and it won't ruin my figure."

What figure? You're round.

"All mice are round!"

But you're like... **really** round.

"How rude!"

I'm just callin' it like I see it.

"That's no way to speak to a lady."

You're a girl?

"You just thought I was pregnant!"

I was being nice. I figured asking if you're pregnant would be less
   offensive than calling you fat.

"How is asking me if I'm pregnant when I'm a boy less offensive?"

But you're not a boy.

"You thought I was a boy!"

But then I thought you were pregnant.

"Shut up and hand me another chip."

They're all gone. We ate them all.

"I don't believe it! I'm still starving."

That's because you have a tapeworm!

"I know..."

Did you know tape worms can grow up to a hundred feet long?

"Oh my God!"

No wonder you're so bloated.

"You have to get this thing out of me!"

I have nothing to do with it!

"I can't get it out on my own."

Sure you can. Just find a chair and press real hard into the back of it...

"Do you see any mouse-size chairs around here? I don't think so! Get over here and grab that."

Grab what?

"That chocolate sprinkle."

Holy crap, I love chocolate sprinkles!

"No, don't eat it!"

Why not?

"You need to put it in front of my mouth so we can coax the tape worm into coming out. Then, grab the worm and we'll run in opposite directions."

Ew!

"I'd do it for you."

I'd never get a tapeworm!

"Sometimes it's not a choice!"

Don't cry.

"Can we just do this?"

If it will make you stop crying.

"Stop stretching."

I need to limber up! We just ate and we're about to sprint 100 feet. If that's not asking for a leg cramp then...

"You'll be fine, sprinkle me!"

Alright, alright. Here we go. C'mon tapeworm. C'mooon. Nice tap–

Hey! What are you doing?

"Hrmph?"

You're biting me!

"I wasn't biting you, I was just closing my mouth around your paw..."

Why would you do that?

"I love chocolate sprinkles."

Come on!

"Okay, sorry. Let's try again."

Here we go. Heeere tapeworm. Got a nice treat for ya... GOT IT!

"KKGGH KKGGGGH!"

What?

"KKGGGH!"

Oh, run! Right!

"KKGGHHGH!"

Gross gross gross gross!

"KKGKGKK!"

IT'S WRAPPING AROUND MY ARM!

"kkkhkggkkkhgk."

How much longer is this thing?

"kgghkgk."

Why won't it just end?

"Pleh! Blech, finally!"

What?

"You can stop running, it's out!"

I can't hear you, you're too far away! Hold on, I'll come over! What did you say?

"I said you can stop running, it's out."

Well obviously.

"Thanks a lot. I owe you one."

More like a hundred. That was the grossest thing I've ever done, and I'm a freakin' rodent.

"It wasn't that bad."

It was pretty bad. I can't believe that thing was in your stomach.

"Ahh! Incoming!"

Run away!

Bad news, Debussy.

"Yes, Admiral."

In light of recent events...

"The horse racing."

Yes, the illegal horse racing. In light of the recent events of your illegal horse racing, I have no other choice but to demote you.

"I understand, sir."

So then, Commander Debussy, may this be a lesson to you. Don't let it happen again.

"Just a moment, is that my new rank?"

Of course, I just said I had to demote you.

"But..."

But what?

"That was already my rank."

Oh I don't think so. How could I demote you to Commander if you weren't higher than Commander before?

"I guess what I mean is that I should be the next rank lower than Commander now."

Are you really trying to get me to demote you even further? That's ridiculous.

"No, I'm just saying that for a demotion, I would have to be lower than Commander now."

But I just demoted you to Commander. Why do you want to be demoted again?

"I don't want to be demoted at all!"

Well that's not going to be happen, as it has already been done, **Commander** Debussy.

"If you say so."

While I'm here, I've been meaning to talk to you about your ship.

"Yes?"

You see, we're in the middle of a war that spans the entire galaxy, fighting to defend freedom and the right to wear short shorts.

"Short shorts?"

That's why I joined the military. Did you know that short shorts are outlawed on Consulate planets?

"I had no idea."

Those damned Connies. If I want to show off my beautiful biker legs, I will, damn it!

"I don't see what this has to do with my ship."

It's filthy, Debussy. You're supposed to be representing the proud and storied military tradition of the Earth Navy. Get your ship clean before your next mission or you're looking at another demotion.

"But if the ship is too clean, surely the glare off the hull will draw unwanted attention to us."

Pride over logic. It's the Earth Navy motto.

"Plus this ship is nearly a mile long! Don't even get me started on its girth... How am I supposed to get it clean that fast?"

Make it happen! You're a Commander for a reason. Command it!

"Is that a Command, sir?"

Yes, that is a command, Commander.

"So you're commanding me, the Commander, to command."

I am commanding you, the Commander, to command, Commander.

"Could there be a commendation in it for me?"

Don't be ridiculous, there will be no commendation for a Commander simply following his commands to command!

"Ha ha, great."

What are you laughing at?

"Forget it."

Fine. Dubussy, get yourself in gear. I don't want to come down here again just to hold your hand.

"Reprimand?"

Yes, a reprimand.

"Will you demand it?"

Yes, I will demand a reprimand for– Wait a second, I see what you're doing. I will have no more of your word play!

"Yes, sir."

Consider this a warning. Any more rhyming, homonyms, alliteration, puns or portmanteaus, well... you know what will happen.

"Yes. Very admirable of you Admiral."

Hm...

"Yes?"

I'm leaving now.

"See you on the other side, sir."

That was...

"Yes?"

That was some kind of a haiku, wasn't it?

"Not at all."

You're skating on thin ice. I'm watching you.

securomax 76

"Hello, I'm looking for a new home security computer system."

All home security systems are run by computers these days.

"What's your point?"

You didn't have to add 'computer' in there. Redundant and repetitive.

"So was that?"

So was what?

"Never mind, I was trying to be specific to help you out, but forget it.
        I need a new security system."

Home or business?

"I just said home!"

No you didn't.

"The first time, when I also said computer."

You should have left that part in, it narrows things down significantly.

"That's exactly why I..."

So, you're looking for a new home security system?

"Exactly. Although, now that I think of it I kind of run my business
        from home... so would you consider a home office as a business?
        You know, as far as security goes."

That's a tough one. What kind of windows do you have?

"None."

Oh, uh... doors?

"Sliding rock slab in the front, drainable lake in the back."

You live in a cave?

"Oh no! No, of course not, I meant... the house. The house part. You
know regular windows, regular doors. Nothing unusual at all."

Great.

"But whatever we pick out will work on a sliding rock slab and a
drainable lake too, right?"

Uh sure... home models are very versatile.

"Good to know."

Did you have any particular model in mind?

"I've read good things about the Securomax 76."

Oh you don't want that.

"Why the devil not?"

How secure do you want to be on a scale of 1 to 10?

"Well a ten obviously."

Obviously. The Securomax 76 will get you about a three, my friend.

"But the reviews..."

Trust me. What you want is one of these systems.

"Okay, tell me about them."

First, the Securomax 80.

"Oh, that must be better than the 76."

Four better. You get motion sensors, electromagnetic deadbolt locks,
and sonic deterrence.

"Wow, that sounds amazing."

It sounds terrible.

"What?"

Compared to this next system. The IntruderDeath.

"That's a bit harsh."

Harsh. But secure as Hell.

"What does it do?"

It kills any intruders. It's right in the name.

"Look, I have the worst luck with these things. I don't want to end up
dead myself. Plus I'm not a real big fan of killing."

Listen, mister...

"Eradicator."

Mister Eradicator, is feeling safe at night knowing you and your family
are completely protected from all the dangers of this dangerous

world important to you?

"I don't have a family."

Then accidental death is a risk you'll have to take to make that level of
security possible.

"Yeah, I don't think so."

Suit yourself. This next system is the perfect fit for you anyway.

"Let's hear it."

The Confusory LT LT.

"What does the LT mean?"

Light.

"And the second one?"

Lite.

"The Confusory Light Light?"

Yes.

"That's confusing."

Exactly.

"So I assume it involves something with a light?"

Kind of.

"And another light?"

The second LT stands for lite. L-i-t-e, you know, like a stripped down
version.

"Why would I want a stripped down version? Show me the Confusory
Light Whole, or whatever you might call it."

Oh no, the Full Confusory Light is only for the most paranoid
customers. Plus it just might make your head explode. I can
hardly wrap my head around it myself, and I have to sell the
damn thing.

"I see. Tell me more about this model."

It's hard to explain. It would be much easier to just show you.

"Show me then."

Unfortunately we don't have an demo hooked up here in the store.

"I need some kind of security today, I leave for vacation tonight. Just
give me the Securomax 80."

No no no, here's what I'll do for you. I'll demonstrate the system at your
home. Full install. If you like it, it's ready to go. If you don't like

it, I'll take it out and you don't pay a dime. Sound good?
"You promise this thing is the real deal?"
Absolutely.
"Fine, I'll do it."
Excellent choice Mister Eradicator.

highered

"Hi, I'm here for an interview."
Ah yes, I've been expecting you! Come with me.
"No problem."
Hey, are you okay?
"I'm fine, I just hit my head in the elevator is all."
Good Golly Miss Molly! That must hurt like the Dickens.
"My name isn't Molly. I'm not even a girl."
It's just a song.
"What song?"
You know. Nananana Good Golly na naaa Miss Molly, nurnana
        nurnooo...
"I haven't heard the song, but I'm pretty sure that isn't how it goes."
Let's get you some ice for that.
"That's not necessary, I'll be okay."
Nonsense! We take great care of our employees here.
"But I'm not an employee yet."
Great news, you're hired! Now where did I put those plastic baggies...
"Really? Just like that?"
Of course!
"When is my first day?"
How soon can you start?
"Uh, well... I didn't really have anything planned after this interview, so
        today I suppose."
Great! Let's get you some ice and we'll send you out to the floor for
        training.
"Wow, this is incredible. Thank you so much!"
No problem. I was impressed with your résumé and you have a com-
        manding yet soothing voice.

"Okay… Thanks."

For Pete's sake, I swear I had a stash of sandwich baggies right here. Right here in this drawer.

"It's okay, my head doesn't even hurt anymore."

Are you sure? That could just be the endorphins from the good news.

"Nope, I'm healthy as a whore."

Excuse me?

"I meant horse. I'm as healthy as a horse. Sorry, I'm a little bit nervous still."

No need to be nervous anymore, relax!

"Yes, I'd love to get in there and dig in."

I like your go-getter attitude. Oh here we go, this should work.

"For...?"

The ice, of course.

"That's an ash tray."

Ash tray, ice dish, it's all just semantics. Here...

"I don't think this is going to work."

We'll just set the edge against your head like so...

"I really don't..."

And flip it real fast!

"Ouch!"

Sorry, that was a bit too fast. But there you go, your wounds are all dressed and you're ready to get started.

"So, is Research and Development on this floor?"

Indeed, but you'll be heading back down to G1.

"What's on G1?"

That's our call center.

"What? I thought I was interviewing for a position in Research and Development!"

Oh goodness, I'm sorry, I didn't mean to mislead you or anything.

"I feel a little deceived, but a job is a job I guess. What kind of call center is it?"

Emergency dispatch.

"That actually sounds kind of interesting. At least it isn't tech support."

Oh it is very interesting. Interesting and important.

"Is there opportunity to grow within the company? Transfer to other
        departments?"

Sure, sure. We can talk about that later. For now, let's get you down
        there and on the phone.

"I'll be taking calls today?"

Of course, what better way to learn than to get right in the thick of it?

"I..."

You'll be fine, I can see it in your eyes. You're a natural operator. We'll
        be in touch.

"Thanks again."

Take care. And whatever you do, don't jump when you reach the bottom
        floor, it can really mess you up.

"I didn't jump, I just..."

It's okay, we all do it. Good luck.

getaway

"DRIVE! GO! GO! GO!"

Where are the custard pies?

"It didn't work out. Let's go!"

What do you mean it didn't work?

"It's complicated."

All you had to do is go in the bakery, flash the gun, grab a stack of pies,
        and come back out. What could have possibly gone wrong?

"They knew the gun wasn't real."

Impossible! I spray-painted it black and everything.

"They saw it dripping."

They... what?

"Well, it's a water gun. Water guns always drip at the wrong time!"

Why did you even put water in it?

"Because it's a water gun!"

So?

"What if something happened?"

Like a tiny fire? A cat tearing the drapes? Wicked witch attack? Idiot.

"You should have said something before..."

I thought it was kind of obvious. I knew it was a mistake to let you be the one to go inside.

"Well at least I'm not a jerk when you come back to the van. That reminds me, Mom gave us a grocery list."

How did being a jerk remind you of the grocery list?

"Jerk spice. It's the second thing on the list."

What the Hell is jerk spice?

"I think it's like posh spice, but even more of a diva."

...

"Don't look at me like that."

Damn it. Alright, give me the gun.

"What are you doing?"

I'm going into that grocery store up ahead and robbing it right.

"I guess I'm back to being 'the sit-in-the-van' guy."

Just be ready when I come back out, alright? Hand over the list.

"Here."

Holy... there are about forty things on here!

"You'll need a cart."

Obviously.

"Won't that be a bit awkward?"

You let me worry about that, Drippy.

"Don't call me that!"

Are you crying? Just what I'd expect from Drippy.

"You know I have a bed wetting problem."

Oh yeah... Sorry, I was only referring to the water g–

"Go get the groceries so we can get on with the job."

Don't cry too hard while I'm gone.

"Shut up."

Hey Greg, come here!

"It's Greg."

I know, I said Greg.

"Oh sorry."

Feast your eyes on this beauty!

"It's a circle."

Not just **any** circle, a **rock** circle.

"Let me guess, you call it that because it's a circle made of rock."

Exactly.

"You should think of a better name."

We'll discuss that later.

"Oh, that's good! Discus!"

It's pronounced 'disc-uss.'

"No, I mean we can call it a discus. We can throw it at things."

Why do you always want to throw everything I make?

"What can I say, your creations typically lend themselves to be thrown."

Forget it, we're not throwing it, and we're not calling it a discuss.

"Discus. So what's the point if we can't throw it?"

Look at it, it's a **perfect** circle! I was just hacking away at some limestone not even thinking, and wham! Perfection.

"You're absolutely right... you carved this freehand?"

Don't you know it.

"Wow that is actually really impressive. What were you thinking of using it for?"

I was thinking I'd just hang it up over the mantle in my cave... Oh don't look, it's them again.

"Who?"

I said don't look!

"Is that some kind of cart?"

Son of a... They stole my rock circle idea!

"Such a stupid name."

Hey you Neanderthals! Hold it, what do you think you're doing?

"Ben, take it easy, you know they can't understand us."

This is ours. OURS. Give it! Now off with you, and learn to speak
      English already!

"That was kind of harsh."

They stole my rock circle idea, Greg. I couldn't let them just walk off
      with this... this...

"Cart."

Right. If anyone asks, we came up with it. But now that I look at it, these
      aren't rock circles...

"Looks like wood."

Guess we can't really call them rock circles after all.

"Surely we can't call them plain old circles."

We have to think of something good. Really good.

"Hmmm..."

Really, really good.

"That's it!"

What?

"Really!"

Really what?

"Really."

You didn't say anything.

"**REALLY**."

Yes, really, now what's your idea for the name?

"Really."

I swear, if you say 'really' one more time, I'm gonna–

"Nooo, we should call them 'reallys'!"

What? Really?

"Really!"

That's stupid. Really is already a real word.

"Really?"

Yes really.

"Oh, obviously. So we need a not real word."

Right.

"Real word. Real word. Word real. Word wood real… Wor... wooreal...
      Wreal... weal!"

Great! But, we can't spell it like that.

"Spell?"

Oh that's right, we can't read or write yet... add that to my to-do list!

"Like the dog?"

No, you're thinking Toto.

"So... like the rock band?"

That's also Toto.

"What are you talking about then?"

To-do list. As in a list of things to do.

"Ohhhh, okay. But how am I supposed to do that if I can't write?"

Shoot.

red, why? not blue

You wanted to see me, Commander?

"Yes."

What can I do for you?

"You've done quite enough already, Lieutenant."

I don't know what you're–

"You know exactly what I'm talking about!"

I–

"We have a mission in less than a week! What are those clowns in inventory doing?"

Every single item requested has been ordered and received, sir!

"Think again. Someone messed up. Big time."

Oh my God, please don't shoot me, I won't let it happen again!

"I'm not going to shoot you, I'm showing you the… Look. Blue. BLUE. **BLUE** lasers?"

Is that a problem?

"You're damn right it's a problem! We use **RED** lasers. It always has been and always will be that way."

Are the red lasers more powerful than the blue lasers, or...

"They're exactly the same in every way except for color."

Then why does it matter?

"The Consolate uses red lasers, and we use blue lasers. It's the law. Simple as that."

Why red?

"They got to pick and chose blue."

That's a shame. Red is just so... angry.

"Regardless, if we get caught using blue lasers I'll be court martialed, damn it! A war criminal for your stupid mistake. You wouldn't want me to get court martialed, would you?"

No, of course not. I'm sorry, Commander, it won't happen again.

"This is your only warning, Lieutenant. Ship these guns back to the factory and make it right."

Yes, sir. But won't that mean we won't have any defenses?

"Temporarily, but so what? We're technically inactive until we leave for battle. In fact, I've ordered a couple of grunts to wash the ship while we're waiting. We can't go anywhere until they're done anyway. Nonetheless, make it quick. The sparkling clean hull may catch the Consulate's attention."

What if they won't take them back?

"Don't be ridiculous, of course they'll take them back!"

But we're at least seven star systems away from their nearest warehouse. They're bound to charge us for the shipping.

"Shipping can't be **that** much."

If we did overnight it could wipe out our entire budget for the rest of the month.

"Then don't ship it overnight."

Right. So... second day?

"Yes, second day, that's fine. Whatever it takes."

Whatever it takes except for overnight.

"Except for overnight."

What abo–

"That's enough, go get this mess sorted out already."

Yes, sir. So I'm ordering... Blue lasers?

"No! We already have blue lasers, get the red lasers! We use the **RED** lasers!"

going down

Hello again. Floor?

"G1 please."

How was the interview?

"Not bad. He hired me, so that's nice."

Oh good for you! Welcome to the company!

"Yeah. I'll be working in the call center."

Oh... that's rough. I'm sorry.

"Why sorry?"

Never mind. Hey, you look a lot sweatier than you were on the way up. You alright?

"Sweaty? Oh no, it's just melted ice."

You mean water?

"Yeah, water."

And what's with the yarmulke?

"It's an ash tray."

Do I even want to ask what you did to get the job...

"Oh, no! No. What? NO. I can't even begin to imagine what kind of mental image you're conjuring."

Something to do with role play.

"Oh God, I can't believe... Have you seen that guy? Not a handsome man by any measure. Not that being handsome would make it any better. Just no. Nothing like that happened or ever will happen. No, no, never, no."

This coming from the guy who enjoyed the expellent retention system so much...

"The what system?"

The funnel and hose.

"Oh that... That stays between us."

I dunno, you're gonna have to take that up with the security camera.

"What?! No! That can't..."

I'm just playing, it's fake. I put that there to keep people from doing embarrassing things in front of me. Not like it worked at all.

"Sorry, it was just so... nice, you know?"

I'm not going to dignify that with a response.

"I'm just sayin'... So, he said I shouldn't jump at the bottom."

You have no idea. We had to scrape up the last guy who tried that. Splattered like pancake batter.

"That's terrible!"

That's why I bring this with me, just in case.

"A spatula?"

I call it mah spatch. No stick coating, lifts guts like nobody's business.

"I think I'm going to..."

Quick! The expellent retention system!

"BLRRGGHHH!"

See, this is what the expellent retention system was built for.

"BLLLRGH!"

Oh, you missed a little bit. The spatch is perfect for this. I'll just collect it all in one puddle and...

"BLLLLLRGH!"

Come on, it's not that gross is it? Actually now that I'm right down next to you, the smell is just... give it here, give it here!

"I can't..."

BLLLLRGH!

"What did you eat today? BLLLRRGH!"

Salmon and– BLRRRRGH!

"Why are you still trying to use the spatula to– BLRRGH!"

The texture is just so fasci– BLLRGH! Oh, here's your floor.

"Ugh, finally. Do you have a towel or something?"

What do I look like, a bathroom attendant?

"Is there a bathroom on this floor?"

We'll have to go back up to G8.

"No thanks! I'll just go outside and find a hose."

Suit yourself. Good luck with the new job!

"Thanks. You should maybe clean up a bit yourself."

Nah, don't worry about me, I'm used to it.

"That's..."

Disturbing? Yes. But at least I don't work in the call center.

"What?"

Er... Nothing! Take care!

groceries

"Can I help you find anything?"

Yeah, where are the pies?

"Two aisles that'a'way!"

Thanks.

"Anything else I can help you with?"

There is one other thing...

"Oh my God, don't shoot me!"

If you want to live, you're going to do exactly what I say. Understood?

"Y-yes..."

My demands are simple.

"I have children!"

Keep your hands where I can see them!

"I'm just getting my wallet, look"

Oh God, don't show me pictures of them.

"There's Wally the Wanderer, Princess Rene, Mr. Gingersnap..."

Those are cats!

"They're my children!"

My demands are simple. I made a list.

"This is just a grocery list."

That's right. Now, we're going to walk around the store all nice-like.

"Okay..."

You're going to put all these items in my cart, walk me to my van, help
        me load up and I'll be on my way. Got it?

"Whatever it to keep you from shooting me."

Don't try any funny business and you'll be fine.

"Okay! Wow this is a really long list. This will probably take a while."

Are you complaining? Because mister bang bang doesn't like whiners.

"No, I was just... Sorry, I'll get started."

Where are you going?

"Over here to get the soda."

We're picking up the pies first!

"Pies aren't even on your list..."

The pies are more important than any list!

"But I'm standing right next to the lime soda."

Fine, grab the soda, but **then** the pie.

"Alright, lime soda. Check. What's jerk spice?"

I have no idea.

"Then why did you even put it on–"

Pie! Now!

"You're the boss."

Aren't you forgetting something?

"What?"

The cart.

"I have to push the cart too?"

I can't push this cart and keep the gun on you at the same time.

"What's wrong with this cart?"

Look at that wheel. It just does whatever the Hell it wants. It's spinning around endlessly. This might be a perpetual motion device.

"You're pushing it wrong."

I'm not even touching it!

"That's the... uh.. roaming feature..."

Roaming is for cell phones not shopping carts. You need some new hardware.

"Hey, did you... *wet yourself*?"

What? Why are you whispering?

"*You have a wet spot around your...*"

Oh crap, I knew I should have emptied it out the window...

"Emptied what out the window?"

None of your business, shut up and start pushin'!

"That's a water pistol, isn't it?"

What? No! What kind of idiot do you think I am? Look, no dripping.

"What about when you pull the trigger?"

Yeah, see, look, if this was a water pistol it would be squirting water at you right now.

"But if it were real, it would be squirting bullets!"

Gotta go.

ughriculture

"Hey, what're you doing with that stick?"

What does it look like I'm doing?

"It looks like you're defiling Mother Earth."

You idiot, I'm sowing seeds!

"That's one huge needle. Where's your thread?"

Sowing, not sewing...

"You just said the same thing twice."

No, I distinctly said sowing, not sewing.

"I hear no difference whatsoever."

Oh never mind! Would you hand me that there?

"Hand you what where?"

That there.

"I don't see anything. My foot?"

You're standing right in it.

"Oh come on, how could you let me step in poop?"

It's not poop, it's manure.

"It's most definitely poop."

Please, Greg, let's be civilized. It's manure, which acts as fertilizer for
the seeds I'm sowing. Would you give me a handful?

"I want to puke from just stepping in it, there's no way I'm picking it
up!"

What if I gave you permission to throw it?

"Now that could be fun– No, you can't trick me! Pick up your own
poop."

Fine, be that way. I'm just trying to bring a little culture into your life.

"More like bringing microbial culture into my life. This is festering with
germs and bacteria."

Don't bring microbial culture into this. Without it I couldn't make the
yogurt you love so dearly!

"Yogurt is made with bacteria?"

Of course.

"I'm going to be sick. I just got done eating a cup of it. Strawberry."

The strawberries aren't made with bacteria.

"But they're an accomplice!"

Get over it and hand me some manure.

"Where did you even come up with this idea?"

Some guy told me.

"What guy?"

Some guy, he stopped by a while ago and said I should give this a try.

"And you went along with it? What'd he look like?"

Oh I dunno... clean cut, snazzy clothes, kind of attractive really...

"Whoa, I don't mean like that."

All I'm saying is that he could probably have any woman he wanted.

"Have you seen our women? They're hairier than we are. ANYONE could have any woman they wanted. Even if they're unwilling it's simply a matter of clubbing and dragging."

Good point.

"So this guy, was he one of us? Or a Neanderthal?"

Well kind of like us, but more... evolved.

"Evolved?"

Yeah.

"What does evolved mean?"

No idea. His word.

"Where'd he come from?"

The Future, wherever that is. I think it's twenty miles South of here, over the mountains.

"Strange. I've never heard of this Future place."

He said we could grow our own food just like this. No more gathering.

"But we'll still have to hunt?"

Oh yeah, we'll definitely still have to hunt.

"If you see him again ask him about the hunting. I hate hunting."

Really? Even with the flaming spears?

"I always take too long to aim so the flame reaches my hand before I can throw. You know what, how about a flaming discus?"

We already talked about this, we're NOT throwing the weal.

"Still haven't figured out a better way to spell it?"

Oh yeah, inventing reading and writing... I thought I asked you to add that to my to-do list.

"I can't write a to-do list when I can't even write to begin with."

No excuses. What do I even pay you for?

"You don't pay me."

Sure I do.

"Chocolate puffs can hardly be considered payment."

Those weren't chocolate puffs.

"What?"

Yeah, that was fertilizer.

"**WHAT?**"

Deer droppings are high in nitrogen, great for cultivating crops.

"**I ATE THOSE!**"

Oh...

"Mixed into a bowl of yogurt..."

With strawberries?

"Yes with strawberries! I'm going to be sick."

Since you're going to throw up anyway, hand me that manure.

gamma raid

"Thank you for calling All Things Laz-ey, your one-stop shop for the galaxy's finest stimulated emissions."

Good afternoon, I need to return a few laser guns.

"They broken?"

No.

"Lose the war before they got there?"

No.

"Why do you need to send them back, then?"

The equipment isn't defective or anything, it's just that they're blue.

"So?"

What do you mean, so?

"What's the big deal? All the lasers are exactly the same."

Only the Consolate is allowed to use blue lasers, didn't you know that?

"Of course, I'm in the laser business, fellah."

Don't fellah me, buddy.

"Don't buddy me, chief."

Don't chief me, pal.

"Hey, HEY now, this is getting out of hand."

All I need is to ship these blue lasers back and get red ones instead.

"Oh, is that all?"

Yes, that's all. When can I expect those red lasers? I'll be postmarking
       the blue lasers lat–

"No need, you already have red lasers."

What are you talking about? I just told you I have blue lasers. Five
       thousand blue lasers.

"Like I said before, all the lasers are exactly the same."

No, these are blue. I need red. **RED**.

"If you took the time to read the user's manual included with each gun
       you would notice that the factory default setting is blue, but is
       customizable by the consumer."

You're kidding me.

"There should be a small dial near the trigger. Just grab a small coin to
       turn it to the left and you're all set for red laser fun."

I'll be damned.

"You're welcome."

Why would you make these guns dual color like this?

"Economics. We can make guns for both sides using only one assembly
       line. Half the factories, half the workers, half the cost. We pass
       the savings on to you."

We appreciate that.

"Our competitors waste their time specializing in either blue or red
       lasers, but here at All Things Laz-ey we cater to all walks of life
       from all corners of the galaxy."

Good to know.

"No siree, our products range from the lasers used to read compact discs,
       to masers used to flash-cook tv dinners, to grasers used to blow
       up planets and stars."

Excuse me?

"Masers used to flash-cook tv dinners."

No, the last thing about blowing up planets and stars. There's something
       that can do that?

"Er, no."

You just said.

"I didn't... I mean, I may have, but it's all part of the pitch. We don't
    really have that..."

Why would you say it then?

"Alright, to be honest I slipped and mentioned the grasers since we've
    already sold a bunch of them today."

To who?

"The Consulate."

The Consulate has weapons that can blow up stars and planets?!

"Yes."

Good gravy, can I get some of those grasers?

"Sure, why not?"

Atta'boy, we'll take twenty.

"Uh… You should probably go with just two."

Why?

"They're pretty big."

How big?

"Really big."

How big is really big?

"Really pretty big."

We'll take two then.

"Great. I'll just enter that order into the computer here..."

Now just to make sure, what color are the grasers?

"What do you mean?"

I just want to make sure I'm getting the right colored grasers so we don't
    have a whole wrong color debacle again.

"Gamma rays are invisible to the human eye."

Ah, I see.

"No, you don't see. That's the point."

Right. So I shouldn't have any problems then?

"Nope. Would you like these shipped next day?"

How much will that cost?

"$38,000 space dollars."

WHAT? That's ridiculous! How much is second day?

"Free."

Are you kidding? I'll take second day shipping. Why do you even offer next day?

"You know people these days, they'll pay anything for instant gratification. You'll get the grasers around next Wednesday."

What? That's like six days, not two!

"We ship them on the second day. After that it's anyone's guess how long they'll actually take to arrive."

Just ship them right now!

"Sure, that'll be next day shipping."

But doesn't that mean you'll ship them tomorrow?

"Oh no, you'll **get** them tomorrow."

That's kind of inconsistent.

"What do you mean?"

One shipping type is named for when I'll receive the shipment, the other is named for when the shipment leaves your facility.

"What would you suggest?"

Call the second day shipping 'sometime next week' shipping and you'll cut out a lot of misunderstandings.

"That doesn't really sound that appealing though."

Well, it isn't an appealing shipping option to begin with. You might as well be up front by having a more accurate name for it.

"It is free though."

Oh yeah... You know, my Commander probably won't be happy with me spending $38,000 just on shipping. Let's go ahead and do the sometime next week shipping option.

"You mean second day shipping."

I refuse to call it that.

"Alright, now I just need a shipping address."

PO Box 3711–

"We can't deliver this to a PO Box."

Why not?

"Do you have any idea how big grasers are?"

Really pretty big.

"Exactly. These suckers weigh over a ton each."

That's a measurement of mass, not volume.

"They're big, alright? Really big."

Really pretty big.

"Exactly."

I'll give you the our direct address, but we better not get any junk mail.

"We don't share our customers' information with anyone."

Yeah, companies always say that but–

"I assure you."

Alright, it'll be Cargo Bay 48, Starship Syrinx, Earth Navy.

"I have no idea where that is."

Exactly, that's why I wanted you to send it to our PO Box, then the post office can teleport it to us.

"Why don't we just teleport it directly to you?"

You can do that?

"Of course."

Why didn't you tell me that in the first place?

"You never asked. All I need is your teleporter's IP address."

Great, I have that right here... it's 53.

"53?"

It's an old teleporter.

"Ancient."

That's only the teleporter in cargo bay... We have three other shiny new teleporters throughout the rest of the ship.

"Yeah, sure."

The ship is mostly brand new, alright?

"Mmm-hmm."

Okay, mostly new. New-ish."

"I'm not judging. The grasers should be showing up in your teleporter in the next ten minutes."

Great, how much is that going to cost us?

"You know what, I feel bad that your teleporter is so old, how's a hundred space dollars sound?"

I disagree with the reasoning, but I accept your offer. Go ahead and charge our account.

"It was great doing business with you today. Thank you for being a valued All Things Laz-ey customer."

You're welcome.

"I'm looking for the call center."

Why are you all wet?

"Long story."

I hate long stories, skip it. You the new guy?

"Yes."

You're in the right place. Here's our handbook. Also, sign all this.

"What is it?"

HR stuff. Don't worry about reading it. Alright, let's get you trained.

"Okay, do you have a pen?"

You can sign that stuff later. Now pay attention, take notes if you need.

"Great, I just need a pen."

I told you, sign that stuff later.

"I know, I need it for notes... never mind."

Here's your workstation. Computer. Keyboard. Mouse. Phone. Simple
        as that. Are you writing this down?

"No, I don't have a pen."

Eh, don't worry about it, we're almost done anyway.

"What do I do?"

It's easy. You'll figure it out.

"Don't I need a headset?"

Oh, here you go. You just need to sign this other paper here agreeing that
        you will pay 70 dollars if you lose it.

"I need a pen."

Look, I don't like lending people my pen, alright? Nobody ever gives it
        back. Or they put it in their mouth. Disgusting.

"Okay, I guess I'll sign this later."

That's the spirit. If you have any problems or questions just raise your
        hand and a supervisor will come over to help you. Good luck.

"Alright."

Why are you holding your hand up like that?

"I have more questions."

No, no, you'll figure it out. Just get started and before long you'll be
        rolling with the best of them.

"How much am I getting paid?"

Answers to questions like that are all in the handbook. I should leave
you to it. I have a meeting to attend.

"Okay, I'll take a few minutes to read all this first..."

No reading on the clock. You can read about that rule in the policies
section.

"I'm not on the clock yet."

You should be! Go auto-in, quick!

"What does that mean?"

It means to auto... in. You know. Auto-in. It's a word.

"I don't think it is."

You'll learn our lingo. The handbook has a glossary.

"It looks like almost the entire thing is a glossary."

We love our synonyms.

"POO?"

Pride. Oratory. Outstanding. It's our motto. Show us your POO.

"That's..."

Don't question the handbook. I need to go, the meeting calls. I don't get
paid the mad bucks for nothing.

"Don't you get paid to train employees?"

I just did. You'll be fine. Just remember the call flow structure.

"What's that?"

It's taped right there on your computer monitor.

"This is a scroll."

Keeps things nice and tidy when not in use. We like to keep things tidy.
Not sanitary though, don't confuse the terms.

"A really, really long scroll."

That's right, 76 easy to remember steps for efficient call flow. Follow
this and your callers will be putty in your hands.

"That seems like a lot of things to remember."

We have people who research these things. It works, trust me. Putty
in your hands! And remember, if you skip any steps you can't
qualify for bonus pay or extra time.

"I'm not really interested in over time."

No, it's not over time. It's extra time. It's a good thing. And you want
your bonus don't you? Without extra time you can't get the

production hours you need to qualify for bonus pay.

"How would I get extra time then?"

You have to sign up for it. But you can only do that if you qualify.

"Qualify?"

You have to meet your production hours.

"But you said I can't meet my production hours unless I have extra time."

It makes sense. Just read the handbook.

"Alright."

Don't read it right now. Call volume is in the red and we need you on the phone. Go get 'em tiger!

which switch

Mister Eradicator, the Confusory LT LT is installed.

"Great, let's see it in action."

All you do to arm the system is a single clap like so...

"So far so good."

Then you have ten seconds to clear the entryway before it's activated.

"Great, simple enough. What just happened?"

It's on.

"The lights turned off."

Exactly. How is anyone supposed to rob a house if they can't see?

"They can just flip the light switch though."

Ah ha, that's the genius of the Confusory LT LT. Give the light switch a try.

"Wait a second, there are hundreds of them!"

Yeap.

"So which switch is which?"

Try that one.

"Which one?"

Any of them.

"Nothing."

Try the one next to it.

"Still nothing."

Try another.

"None of them work! Okay, maybe this one will..."

You see, when the Confuser LT LT is activated, none of the switches
work. The computer detects when more than one switch toggle
takes place and contacts the authorities. The criminal will be
kept occupied trying to find the correct switch long enough for
police to arrive and arrest the perpetrator.

"That's genius. But how do I disarm it?"

Clap twice like so.

"Nothing happened."

The system disarmed.

"Shouldn't it have turned on the lights?"

You still have to use the light switch to do that.

"But the clap to arm turned the lights off."

Right.

"So..."

I don't follow.

"Shouldn't deactivating the system turn the lights back on?"

No, you can just use the switch.

"Oh. Okay, now which switch do I use when it isn't armed?"

Any of them.

"Now wait a second, I don't think robbers even turn on lights when they
break into a place."

Sure they do. Strange new environment in the dark? Might as well be a
mine field. Every piece of furniture lies in wait, just aching for
the opportunity to take someone out. No, lights are the first thing
any robber needs for a robbery. Safety first, robbers especially.
They don't get workman's comp you know.

"I guess I could see that."

So we have a deal?

"What kind of return policy do you have?"

I've never had anyone return their security system, so I'm not sure.

"Good enough for me."

You won't be disappointed. If you are, you can come back and beat me
up. But really, please don't beat me up. Or at least take off those
metal gloves you're wearing when you do.

"They're gauntlets."

A gauntlet is a type of glove, no need to correct me.

"I'll correct your face."

Whoa, whoa, whoa! I'm gonna get going. Enjoy the Confusor LT LT.

"You better hope I do."

detail detail

"How does the Commander expect us to wash this thing? It's at least a
    mile long."

Not to mention the girth.

"We're gonna need a really long hose."

Yeah.

"Do we even have any hoses?"

The greenhouse deck might have some.

"I hate the guys on the greenhouse deck. 'Oh look at me, I grow veg-
    etables, you should worship me because you have baby corn and
    tomatoes.' What about in the janitor's closet?"

Looked in there on the way out here. Nothin'.

"Well shoot, what are we supposed to do?"

How about this, we find a planet made entirely out of soapy water...

"Yeah..."

Then a planet made entirely out of clean water to rinse.

"I gotcha."

And end with a planet made of chamois cloth.

"You forgot the planet to sanitize! Wait, what am I even saying, that
    whole idea is ridiculous. How about we feed the Commander
    images of the ship from right after we left the port?"

Genius! But we'll have to hack into the main frame for that.

"Oh, I've got a guy..."

What're you doing?

"Morse code, don't want the bridge catching on."

Of course.

"Mmm-hmm, yeah yeah I see, excellent..."

What's he saying?

"Spaghetti and meatballs for dinner in the mess hall."

No, about hacking into the mainframe!

"Right, sorry. I love spaghetti and meatballs."

It's fine.

"Especially when they use oregano. Delightful. Sprinkle a little bit of parmesan on top, real Parmesan not that powdery crap. Maybe some baby corn on the side–"

Mainframe! Hack! Images!

"Sorry again, I just really love sp–"

Ask him already!

"Okay he says he'll have it tapped in within the next five minutes. Just in time to head to the mess hall for some oh so delicious Italian cuisine."

Fantastic, now we just sit back and wait?

"Yeap."

What's that sound?

"Sounds like the alarm system."

Do you think...

"Hold on, I'm getting another Morse code message."

Yeah?

"He says he set off the alarm system, they know it was him, and he's being taken to the brig."

How is he–

"Shush! Oh that's a relief."

What?

"Spaghetti is still on and they're bringing him a bowl of it. How nice of them. You know, the cooks down in the brig are actually pretty nice–"

Enough! What are we supposed to do now?

"I guess we should actually clean the ship. What about limes?"

Limes?

"I heard we have a massive surplus of limes since nobody on the crew likes them except the Commander. The citrus acid is great for cleaning rusty steel."

That sounds perfect! Let's get the limes out here.

"We'll have to wear protective clothing because of the acid."

We're already wearing space suits.

"Oh right. We're all set to go then. I'll just send a text to Bob in the mess
hall to let him know we need those limes..."

You better not be–

"He says this is the best batch of spaghetti and meatballs he's made yet!
Spaghetti sauce made with fresh tomatoes and spices..."

Come on!

"And fresh baby corn! Yes!"

Limes! Limes! Limes!

"Why would I lie abotu spaghetti?"

No, liMMMMMes!

"Right, sorry, I just–"

Love spaghetti, I know. The sooner we get this ship clean, the sooner we
can go inside and eat.

"He's sending out the limes now."

Great, it's about t–AAHHHH!

"What are you doing?"

How was I supposed to know he would send them out of the bay I was
holding on to! Quick, we have to grab these limes before they
drift off into space.

"I probably should have asked for them in a bag."

You think?

dumbesticated

"Ah! Wolf! Wolf! Kill it!"

Calm down, it's perfectly safe.

"How do you expect me to calm down? There's a wild animal sitting on
   your lap!"

Remember what you said about hunting?

"No."

The other day, when I was planting seeds I said we wouldn't have to
   gather anymore, you asked if we would still have to hunt.

"Oh yeah, hunting is so stupid and time consuming. I'd much rather
   gather than hunt any day."

Well now we won't need to hunt either!

"Is that so?"

Oh yeah, I saw that handsome guy again and asked him what we could
   do about the whole hunting situation.

"He told you to put a wolf on your lap? Right next to your business..."

He told me how to domesticate animals.

"Of course! That's so obvious. We raise the wolf here in the cave, then
   eat it whenever we want!"

What? No! We're not eating Ralphie!

"Obviously we can't now that you've named him."

Yeah, isn't he the cutest?

"Is that a rabbit leg hanging out of his mouth?"

Oh yeah! Want some rabbit? I had to let him have his fair share.

"Wait, so we're not eating the wolf?"

Ralphie.

"So we're not eating Ralphie?"

Nope, he'll be doing the hunting for us. Isn't that wonderful?

"How can you trust him?"

He's domesticated!

"If he's domesticated, does he still have his cunning animal instincts?"

Uh, maybe.

"The instincts that allow him to track and kill even the wiliest of
   prey?"

I'm sure his instincts are in his noggin somewhere.

"And how will we know he doesn't just kill something, eat it out there, then come back and pretend he didn't find anything?"

We'll have to go out with him.

"What? What's the point of having him hunt for us if we still have to go out and supervise?"

It could be fun. We can play games with him and stuff while we're looking for prey.

"What kind of games?"

I dunno... fetch?

"That's not a word."

Sure it is, it means to bring something back after it has been thrown.

"You're just making this up as you go aren't you."

No!

"So what can we throw to him?"

A stick?

"I don't think he's fast enough to catch a stick."

He doesn't have to catch it, he can just pick it up off the ground.

"That's boring. I want to see him jump in the air and catch something."

There has to be something that doesn't fall down as fast as a stick.

"Leaves?"

You're an idiot.

"I know, the discus!"

We've been over this a hundred time, it's called a weal, and we're NOT going to throw it.

"Come on, you haven't found any other use for it."

Hmm.

"Let's just try it."

Fine. But if it doesn't work we're never to speak of throwing the weal again, okay?

"Deal. Bring Ralphie outside, I'll grab the discus."

Weal.

"Here Ralphie, here boy! See the discus?"

Weal. Ralphie, it's a weal.

"Go get it!"

Oh wow, that flies pretty well.

"And look at that! He caught it!"

I've gotta admit, pretty good idea.

"I told you! Good boy, Ralphie!"

Let me try! Go get it!

"Oh! It hit him in the head..."

Crap!

"Is he okay?"

He's unconscious.

"Maybe we shouldn't use the discus made of stone. Should we call a vet or something?"

He's the first domesticated animal, there's no such thing as a vet yet.

"Now is a good time to become one. I think he might need stitches. You should go get your sewing equipment."

Wrong kind of sowing.

holy water

Good sesh, Luke.

"Not so bad yourself old man. I was holding back a little at the end."

Bull, I saw you struggling. Did your tail cramp up?

"You know I don't use my tail for swimming! That wouldn't be fair."

Since when do you care about being fair?

"Me? Not fair? Last time I checked Heaven was harder than Hell to get into."

That's limbo department's fault.

"It's not like you make it any easier. You know I got a guy who got sent to Hell because he fell off a toilet. What's with that?"

Oh yeah, Pete was telling me all about it. Guy took forever and a day to accept that he died. I guess I should take a second look at our embarrassing death policy...

"No kidding. You could stand to be a little more lenient. some people die for peanuts these days!"

Food allergies build character.

"And it builds the crowds of souls lining up to complain that they died for a stupid reason and got sent to Hell for it. It's not my fault they suck at limbo. Don't get me wrong, I'll take the sould but I could do without the whining."

You made that toilet guy your assistant, didn't you?

"Yeah, so?"

Have him deal with them.

"He has enough on his plate, most of his day is spent dousing souls with lighter fluid."

Oh what the Hell, Luke? That's cruel.

"Would you rather deal with all those souls?"

Sure. They would never complain in Heaven.

"Maybe, but sure as Hell all your perfect angels would start complaining that they're trashing the place."

Nah, I don't think that would happen.

"Hey, let's ah, continue this conversation later."

What, why?

"I have a rule. Don't make conversation or eye contact with anyone while nude."

Oh I didn't know, so–

"Ah ah ah, a response creates a conversation. I'm about to slide off my trunks, so anything we say from here out must be stand alone statements. If we work together we can get through this without incident."

So, it's okay if I make standalone statements.

"This water is freezing."

Everything below boiling is freezing to you.

"Hey, I said no conversation!"

You're making eye contact.

"No I'm not!"

Hey, stop checking out my private parts!

"Am not! I am clearly averting my eyes if anything."

But I'm everywhere.

"Your crotch is everywhere?"

If I'm everywhere, so is my crotch.

"That makes sense in a weird messed up way. So... your junk is in your mouth?"

WHAT?

"Your mouth is everywhere too, right?"

Yes.

"So if your mouth is everywhere, and your crotch is everywhere, then your junk must be in your mouth."

No! That's not how it works.

"It must be. Your rules."

Well if my crotch everywhere, it must be in your mouth too!

"Gross, stop putting your stuff in my mouth!"

I knew there was a reason I banned you from Heaven, you're such a degenerate. Hey, we're having a conversation in the nude.

"Damn it! You tricked me!"

I'm surprised you didn't catch on sooner.

"This ends now, no more conversation."

Fine.

"Fine. Hey, where'd you go? God? Where are you?"

god particle

Hello?

"What the... Who are you?"

Where am I?

"How did you get in there?"

In where? What's going on here?

"You're in a particle accelerator tunnel."

A what-a what tunnel?

"A particle accelerator tunnel. How did you get in there?"

You tell me, I have no idea.

"We need to get you out of there, it's dangerous. You're lucky our last experiment just finished, or else you'd be a goner."

What experiment?

"To detect the Higgs boson."

I don't know what that is.

"It's a– look, we need to get you out of there. How did you get in?"

I keep telling you, I don't know.

"Do you at least know who you are?"

Of course. I am God.

"You're full of it. We need to get you out of there, we have more tests to
        run. We're on the brink of detecting a Higgs boson."

Wait, did you say Higgs boson?

"Yes. You said you didn't know what that was."

I thought you said 'Higgons' boson.

"No, that isn't even a thing."

I know it isn't a thing, that's why I said I didn't know what it was. Well,
        you probably shouldn't do the experiment again.

"What? Why?"

It was successful already.

"What are you talking about?"

I'm God. I'm the 'God Particle'... more or less.

"No, that doesn't even make sense. There are some workers opening up
        the tunnel near you right now, head over to them and get out of
        there."

I'm not crazy, I'm God. It's true.

"Even if it was true, and it was a success, we still have to do the experi-
        ment again to verify that it is indeed repeatable."

You don't want to do that.

"Why not?"

There's only one God, me. So if you try to reproduce me, well...

"Well?"

The next guy will come.

"What next guy?"

You know. Satan.

"You're nuts."

You believe me about being God, but you don't believe Satan is next?
        Go ahead. Summon the Prince of Darkness. See what I care.

"Maybe we will!"

Okay then.

"Hold onto your robe, old man."

I'm not wearing a robe.

"Hold onto whatever you're wearing then."

I'm not wearing anything.

"What? Why are you naked?"

I was in the locker room at the rec center when you made me pop up
here.

"Ew. Old man balls. Those have to go."

You don't know what you're starting!

"Science marches on."

No, wait! Will this hurt?

"You're God apparently, so you can't get hurt."

How would you know? Hold on a minute! I changed my mind! Get me
out of here!

"Too late, the accelerator's winding up."

See here young man, I can make sure you don't get into Heaven with
this kind of behavior.

"Just one more seco–"

satan particle

It stinks to High Heaven in here. What is this place?

"God?"

What? No, I'm Satan. Who the Hell are you?

"I'm a scientist."

Ah, one of those. Why does this place smell so bad?

"I don't know."

What do you mean you don't know, you're a scientist. You're supposed
to know such things.

"I'm not that kind of scientist."

The kind that knows things?

"That kind that knows about smells."

Figures.

"Are you the only one in there?"

Should I not be?

"Just a second ago God was–"

There you go with that God business again. God this, God that. He's not
the only all powerful being around, you know.

"He was right where you're standing just a moment ago, before we ran
the experiment again."

Which experiment?

"We're attempting to use this particle accelerator to recreate the conditions of the big bang."

Oh! You're one of those God Particle guys huh? This must be where God vanished off to...

"We don't actually call it the God Particle, but yes. I'm one of 'those' guys."

Where's God now?

"I don't know. I thought you would know."

How would I know? I just got here! I never thought you guys would pull it off, but I'm glad you finally did it.

"Did what?"

You summoned me. Now I can bring this stinky world to an end.

"This accelerator can't cause the end of the world."

Everyone's been saying you'll create a black hole that will devour the planet.

"Sensationalist media. Creating a black hole this way is impossible."

You've got Satan here in your stinky tube thing; I think you need to revise your standard of impossible. Hey, are you typing over there?

"No, of course not."

I hear the clickety-clack of a computer keyboard. Ears like a canine, I hear everything. What do you think you're doing?

"Nothing. I am doing... nothing... at... all."

You're pausing to type as you talk, who do you think you're fooling?

"I'm... not... pausing... to type... I just... talk like this... normally."

You really are a scientist; your 'speaking-while-doing-other-things' skills are absolutely terrible. That comes from lifelong lack of friends to talk to.

"Shut... up."

Poor little scientist, always alone with his computers and books and other science related things.

"You're... going to... regret... those words."

I know what you're doing. You're running the experiment again, aren't you? Well think again. If smashing God with particles summoned me, just imagine what will happen when you smash me!

"What are you talking about? What comes next?"

Not what. Who.

"WHO comes next?"

I really shouldn't be talking about this.

"I'll just find... out... for... myself."

You really don't want to do th–

santa particle

How DARE you!

"Holy crap, who are you?"

I'm Santa.

"As in Santa Claus?"

Duh. Stupid mortal.

"I'm a scientist. I'm not stupid."

You're obviously stupid enough to summon me.

"I'm not really sure what to say to that. I did just rid the threat of Satan come to Earth."

Ho ho ho, Satan? You're afraid of Satan? He's a wimp. I tell Satan what to do, buddy.

"What? Well then I'll just get God back and he'll..."

Ho ho ho! Such a clueless little man. I tell God what to do too. You see, I'm behind it all. But I'm busy, and you're wasting my time, which makes me angry. There's no worse Santa than an angry Santa.

"Look, I'm just going to run the experiment again and all of this will be over."

That's not how it works, I'm here to stay.

"Hey, stop breaking things in there!"

You can't tell me what to do. I'm Santa, damn it.

"How are we even talking then? Couldn't you just make me shut up so you could go on your way to do whatever it is you do?"

That would be kind of boring, wouldn't it? No, I always make sure the one who summons me knows exactly how much they screwed up. I remember the last time like it was just yesterday... That was back when there were all these giant lizard people.

"Dinosaurs?"

Yeah, that's what you call them isn't it? Anyway, they did this exact
same thing back then.

"Summoned an almighty being using a particle accelerator?"

They sure did. It didn't go well.

"You're what killed off the dinosaurs?"

Of course, well not directly, what's the fun in that? They were even
worse to talk to than you are. Always screeching about this or
that. They had to go, or else I knew they'd keep bringing me
back again and again to complain about something. 'My front
legs are too short, it's too muggy, there are too many mice.'
Bunch of whiners.

"I can imagine."

You monkeys are just as bad. If you don't mind, I'm off to teach this
wretched planet a lesson.

"Are you going to kill us all? Like the dinosaurs?"

I was planning on it. I should get going, lots of work to do, carnage to
watch, weapons to make.

"Weapons? I thought you made toys."

Pfft, toys. Child's play. Times like these I make weapons!

"What kind of weapons?"

You'll find out soon enough. Which way is North?

"You really live at the North Pole?"

Only when idiots like you drag me all the way to this stupid planet...
where exactly are we anyway?

"Switzerland."

Switzerland? Pfft, worthless! I'm out of here.

"How long do we have before the apocalypse?"

It depends on how fast their space ship is.

"Whose space ship?"

Ho ho ho!

night lights

How's surveillance going?

"Very well. The humans have no idea we're here."

Fantastic. Wait, why is that one looking at us?

"What are you talking about?"

That one. He's looking right at us.

"Impossible! Our ship is painted entirely black."

Are you sure it's night time right now?

"Yeah, look, it's dark outside."

Hmm, maybe he's just looking at a moth or something. Hold on, that one is looking at us too.

"Maybe there's a really big moth?"

That's absurd. There's another one! In fact, it seems that every single human down there is looking right at us. What's going on here?

"I don't know. There's no way they can see us, our stealth technology is the best in the universe!"

You mean the black paint?

"Yes, the blackest paint in the universe!"

It has to be something else then...

"Maybe there's an even bigger ship behind us?"

Impossible!

"I'll turn us around just to make sure... Nothing there."

I have a feeling these humans are up to something.

"There are even more of them looking now!"

Okay, let's try something. Move to our left real quick.

"How quick?"

Impossibly quick. We'll be able to tell by their reaction if it really is us they're looking at.

"Here it goes..."

Ha ha ha, look at them! Go back, go back. They're like dogs looking at us wave a tennis ball!

"Uh, that means they can see us."

Crap. How can this be?

"Beats me."

Maybe the paint is too black?

"There's no such thing as too black. Black holes are the blackest thing in the universe and you can't see them, so logically..."

What does that light there mean?

"Which one?"

By your left hand.

"That's for the headlights."

So when it's lit up like that it means...

"Oh crap, the headlights are on!"

Turn them off, turn them off!

"They won't shut off! The button is broken!"

What kind of ship are we running?

"Crumbs must be jamming it!"

Crumbs? Why were you eating in here?

"I'm usually very careful!"

It wasn't a one time occurrence?

"We have more important problems at the moment!"

Yes, I know, problems that were directly caused by you eating in here!

"Hold on, I have some air duster here somewhere."

We don't need air duster, we need button duster.

"It doesn't dust the air, it uses compressed air to blow dust off of electronics."

That's brilliant. Who came up with that?

"Believe it or not the humans did."

No way, they're smarter than I thought.

"I know, right?"

So where is it?

"Someone must have taken my last bottle."

What? Who would dare steal a tool so vital to our operations?

"Some of the crew likes to sneak up and blow it on the back of each other's necks. They nearly jump out of their skin."

That's hilarious.

"I know, what can't air duster be used for?"

Apparently nothing! Too bad we can't find any. Everyone down there is still staring at us.

"What can we do?"

I know! Where's the fuse box?

"Of course! Over there under the dashboard."

I can't reach it.

"Lay on your back."

Okay... Now what? I can't see a thing.

"Do you see the red fuse with a '20' on it?"

I just said I can't see a thing!

"Here, use my phone."

The screen isn't bright enough.

"Turn the brightness up."

How do I do that?

"Click on the menu button."

Which one's the menu button?

"The one that says menu."

I can't see it!

"Here, use this flashlight."

Great, alright, there's the menu button...

"Okay, that should take you to the main menu."

Yeah, I'm there.

"Now select settings."

Alright.

"Then scroll down to brightness."

Oh yeah, I got it. Great. Here's your flashlight back.

"Do you see the fuse I was talking about?"

Sure do.

"Yank that sucker out."

Alright, let me get a good gri–

"Oh wait, wait, not the red fuse, the blue one."

Make up your mind!

"I'm pretty sure it's the blue one."

There are three blue ones.

"What number?

Three.

"No, what number is written on them?"

Oh, right. They all say '15'.

"Crap. I guess you'll have to unplug all of them."

Are you sure?

"It's our only option."

Okay then... OUCH!

"What happened?"

It shocked me!

"What's that smell?"

The whole fuse box is fried.

"Don't worry about it, the important thing is that the humans can't see
    us now."

Ha ha, yeah. They sure look confused.

"As far as they can tell we just vanished into thin air."

Brilliant. Take us to the next surveillance site then.

"Uh oh."

That isn't what I want to hear. What now?

"The controls aren't working! That fuse box must have been for the
    navigation computer too. We can't move!"

Shoot! How are we supposed to invade now? Our reconnaissance is
    incomplete!

"We'll just have to start attacking sooner than we planned. Hopefully
    the weapon controls are wired separately."

Try the grascr. Low power, just in case.

"The gimbals seem to work."

We have gumballs?

"No, gimbals!"

I want a gumball.

"We'll get gumballs later. Now, what's a good test target... Here we go...
    yeah!"

Bull's eye! Take over their broadcasting frequencies ASAP, there's no
    time to waste!

"Already on it. Get yourself into makeup before you get on camera, will
    you? You look terrible."

You're one to talk.

"Why I oughtta."

you foe

"This is nine hundred and eleven, what is your emergency?"

Uh... is this 9-1-1?

"Yes, nine hundred and... oh right, 9-1-1. Sorry about that."

I'm callin' cuz me and my wife just saw a you foe.

"Uh... a what?"

Y'know, a you foe!

"I'm looking through my handbook and I don't see anything about–"

A flyin' saucer, durn it!

"Ohhh, you mean a U-F-O."

I know how to spell it, I ain't no dummy. Dummy.

"Sorry. Tell me exactly happened with this... you foe."

We was out havin' supper on the back porch when Greta, that's my wife, saw these lights just floatin' out there in space.

"I see."

We was pointin', looked over at our neighbors and they was pointin' too. Then poof.

"Poof?"

Yeah, poof. Lights went out.

"The lights in your house?"

No! The lights in the sky! The you foe lights!

"It disappeared?"

Clear as a badger on Saturday morning.

"I'm not sure I know what that means."

It dispeered, awright?

"Great, er, thank you for giving me that information. Let me just put that into... the... computer..."

Hurry, my wife's scared we're gonna be inducted.

"Abducted?"

Yeah, that!

"Hmm."

Hmm what?

"I'm sorry, this is my first day and I'm not really sure how to use the computer yet."

What?

"You're probably better off hanging up and calling again. I'm terribly sorry."

This is ridiculous! Me and my wife are sittin' ducks about to get conducted–

"Abducted."

And the almighty 9-1-1 operator doesn't even know how to work a gosh durn computer!

"I know how to use computers, just not this one."

Even I know how to use a computer, and I hunt possum out in the thicket every night!

"I understand you're upset. Would it be okay if I put you on hold for one or two minutes while I speak to a supervisor?"

I guess I got no choice.

"Hey, over here. I have a question! Hey! HEY! HEY!!! Damn it. Thank you for holding."

Well?

"I couldn't find an answer for you..."

What?

"I'm sorry, it looks like your best bet is going to be to call back and hopefully the next agent you talk to will be better than me."

Fine.

"Do you need the number?"

No! Bye.

"Man, this job is hard without proper traini– This is nine hundred and eleve– errr, 9-1-1, what is your emergency?"

You again!

"What are the chances?"

Look, can you just send a squad car out here or something?

"I think so... can you just confirm your location?"

I'm on my porch!

"Where is your porch?"

Outside my house!

"And where is your house?"

Can't you GPS us or somethin'? I know the government is watchin' us.

"It doesn't really work like that."

Bull doggy! Send a squad car out here right away. We'll be holed up in
      my den. Tell the off'sir to knock like this before he comes in so I
      don't shoot 'im. Tap tap ta-tap taptap tap ta-ta-tap ta-tap tap.

"I think I'm losing you sir, there's some kind of tapping sound on the
      line."

I'm doin' the secret knock! Are you payin' any attention? Here it is
      again. Tap tap ta-tap taptap tap ta-ta-tap ta-tap tap. Repeat it
      back to me.

"Ta-tap ta-tap tap tap tap tap ta-tap ta-tap tap. Was that it?"

No no no, like this. Tap tap ta-tap taptap tap ta-ta-tap ta-tap tap.

"This? Tap tap ta-tap taptap tap tap ta-tap ta-tap tap."

You're waiting too long between the 8th and 9th knock, what are you
      some kind of square?

"No, I'm very hip."

Hip my left hip! Try it again. It's a simple swing rhythm.

"Okay, so... Tap tap ta-tap taptap tap ta-ta-tap ta-taptap."

Close enough. Make sure you tell the off'sir to use that knock exac–
      Oh sweet baby corn!

"What was that sound?"

The town's water tower jis' sploded! Water everywhere! Send all the
      cops you got, it's gettin' scary down here!

"This is starting to sound serious."

Durn right it's serious! You better get yer tail into a bomb shelter right
      quick.

"Thanks, I'll work on that."

Who knows how many other you foes there are waitin' to evade and
      deduct us all!

"Invade and abduct."

That's what I said! I gotta go push the frig'rator over in front of our
      door. B'bye.

"Good bye."

greetings earth

Are we ready to broadcast?

"Yes, I'll give you a countdown, and then begin."

Great.

"And five, four, three, two, one."

...

"Are you going to start?"

You didn't finish the countdown.

"We're broadcasting right now!"

What? You didn't say zero!

"You don't say zero in a countdown!"

At least say 'blast off' or something, how am I supposed to know when
       to start?

"You start after one."

I've told you, you need to be explicit with me. I don't have time to read
       between lines.

"We're still broadcasting."

Oh jeez, why didn't you say so?

"I did."

Hello humans.

"Keep going."

I was waiting for a rcsponse.

"They can't talk back to you, just make the speech."

That's going to really throw me off. Okay, hello humans.

"You did that part already."

We are here to destroy your pitiful species. We've seen what you're
       capable of, and what kind of evil you represent.

"Doing great."

We have been living among you for years. Decades. Cent'ries. Watch-
       ing. Waiting. You have treated us with disrespect, as if we carry
       some kind of disease.

"Perfect."

In a way you were right, because now we bring to you destruction, pain,
       and other unpleasant things that we're capable of but best go
       unsaid for the sake of this speech. We have no demands and are

accepting no apologies. The apocalypse begins at sunrise.

"Great."

I thought that went pretty well. What did you think?

"We're still broadcasting."

Well stop it!

"Sorry, okay now we're off the air. All things considered, not bad."

What do you mean all things considered?

"Well most of it was us talking about the countdown and whether or not we were broadcasting."

Think we came across as unprofessional?

"Maybe a little bit."

I feel like we could do it a lot better if we did it again.

"But everyone already saw what we just–"

I want to do it again.

"Okay, okay. Same script?"

I thought it worked reasonably well as written, but try not to say anything while I'm talking this time. That threw me off.

"Sorry, I'll be quiet this time."

Great, I'm ready. What are you doing with your hands there?

"I was counting down. I thought you didn't want me talking this time."

Still say the count down, I don't understand your fancy sign language.

"Five, four, three, two, one."

...

"Blast off."

Hello humans. We are here to destroy your pitiful species. We've seen what you're capable of, and what kind of evil you represent. We have been living among you for years. Decades. Cent'ries. Watching. Waiting. You have treated us with disrespect, as if we carry some kind of disease. In a way you were right, because now we bring to you destruction, pain, and other unpleasant things that we're capable of but best go unsaid for the sake of this speech. We have no demands and are accepting no apologies. The apocalypse begins at sunrise.

"Very well done."

I said don't talk!

"We're off the air now."

Oh. How was it that time?

"Brilliant, but you kind of pronounced the word 'centuries' funny."

What do you mean? How did I say it?

"Kind of sounded like 'sentries.'"

Isn't that how I said it the first time?

"Yeah you kind of did. I didn't want to say anything because the rest of
the speech that first time was so bad anyway."

What the Hell? How should I pronounce it?

"Cent-oo-ries."

With emphasis on the 'u' like that? Kind of weird.

"No, no, I was just emphasizing that there are three syllables. It's more
like cent-oo-ries than sent-oo-ries."

You just said it exactly the same way.

"Cent-oooo-ries. Sent-oo-ries. Crap, I can't say it any other way now.
Cent-oo-ries. This is going to drive me crazy."

Cent-oo-ries. Damn, now I'm saying it that way.

"This isn't good."

We can work through this together. Scent. Trees. Scent. Trees.

"No, I don't want to pronounce it that way. It's wrong."

It's less wrong than your way.

"Fine, but this is only temporary."

Scent.

"Scent."

Trees.

"Trees."

Cent'ries.

"Cent-oo-ries."

Damn it!

"Forget it, how often do we use that word anyway?"

Only like once or twice a cent'ry.

"Cent-oo-ree."

Sentry.

"Bah. What time is it?"

Half past ten.

"Great, plenty of time before dawn."

Alright, I'm going to go take a nap.

"That sounds like a great idea. I'll set the alarm for five o'clock."

Wake me up if I'm not awake when you get up.

"See you at five."

Sweet dreams.

"Don't be weird."

shelter

Alright, what is it new guy? Why am I not seeing putty in your hands?

"What?"

Putty in the hands!

"Uh, I was just wondering if I could have the rest of the day off. I'm feeling kind of sick."

You're asking to go home sick on your first day? The nerve! You don't even look sick.

"It's my stomach. Oh. Ohhhhh, oh. The pain."

I don't believe you. What's really going on? Can't handle the pressure?

"No, it's... I got a call from this guy who said the aliens are invading."

Which aliens?

"THE aliens."

From mexi–

"Outer spa–"

Outer space, of course. So what does this have to do with anything?

"I need to find somewhere safe."

Safe? At home? Ha! Do you have any idea how safe this building is?

"How safe is it?"

Safer than a safe. Now that's safe. I mean, we have an elevator that goes into space. If that isn't something that demands the highest level of security, I don't know what is.

"Good point. So is there somewhere we should gather?"

What do you mean?

"Like a safe area for times of crisis."

Don't be silly, everywhere in this building is the safest place to be. We're an emergency call center. In an emergency, we're who everyone relies on. If we had to get off the phones to go gather somewhere safe anytime an emergency happened, well that would be kind of silly wouldn't it?

"So... I should stay on the phone?"

Absolutely.

"Just wonderful."

Hey, you should be glad you even have a job. Don't complain.

"Speaking of the job, this is really rough without getting any kind of training."

You got plenty of training. Some people at other companies would kill for a manual as thorough as this one.

"There's nothing at all in here about you foes."

About what?

"Er, UFOs."

We can't cover everything in the manual, the emergency possibilities are endless.

"But there's an entire section about dogs choking on cat toys."

That's actually one of our most common calls.

"There's even a section on Bigfoot."

Also very common, especially in these parts.

"Bigfoot, seriously?"

Seriously. All I'm saying is keep your doors locked when you're driving home after dark.

"What'll that do?"

Bigfoot is notorious for car theft. In fact there's a warrant out for his arrest so make sure you send a squad car immediately if you get a sighting.

"But what about UFOs?"

What about them?

"What should I tell people? I just kind of winged it with that last guy, and I expect we'll be getting a lot more calls about it."

Yeah... that message from the aliens probably won't help either.

"What message?"

They took over all the TV stations just a few minutes ago. Said the apocalypse starts at dawn.

"What? I've really gotta get out of here then!"

No way, the phones are ringing off the hook because of this. In fact,
    I don't even know why I've let you keep me here talking to you
    for so long! Get back on the phone and strap in, it's going to be
    a long night.

"But I really..."

Back on the phone, we just went into the rosewood!

"The rosewood?"

It's like being in the red, but darker.

"It actually sounds kind of pleasant."

There's the call volume danger level color chart. Does that color look
    pleasant to you?

"It looks black."

It's the black of red.

"I'm pretty sure it's just plain black."

No the next one down is black.

"They're both pretty black."

You just need better light and you would see the hint of red...

"That's another thing, the lighting in here is terrible."

You just told me that aliens are invading, and you're complaining about
    the ambient light? Get back to work!

"Can I at least use the bathroom real quick?"

If what you say is true, I really wouldn't recommend being in the
    bathroom right now.

"I thought almost all bathrooms served as tornado shelters."

Tornado shelters? Yes. Earthquake shelters? Maybe. Alien invasion
    shelters? Oh God no.

"What's so different about alien invasions?"

Probing. You don't want to get caught with your pants down.

"Uh..."

I'm just looking out for your safety. Feel free to put yourself in the
    line of danger, but know that it will really hurt your adherence
    stats. I would recommend that you stay on the phone until your
    scheduled break time.

"If you say so."

worry some

Hey George, pass the chips.

"After what was just on TV all you can think about are chips?"

Yeah, I'm hungry.

"Aliens are going to destroy the world at dawn!"

I'm not too worried about it.

"Why not?"

Pass the chips and I'll tell you.

"Here. So tell me."

Well, you know how I got these chips.

"I just handed them to you."

I mean originally. Your company, Time Chips Inc.

"I still don't fully understand that whole thing."

Future you stole my time machine...

"You have a time machine?"

Future me has a time machine. Or... one, until you stole it.

"You mean... will have, until I steal it."

Let's not get bogged down in tenses.

"I'm tense enough as it is."

Anyway, your company delivers chips to the exact place and time that
     they're wanted, even before the customer knows that they want
     anything.

"What's your point?"

Well, surely one of our future selves is already all over solving this alien
     invasion problem.

"Do you really think either one of us is that heroic?"

You said when future me came back I was wearing spandex pants.

"Are you saying you were some kind of super hero?"

No, just that it takes courage to wear something so snug out in public.

"Especially with the situation you have going on."

Shut up!

"Just sayin'."

My point is this alien invasion thing will work itself out. If nothing else,
     future us will at least make sure that present us are safe.

"You're really sure about this aren't you?"

Super sure.

"Alright, what should we do then?"

Play some video games?

"That works for me."

pre hysteria

What is that there on the shelf?

"Oh, that's just a television. We're getting reception now. That must mean we're getting pretty close to shore."

Fascinating, so that's what a television looks like. What is this program all about?

"Looks like a news report."

Their mouths are moving... Should there be sound?

"Yeah, I'll turn up the volume."

You know, seeing one of these in action makes me regret not staying thawed back when Johnson paid me a visit.

"Well, what's done is done."

Indeed. This woman seems worried. More worried than you were back in the ice cave.

"I wasn't worried."

You were shaking in your boots.

"It was an ice cave. It was cold!"

Those were shivers of anxiety.

"Hold up, what's that?"

It looks oddly familiar.

"They're saying it's some kind of UFO."

Dear God. I've seen that before!

"What? That's impossible!"

Yes, yes, before I froze myself.

"You froze yourself?"

We had reason to believe the end of the world was near, so a select few of use froze ourselves to preserve the species.

"Wow. That's intense."

All because of that. That... UFO.

"So what happened?"

I can't say for sure, I was unconscious before anything happened, but obviously it turned out badly. Thiss UFO must be stopped.

"Obviously, but what are we supposed to do?"

I must speak to your President as soon as possible.

"I don't think that's possible."

I'm a dinosaur damn it! You don't think the President will find the time to speak to a dinosaur?

"Yeah, he probably would."

Make it happen.

"What happens after that?"

Don't you worry about that.

"I'm not worried."

You're shaking in your boots again.

"I don't have my sea legs yet!"

Tremors of apprehension.

"If my legs weren't wobbly I'd come over there..."

I could eat you up in two bites. Maybe one if I stretched first. Just calm down and change the channel. See if you can find some cartoons. I'd like to see Gertie in action.

"That probably won't be playing on any channels."

I want to see Gertie the Dinosaur. Now.

"Hey, Rapido, my main man, how's it goin'?"

Hi... I'm sorry but do I know you?

"It's me, Captain Wham! But you can call me Whilliam. With an 'h.'
        Wham is short for Whilliam."

I get it. What do you want?

"I'm sure you heard about the 'alien invasion' through SuperBook."

I don't use SuperBook, I prefer Hero In. It's less flashy, much more
        professional.

"You mean heroin?"

What?

"The website, it's called heroin, I thought."

No, Hero In. Two words. It's like you're a hero and you're plugged in.
        Hero In.

"Really? I always avoided that site since I thought it was for heroin."

Well, heroines can use it too.

"What?"

You know. The lady heroes.

"I was talking about heroin. The drug."

Oh wow, yeah, that's a terrible name for a social networking site.

"Yeah, right?"

I think I'll set up a SuperBook account when I get back home.

"It's great. I like the games. MafiaBoss is so awesome."

I'm not really into that.

"You can invite all your friends to get more points, and you can do all
        kinds of stuff."

Isn't it just clicking links over and over?

"No! There's action, and buying stuff, and..."

So it's like a flash game then?

"Kind of. I mean it's all text based but..."

So you click on links that take you to more text.

"There's some pictures too! And numbers!"

Idiot. So what did you want?

"Oh right, the alien invasion."

What about it?

"Well, my sidekick Little Whammy and I have been at odds lately and started seeing a therapist. Lovely guy, kind of smells like old people, but sharp as a tack."

What does this have to do with me?

"Our therapist thought it might be beneficial for us to do more away from each other, in groups."

I'm not into bowling.

"No, super hero stuff, obviously."

I'm not into super bowling.

"I mean saving the world! I thought this alien invasion was the perfect opportunity."

Oh. Yeah, not into that either.

"But you're the fastest man on the planet!"

That's true, but my answer is still no.

"C'mon Rapido, we need you. Sure, I do have super speed, but not the **superest** speed."

That's not a word.

"Damn it man, I'm a super hero not an English professor."

It's been a bad week, alright? I've been sick and I'm just not in the mood to talk about anything. So if you wouldn't mind, leave me alone.

"That sucks, man! What's going on? I'm here for ya, that's what pals are for!"

You're not my pal. We just met.

"Seriously, if you don't join the Crime Brigade my therapist will not get off my back and Little Whammy's going to leave me when this is all over. I can't go it alone, I have no idea how to read a map! Not to mention the aliens man. The ALIENS!"

You're not going to leave me alone until I say yes, are you?

"That was the plan."

Fine, I'll join your little 'Crime Brigade' under two conditions.

"Sure."

First, there has to be a better name for the group than 'Crime Brigade.' It sounds like a stupid team name from your MafiaBoss game.

"Actually, that's my 'family' name in MafiaBoss."

I figured.

"And the second condition?"

You need to promise that you will never, **ever** send me MafiaBoss invitations. In fact, I never want to hear about that stupid game again.

"Not even a wall post?"

I swear I will punch your face at the speed of sound.

"You drive a hard bargain, but you're in. Welcome to the Crim–"

Ah ah ah.

"Super hero group whose name is to be determined."

Better already.

crackow!

"Stop shooting at me!"

Who goes there?

"Please lower your gun, sir. I'm a police officer."

Prove it.

"Look, here's my badge."

You could be one a'dem aliens!

"My grandparents came to this country in the 1930's, I am NOT an..."

SPACE alien, dummy! From the you foe!

"The what?"

The flyin' saucer!

"Oh right, that's what you called about."

What call?

"There was a 9-1-1 call from this address a few minutes ago."

How d'you know about that?

"I'm a police officer. I was sent here to help you."

Nuh uh, no way. You tapped the phone line or used one of yer fancy listening dishes! Get the Hell outta here before I shoot you!

"You don't understand, I'm not an alien!"

Oh I understand plenty, ette.

"Ette?"

Ette!

"What are you talking about?"

ETTE!

"Can you spell that for me?"

E-T, ya dummy. Ette.

"You mean just E.T."

I know, I just spelled it for ya!

"It's short for Extra Terrestrial."

I know what an ette is, don't you talk down t'me!

"I'm not trying to offend you, I'm just trying to serve and protect."

Yeah, if by that you mean probin' me 'n my wife!

"Your wife is here too?"

Wouldn't you like to know?

"I'm not going to hurt you."

Dagtootin' you're not. I don't hesitate shootin' possum, I sure as heck ain't done gonna hesitate shootin' you, ya filthy ette.

"How can I convince you that I'm on your side?"

If you was on my side, you would know the knock.

"The what?"

The knock! I'm not splaynin' it, you oughtta know!

"I have no idea what you're talking about."

Then you leave me no choice.

"Ah! Good God, stop shooting!"

I'll stop shootin' as soon as you and yer friends leave my planet!

"My hat! It's ruined!"

I was aimin' for yer face! Now git!

"Fine, I didn't really want to help you anyway, you crazy old man!"

I knew it, I knew you was from the you foe, ye stinkin' ette!

This is 9-1-1, what's your emergency?

"Hi, uh... I'm covered in blood..."

Okay, can you tell me what happened?

"And I'm naked."

Excuse me?

"I'm covered in blood and naked."

Okay... What happened?

"No idea. I woke up like this a minute ago and found this emergency
       call box on a highway outside the forest."

Are you injured?

"Not hurt... the blood isn't mine."

Is someone near you injured?"

"Caribou. Full grown male. Tastes... Great..."

Uh...

"Sorry. Don't know what came over me. So confu- fuu- arooooooo!"

Is this a crank call?

"Arooooo!"

Please stop howling, I can't help you unless I know what's wrong.

"Don't know what's grrrrrr."

Don't grumble, I'm trying to help. Listen, I'll just send a squad ca–

" Police can't be involved."

Then why did you call 9-1-1?

"Would you look something u-rooooo! For me?"

Why do you keep howling?

"I'm beginning to suspect I might be a grrrrr arooo!"

Be a what? Please stop sniffing into the receiver.

"That's MY caribou, stay away!"

Hey, I'm not trying to take your Caribou.

"Not you! Get out of here! Shoo! GRRRR! AROOOOO!"

Are you there?

"Yes, sorry. Damned scavengers were picking at my caribou."

This is the weirdest damn day... so the caribou is yours?

"Of course! I killed it with my own two... paws?!"

No need to panic, we'll get you some help.

"What the Hell is happening to-roooo!"
Just stay put so we can find yo... Are you there? Hello? Great, he's prob-
       ably off chasing a rabbit.

"Arooooooooooooooooooo!"

oh deer

That did not go well.
"I knew you wouldn't do any better than I did."
It's this damn water pistol. We need a real gun.
"Whoa whoa whoa, we're not armed robbers."
But maybe we should be.
"We can argue about this all day, let's just go before the cops arrive."
Let's head to the site. I'm willing to let the pie slide for this job.
"Where exactly are we going, anyway?"
Oh this is the jackpot of burglaries.
"Yeah?"
You ever heard of The Eradicator?
"That ridiculous super villain?"
Exactly. His real name is Bucky Rimbleton.
"Ha ha, what a silly name."
And he's a millionaire.
"No joke. So why him?"
I heard through the grapevine that he's been having problems with his
       security system lately.
"That's perfect!"
Yeap.
"So where is his place?"
No idea.
"You didn't get an address?"
It's a secret hideout, I figured it was an undisclosed location.
"What about your grapevine? Isn't that the kind of thing grapevines are
       for?"
They said it's somewhere outside of town.
"Gee, that helps."
Here, I'll get on the highway going into the mountains. That's where I'd

build my secret hideout if I had one.

"Makes sense."

Keep your eyes peeled for any signs of a secret hideout.

"I'll have a look at the map. Maybe we can narrow it down a bit."

Careful, careful, careful.

"Oh, that is not how this unfolds."

You better not tear it, that map was expensive!

"You didn't steal this?"

No. I had a moment of weakness!

"Alright, I think I figured out how to... there we go."

You better remember how to fold that back up.

"Let's see, it's probably not in the national park."

Maybe where all the fancy mountain homes are?

"Where are those?"

You know, off exit 108.

"Show me on the map."

What kind of navigator are you?

"I'm not the navigator, I'm the sit in the van guy!"

Part of sitting in the van entails navigating!

"Just show me where you're talking about."

Look, it's right there after the lakes.

"Those are lakes?"

The blue things? Yes, those are lakes. What kind of...

"Watch out!"

Holy crap! What the Hell was that?

"I think you just hit Bigfoot!"

Don't be ridiculous!

"What are you doing?"

I'm stopping.

"No way! We already have the cops after us, we have to keep going!"

But what if we killed him?

"As far as we know it was a log."

You said it was Bigfoot!

"I was panicked and surprised. And it's dark out."

I looked up and saw right into its eyes.

"It was a log."

I really don't feel good about this.

"Like you said we're on the mission of a lifetime, put it out of your mind
        and drive. If he's having problems with his security system we
        don't know how long we have until it's back up and running."

Fine.

"What are you doing?"

I'm turning around, we have to check on whatever we hit.

"I'm telling you it was just a log!"

I looked into its eyes. I peered into its soul.

"Fine, it was just a deer, then."

Oh my God, a deer! Poor deer!

"Are you kidding me?"

I'm going back.

"But we're almost there!"

But deer are so cute.

"For crying out loud. The cops are after us!"

A deer. A deeeeeeer!

"Fine, but hurry up."

Aren't you getting out with me?

"Why?"

So you can see the deer!

"I've seen deer before."

Come on.

"No."

Come ooooon.

"You're so annoying."

Alright! Let's go look at the deer!

"This is ridiculous."

Where did it go?

"There's nothing in the road."

It must have bounded off into the woods.

"Oh God, get back in the van!"

What?

"It's coming right for us!"

Holy crap!

"Start the van!"

It won't start!

"Why did you even turn it off?"

Oh my God! It's clawing at the door!

"Let off the clutch a little!"

Stop telling me how to drive!

"Just tap the gas pedal!"

I'm trying to!

"Floor it!"

What. The. Hell.

"I told you we shouldn't have stopped."

That was not a deer.

spats spat

Commander Debussy?

"Who's askin'?"

The name's George. I'm from the future. Er, well, my future. I'm from
    your past. Sorry, I'm used to going back in time for this kind of
    thing.

"Yeah, those spandex spats of yours went out of style twenty years
    ago."

I don't think you mean spats.

"Sure I do."

A type of shoe accessory that covers the ankle?

"Uh, no. It's what we call tights. Duh."

What do you call spats then?

"Horsey foot covers."

What?

"You know, because they look like those foot covers that horses wear."

What do you know about horses?

"Hey, you're talking to the king of interstellar horse racing. Got a track in
    the cargo bay and everything. Don't tell my superiors though."

Aren't those things horses wear called spats too?

"Horsey foot covers is much clearer. Don't you know how many people thought spats were pants?"

I've never encountered anyone who thought that.

"Believe me, I talk about spats, or rather horsey foot covers, all the time. I always have to explain what they are when I say spats. Luckily a few years ago someone decided to just change what the words meant."

Who decided that?

"I did."

You can't just choose what words mean!

"Let's not argue about it, Spats."

You better not call me that.

"What brings you here?"

I need your help. Well, more generally, your star ship's help. There's an alien invasion about to take place in the twenty first century. Only your ship can prevent the world from ending.

"We're getting ready for our own war here; I don't have time for shenanigans from a spat-wearing hippy."

What? I don't even have long hair.

"I was referring to your wide pelvis. You would make an excellent mother. If you weren't so obviously a guy. I think."

Look, I have a time machine so you have all the time in the world.

"Where?"

Here.

"That?"

This.

"How is that little thing supposed to send an entire ship back in time?"

I hadn't thought of that...

"And you said only this ship can do it. Why this ship? This ship is hardly top of the line. We have one of the first teleporters ever made, for crying out loud! Why not go further into the future and recruit a better ship?"

It has to be your ship because that's how history happened, and that's how it always has to happen.

"So you're saying victory is a sure deal?"

Yeah. See, look at this newspaper clipping.

"Paper? Wow that's old."

Your ship fought off the aliens and saved the world.

"Spoiler alert."

Will you help me or not?

"It sounds like we have nothing to lose so... sure, why not? But you have
to find a way to send this whole ship back in time."

Yeah... do you have any ideas?

"I'm sure you've heard the legend of the greatest inventor in history."

That rings a bell.

"Archaeologists found his skeleton next to the earliest evidence of the
wheel, fire, agriculture, domesticated animals, and what might
be a rocket pack."

What? That's kind of a big leap.

"Exactly why he might be the solution to our problem. He might have the
answers we need to get this whole ship moving through time."

It's worth a shot. I'll be back in a minute.

"You can take it a little longer than that."

I didn't mean literally, though I could if that's what you'd like.

"No, no, take your time."

It won't be rushing me or anything; I have a time machine after all.

"I need time to prepare the crew. No sense for you to come back so
quickly just to stand around waiting."

Of course. We'll make it an hour then?

"Too long."

Thirty minutes?

"Make it thirty five."

Great, see you in thirty-five minutes.

"We'll be waiting for you."

Should I come back sooner? I don't want to make you wait on me.

"It was a figure of speech."

You sure?

"Somewhat."

Great. See you then.

"Take care."

robed the wrong way

"Hey are you... I can't quite put my finger on it."

Jesus?

"Yeah!"

I get that a lot.

"So you aren't really him then."

No, I am.

"Whaaaat!"

What can I say.

"What luck! The names Whilliam, with an H, but you can call me Captain Wham. Or just Wham. Whatever you want, Jesus."

Please, call me Chuy. Chuy Cristo.

"Uh..."

You have a problem with that? I'm trying to go for a different image this time around. Not going to make a big impact with my return if I don't have some pizzazz.

"You look exactly the same as the pictures I've seen."

I haven't gotten around to getting new clothes yet.

"Let's get you hooked up then!"

What's happening here?

"You have the amazing opportunity to join me and my super gathering of... super hero team fighters... to fight the alien invasion and save the world!"

Ha, you're worried about that?

"What do you mean? Alien invasion! End of times! Apocalypse!"

Those aliens are the least of your worries. Look, I'll join your team because I'm the friendly type, but I'm calling the shots.

"I don't know about that."

Come on. I'm the son of God. You can trust me.

"How do I know you're not just some filthy guy in a bath robe?"

Do you have a bottle of water?

"I do."

Hold it out for me.

"Alright..."

Bam. There you go.

"What the... cola?"

Have a taste.

"Oh gross, lime flavored!"

I thought that was popular.

"Stick to wine."

Do you believe me now?

"Yeah, close enough I guess. So what's the real threat if the aliens are
        nothing to worry about?"

Santa.

"Satan?"

Claus.

"The claws of Satan?"

No! Santa Claus.

"Jolly fat man who brings gifts for good children?"

Yeap.

"Get out of town!"

Cross my heart. Hope to die.

"You already kind of did that."

It wasn't as bad as you would think.

"So where can we find Santa Claus?"

The North Pole.

"Of course. I guess we'll need to get you some winter duds then."

Duds?

"Yeah, duds. Threads. Clothing."

I know what the word means, but come on, 'duds'?

"I'm hip, man."

Dork.

"What do you know about fashion?"

Don't make me regret joining your team.

"Fine, let's get you some winter attire."

I was thinking mukluks. They still make those?

"And I'm the dork?"

What? Mukluks are excellent footwear for snow.

"Let's just focus on getting you dressed for action. There's a world that
        needs saving."

Agreed. Hey, I'm parched. Can I have a swig of that?

"Oh I see how it is. You only turned my water into lime cola so you
    could drink it yourself."

I only need a sip or two.

"I've heard that before. There's a convenience store on the corner. You
    can get a drink there on the way to the coat factory."

The coat factory? But I need mukluks!

"They don't sell JUST coats."

That's a stupid name then.

"Nobody's perfect."

I beg to differ.

dispatched

"This is 9-1-1, what's your emergency?"

I'm hurt bad. Real bad.

"What happened?"

I just got hit by a van on the highway.

"Oh God, are you okay?"

Yeah, I'm perfectly fine. That's why I thought I'd call 9-1-1. Idiot.

"Hey now, no need to get snippy."

You'd be snippy too if you just got hit by a van!

"Yes, I absolutely understand, I'm sorry to hear that."

You can't even begin to understand. Getting hit by a van on the highway
    hurts like a bitch.

"Where are you?"

I don't know. Can't you tell what call box I'm calling from? I'm here on
    the side of some highway.

"Of course. What kind of car are you in."

I'm not in a car.

"But you collided with a van on the highway."

A van collided with ME.

"Right. So you were driving a–"

I was walking.

"You got hit on foot?"

Yes.

"Wow, I'm amazed that you're even alive, let alone able to speak."

You're not the only one.

"What?"

Never mind. Just send an ambulance.

"Sure, I'll send an ambulance your way. Good luck and goodbye."

Is that part of your closing script?

"No, I was feeling a little ambitious, thought I'd ad lib the goodbye."

Terrible, stick with the script.

"Thank you for being a valued 9-1-1 customer."

Oh God, never mind. Never use the script again.

"I know, right? The ambulance should be there soon."

I hope so, I'm bleeding something fierce.

livestock

Problem solved, Commander.

"That was fast Lieutenant. Please don't tell me you used up our budget for overnight shipping."

No sir, we already have red lasers.

"Are you blind? Blue, BLUE! We've already discussed this."

Just give me a moment...

"These aren't coin operated, what do you think you're doing? Well slap my hindquarters and label me slack jawed. How come we didn't know about this feature?"

Apparently it's all right there in the user's manual.

"Nobody ever reads the user's manual for a gun. Point and click. Easier to use than an mp3 player."

What's an mp3 player?

"Oh forget it, you're too young. Now go tell the crew so we can get back on track."

There is one other thing.

"What?"

I ordered us something extra. Something better.

"What did you buy now?"

Grasers.

"Like cows?"

What?

"Cows. They graze on pastures."

Not grazers, grasers.

"I don't follow. We're going to moo them to death?"

No.

"Milk them to death?"

No. Grasers. With an s.

"Of course there's an s, it's plural. Nothing we can do with just one cow. But we get thousands of them and we could really pull something off. Genius. But do we have enough hay? The horses have to eat too, you know."

I didn't order cows.

"Goats then? Not quite as good, but studies show people get less emotionally attached to goats so that may be for the better."

I didn't order goats either.

"How ab-"

Nor sheep, nor bison, nor any other grass-eating animal. I ordered GRASERS. G-R-A-S-E-R-S.

"Oh. What's that?"

I'm not entirely clear on the specifics, but apparently they can blow up planets and stars.

"Wow, entire planets?"

And stars.

"That's a little bit over the top, isn't it?"

Well... the Consulate has them.

"Holy handbag, how come we didn't know about this?"

It was probably a secret.

"And how did you find out?"

The guy I buy our lasers from let it slip.

"That sounds awfully convenient. Sounds like a set up. Call him back and cancel that order immediately."

We already have the grasers.

"What? That was fast. Suspiciously fast."

They sent them through the teleporter.

"Hmm, I see. I guess we may as well keep them for now."

Shall I have them installed?

"No, not now. We have more pressing matters."

Yes Commander?

"Tell the crew we're going on a mission before the mission."

A pre-mission mission?

"Exactly."

Very well, when will this pre-mission take place?

"Uh... in about twenty minutes."

What? That's hardly enough time!

"I asked for thirty-five but I've been waiting for you to get back from calling the laser folks."

You could have let me know before we started discussing the grasers!

"I don't need your sass, get the crew ready, time's a wastin'."

The ship hasn't finished being cleaned yet!

"I wouldn't worry about that, the ship didn't look very clean in the news clippings."

What are you talking about?

"This isn't an official mission per se, so the shininess of our hull is the last priority. Tell the cleaning crew they have my permission to take a load off for now."

So you're giving permission for pretermission for the duration of the pre-mission mission.

"You got it."

This isn't about a horse race, is it?

"I wish. No, this is something more down to Earth."

Say no more, we'll be ready for action in twenty.

"More like eighteen now."

Eighteen it is.

"Hey one more thing."

Yes?

"Do you know where all the limes went? I've had a hankerin' for a wedge of lime to squeeze into my cola but it's like they all just up and jumped out the air lock or something."

I really don't understand your taste sir, but I will look into it for you.

"You're a good man."

oval

Mister President, thank you for making the time to speak with me.

"Of course, this is a matter of national and international security. Plus a
     talking dinosaur? That's pretty damn cool."

I figured as much.

"This alien invasion thing. We don't have much time. Lay it out for
     me."

I can't say for sure, but I think that these aliens are the same beings who
     wiped out the dinosaurs sixty-five million years ago.

"I thought that was a meteor."

That's a possibility, but there is no way to be sure.

"I don't think this is the kind of thing I should act on just because of a
     hunch."

A hunch from a dinosaur.

"A hunch nonetheless."

The most important hunch in history, as far as I'm concerned.

"Now you listen here, before I got into politics I was studying to be
     a paleontologist. All scientific evidence to date points to the
     dinosaurs being wiped out by a massive meteor strike and
     the ensuing debris cloud and global climate change. Now I'm
     supposed to believe that it was some alien spacecraft caused the
     mass extinction?"

You call it extinction, I call it genocide. Surely, the aliens directed the
     meteor at the Earth.

"Hey, watch your tail please."

What? Oh sorry.

"Lots of expensive vases and paintings in here."

I didn't mean any harm.

"No of course you didn't, just be careful."

I'll try to control my wagging.

"So what do you propose we do?"

I'm not quite sure yet, I'm still having trouble remembering everything
     from before I went into suspended animation.

"Whatever we can do to help you remember, please don't hesitate to
     ask. Until then, I have other things to attend to."

Of course. I'll just wait in the lobby for now then?

"Uh, yeah, I think it's probably best you went on the lawn."

It's dark outside! And cold! I'm not some pet.

"Nothing personal, it's just..."

It's just what?

"There are so many fragile items in the lobby I don't want to risk it."

I told you, I can control my– whoops.

"The Abraham Lincoln painting!"

Sorry. I'll be out on the lawn.

"Yeah. Great. Let us know when you remember anything else."

clock around the rock

Whoa, ease up on the spear!

"Hey! It's you again! My handsome friend from the future!"

What? I've been here before?

"Yeah, you were here just last week!"

I don't remember that. Are you Bongo?

"Benjamin."

Ah, right. The greatest inventor in history, yes?

"I'm blushing!"

I'm here because I need your help.

"Sure, anything for you!"

Long story, but it boils down to this. I need a time machine that can transport an entire space ship through time and space.

"A what that can what an entire what through what?"

A time machine that can...

"I heard what you said, but I don't understand any of those words."

But you're the greatest inventor of all time! I thought you knew all about this kind of thing.

"I only know what you've been teaching me."

What?

"You've been teaching me how to do and make all these things, and I just wanted to make my friend Greg think I'm smart so... I told him I was inventing them. I'm a fraud!"

Hey, hey, hey, don't cry. I hate crying.

"You hate me, don't you?"

I don't hate you.

"I'm just a stupid cave man."

You're not stupid.

"Really? You think so?"

Sure, if I've been teaching you all this time, you must be smart enough
to learn.

"Uh huh."

Look, I promise I'll keep teaching you these things, but right now I
don't have any time to waste.

"There's that time word again. What is that?"

You know, time. Like a clock.

"A what?"

Oh... right. You see a clock is round like this.

"Oh! A weal!"

Kind of.

"I get ya. Please don't tell me you throw clocks, I wouldn't hear the end
of it from Greg."

No? Forget about that. Obviously you can't help me with what I need,
but I'll be back soon okay?

"Wait, you said something about this time stuff before. You asked me to
remember so... yes of course, I drew a picture of what you told
me in my cave."

Lead the way.

"Please excuse the mess. Greg just loves throwing things around."

Room-mates. Typical.

"Here it is."

Is that a dinosaur?

"Yes."

Is he holding a clock?

"It's a rock. I thought that's what you said he gave you the first time you
explained it to me."

Wait, you just used the word time.

"Yeah..."

And you mentioned that I was here a week ago.

"Right. Oh THAT'S what you meant by time?"

Yes!

"You can travel through time?"

Yes.

"No wonder you don't remember me, you just haven't gone back to last week yet! You have to teach me how to time travel!"

All in good time.

"Ha ha, good one."

Thanks for showing me this drawing. I have to go back in time to find this dinosaur!

"Hey, can I still tell Greg that I came up with all the stuff you taught me?"

Sure. In fact, tell him I said you're the greatest inventor in history, and I should know.

"You rock!"

Ha ha, good one. See you around Benjamin.

p'leece pullover

"License and registration please."

What seems to be the problem, officer?

"I think you know."

I may have been speeding a little bit.

"More like a lottle bit. You were going 15 over the speed limit."

Oh.

"In some kind of rush?"

Not really, I guess my speedometer must be broken.

"Also you were driving with your lights off."

I thought it was dangerous to have the lights on inside a vehicle while driving.

"Not the dome light, your headlights."

Oh, was I? The fuses must have gone out. Damn fuse box, goes out all the time.

"That's endangerment."

Is that a thing?

"Sure, why not? What's your friend there's deal?"

He's my brother.

"Whatever, why is he being so suspiciously quiet?"

He's deaf. And he can read lips, you know.

"What's he doing?"

He's signing. Says he's offended.

"No he didn't"

Yes he did.

"I grew up with my deaf cousin back in Buckley Green. Your brother there definitely just signed that he wants a cup of decaf."

Let me guess, American Sign Language?

"Of course."

Well there you go, my brother only signs in Chinese.

"What? You guys aren't Chinese."

My parents bought the wrong sign language book.

"I'm going to have to write you a ticket."

Oh come on, I didn't mean to do it.

"No excuses. I'll be right back, don't go anywhere."

Alright. Idiot, I thought you knew sign language. You don't have to sign now, he's in his–

"Who is Bertha?"

Oh hi, that's our mother.

"Right, and she gave you permission to use her van?"

Of course!

"This van was reported stolen earlier tonight."

That's ridiculous! She knew we were going out to get groceries.

"Groceries huh? You know there have been a couple attempted robberies tonight, both involving a van just like this one."

You think we did it? We're just enjoying a brisk night time drive through the mountains.

"I thought you said you were out getting groceries?"

Yeah, that was earlier, now we're out on a brisk night time drive.

"Where are they?"

Who?

"The groceries. I don't see any in the back there."

Oh, we ate them.

"Really."

Yeap, we were really hungry.

"Step out of the vehicle for me."

Hey, you have no reason to do this.

"Just put your hands on the hood of the vehicle and– Woah, what's this about?"

What?

"Where you in some kind of wreck?"

Not that we know of.

"The headlights are smashed and this is... blood."

We have no idea how that got there!

"Alright, I'm taking you in."

What? Why?!

"Clearly you've been involved in a hit and run, not to mention the countless number of other offenses you've managed to tally up tonight."

You'll be hearing from our lawyer!

"You don't have a lawyer."

Yeah, we don't have a lawyer.

"Watch your head."

I don't need your help getting in the back of a car oka– OW!

"I told you to watch your head."

You pushed my head into the door frame on purpose.

"Maybe I did. It's your word against mine."

Brutality!

"Make like your brother and shut up, alright?"

Oh no you didn't, you really made him mad now!

rock of ages

Man, all this time travel is making my stomach churn. I guess I'll have some chips while I'm looking around...

"Looking for someone?"

AHHH! PLEASE DON'T EAT ME, PLEASE DON'T EAT ME! PLEASE. DON'T. EAT. MEEEEEEEEE.

"What was that all about?"

I sing when I get scared.

"You dropped your chips."

I'll pick them up later.

"You better. All this jungle needs is a litter bug."

I understand.

"You know what we do to litter bugs?"

...Eat them?

"We SQUASH them. And then eat them. Makes a lovely sandwich spread, goes great on rye..."

Listen, I'm looking for the greatest inventor of all time. He looks like this.

"What a crude drawing. No, no, he doesn't look familiar."

Wait a second... this is you, isn't it?

"Well I am an inventor. I wouldn't say the greatest though."

Finally! Do you have any idea how many time jumps I've gone through to find you?

"Two hundred."

That's... well no, just five. It's still a lot though.

"Huh, I thought..."

Listen, I need your help.

"Of course you do."

I'm from the future.

"Obviously."

And aliens are about to attack the Earth.

"Aliens. Right."

Our only chance is if this space ship from our future goes back in time to defeat the aliens.

"You clearly have a time machine, so what do you need me for?"

My time machine only transports one or two people, not a mile long
    space ship.

"Ah yes, of course. I have just what you need."

Really?

"Yes, really. Come on the other side of this tree here. I've been working
    on this for a while now."

Alright... okay, now what?

"This is it."

Where? I can't see it.

"This."

You're kidding me! That's just a rock!

"You're from the future, right? So you've heard about dinosaurs?"

Of course.

"Fossils and all that?"

Yeah.

"And has anyone ever found machines, gadgets, or tools alongside those
    fossils?"

No.

"Of course not, you're looking for tools like the ones you use. See these
    stubby arms? We can't do crap with these. That's why we use
    psychic powers to tap straight into the power of nature."

Uh...

"Here, watch. I just close my eyes and..."

Holy crap, take us back, take us back!

"Here we are on primordial Earth. The crust has yet to cool, and the
    atmosphere is full of sulfur and carbon dioxide."

It's Hellish! How are we not burning or suffocating?

"I'm keeping us safe in a bubble of protection."

That's the lamest name for something so cool.

"It was a description, not a name. Figured I would save some time by
    not having to explain what a Shialabuff was, but now I've wast-
    ed just as much time."

Shialabuff? That's not bad.

"Let's go back to my time, shall we?"

I'm all for it. Wow, it doesn't even make me want to throw up like my time machine.

"Of course not, it's all natural. Good for the Earth, good for the body."

Can you come with me?

"You don't need me. In fact, I'm already there."

What do you mean?

"You'll find me at the White House."

Wait! How do I use this?

"Just close your eyes and imagine. The rock will take care of the rest."

So, do I hold it like this, or...

"No, you don't have to hold it over your head, it isn't Excalibur."

I just thought it looked kind of cool.

"In those spats? I don't think so."

They're **tights**, not **spats**!

"Whatever you say. In fact, you should probably take advantage of the rock and hold it in front of your uh... package."

I take pride in my body, alright?

"Good luck. Don't forget to pick up your trash."

Right, sorry. Oh what the hell? All the chips are gone!

"One of those pipsqueaks must have eaten them. Damn it!"

And what... the hell... is this?

"Disgusting! don't throw it at me!"

That was like a giant booger.

"Please don't describe it."

I think I'm going to throw up.

"At least it won't be from the time travel. You better get going."

See you later I guess.

"Something like that."

What now?

"Yeah, I can't do this anymore."

Raising your hand is standard etiquette.

"No, this. I can't do this job anymore."

What? So you're quitting?

"This is the weirdest and most stressful damn job I've ever head."

I'm hurt.

"And I didn't even come here to interview for this position! I have a
degree in mechanical engineering for crying out loud."

Hey, we all have degrees here.

"In what?"

I have a management certificate. It's like a degree.

"You're an idiot."

Hey! Would an idiot be able to lead a team of twenty on the swing
shift?

"A monkey would be more helpful than you."

Hey, I don't need to be helpful, that's what the handbook is for.

"Then what are you here for?"

To lead! Without a leader, there is no direction, and without direction,
nothing gets done.

"Couldn't they just put directions in the handbook?"

Actually there are, right there on page five. Oh. I see.

"Sorry, but I'm out of here."

My life is pointless. This is the best thing I'll ever achieve. A team
leader at a call center.

"Uh..."

I don't even have a girlfriend, I spend all my time here! Sure, I make
quite a bit of money, but at what expense?

"Maybe you should go take a break."

I want to have kids damn it! You have to help me.

"I'm not having your children. I'm not even a girl!"

Help me find some direction. Be my leader!

"Get with it man! Where would you be without this company? You
probably started here fresh out of high school."

Yeah.

"No other prospects.

Yeah.

"Nobody was going to put you through college, hell, you didn't have the
         test scores to go anywhere but community college anyway."

You're right.

"But here you are, because of this call center. You're the king of your
         little world now, and no one can take that away from you."

Well, the Director could.

"The Director would be lost without you."

Yeah... Yeah! I'm the king of this little world! Bow before me!

"That being said, I'm out of here. Sorry."

Hey don't even worry about it, like five people quit every week. Why do
         you think we put so little effort into training?

"I figured."

Hey, aren't you forgetting something?

"Uh... long live the king?"

No, your headset. Hand it here.

"I kind of drew all over it with a silver marker."

Don't worry about it, we'll just hand it over to the next hire. They won't
         even notice.

"Alright, well... Goodbye."

Be gone, peasant!

"Come on, really?"

So it shall be done!

rock it, man

What are you looking so smug about?

"I'll have you know that I saw my friend from the future again."

So? Did he tell you to play in more poop?

"No. nothing about agriculture. Actually, he told me to tell you that I'm
the greatest inventor of all time."

Manure.

"He ought to know, he's from the future!"

So what if he's from the town over the mountains.

"No, the future as in... tomorrow. And beyond!"

I don't understand.

"He used a time machine to travel back in time. A time machine that I
invented for him of course."

You never said anything about a time machine!

"Well, now I can finally tell you."

What's a machine?

"I'm.. it's a thing. That does stuff. It's too complicated to explain."

So I guess a time machine is beyond complicated.

"You have no idea."

You're making all of this up!

"I am not!"

Then show me this time machine.

"I can't. He has it."

Why did you give it to him?

"He has important things to do."

Such as?

"Errands."

Yeah right.

"It involves dinosaurs."

Ha, I told you there were dinosaurs around here!

"Not here, in the past!"

What's the past?

"You know, like yesterday, or the day before. Stuff that happened before
now is the past."

I remember seeing a dinosaur down in the stream.

"That was a frog!"

Frogs don't live in the water! I asked around!

"You're thinking of toads."

What the heck is a toad?

"It's like a frog, but it lives on dry land."

No, that's a frog! Dinosaurs live in the water!

"Come here."

Don't show me your stupid drawings again. All you do is draw, why
        don't you figure out how to write words already?

"Look, that is a dinosaur. Docs it look anything like the 'dinosaur' you
        saw in the stream?"

Well... no, but there are all kinds of dinosaurs aren't there?

"Sure, but not frog dinosaurs."

Is that dinosaur holding a discus?

"No, it's a clock."

What's a clock?

"It's a weal that keeps track of time."

Oh, so it's okay for you to go calling the weal other things, but I'm not
        allowed to call it a discus?

"Actually that's what my future friend called it."

Future friend this, future friend that. It's been all about him lately!

"That's not true."

Wait a second, HE called it a clock?

"Uh, yeah..."

And HE told you to try the poop in the field?

"Agriculture. Yes."

And HE has a time machine?

"Yes."

I see what's going on. You're not an inventor at all!

"You take that back!"

This guy, your future friend, he's been telling you how to do everything.
        You couldn't invent a paper bag!

"Paper bag? That sounds like a great idea."

I know it is, and I'm the one that came up with it because I'm a real
        inventor! Look at this I made today.

"Whoa, what is that?"

It's a jet pack. That's right, you don't even know what that means do you? You're too busy with your future friend to care about what I have going on!

"What does it do?"

It makes me fly, that's what it does. Watch.

"Wow, that's amazing? But what's that coming out of the bottom?"

Well, it's fire...

"Ah ha! I invented fire. All you did was steal MY invention and put it in a bag!"

It's a lot more complicated than that. It is in fact rocket science.

"Oh, is that what that phrase means?"

It does now. You know what, if you hadn't invented fire I would have never been inspired to make this. I'm sorry for getting upset.

"It's okay."

Grab on, let's go for a ride.

"Is it safe?"

Who knows?

"What have we got to lose."

Here we go!

"Oh my... this is incredible! What's that noise?"

Uh oh, that's th– AAAHHH!!

durnk

"Hey, Lady Love Lumps?"

Yeshh.

"It's me, Captain Wham."

Heeeeeeyyyy! Wherr'rrre you?

"I'm at the coat factory."

Youwer sposed t'be HERE!

"I know, I know, I'm sorry I can't make it."

Whateverrr.

"I'm getting together a group of super herocs to battle the aliens. I was
      wondering if you were in."

Kayos. Icon dewthat.

"Are you drunk?"

Yeha.

"..."

DURNK!!!

"Why are you drunk?"

I havs, I... Havs just a sec.

"Okay..."

Srry, had to threw up.

"Why are you drunk?"

I had SO MUCH t'drink. Ohmigod.

"Listen, I just wanted to call to say I'm sorry that I can't be there and
      ask if–"

Ohhhhh don't be surry. I understand. Purfectly understurblegurble.

"I'm a bit concerned about you being drunk, though."

Yeassyayyysss!

"I was under the impression that tonight was your WeeboWareTM par-
      ty."

WEEEEBO! Yesh, WeeboWare purty hurdy!

"So... WeeboWareTM parties just mean getting plastered."

Bingo! Thurs a reasin WeeboWare is purfectly pronunsububble whale
      drunk. WE gets drink'nd tlk about WeeboWare prawdics.

"Do you think you're in good enough shape to save the world?"

Yeaaaaaaaa... Icon dewthat noproblim. All jis drive over thur ritnow.

"No no no, don't drive. I'll come pick you up."

Inde Wham-Mobul?

"Of course."

Uuuuccch.

"What's wrong with the Wham-Mobile?"

Itsoooo ugly.

"It's not about looks, it's about functionality."

Funshunutter mayass! Yule never geta gurlfurnd drivin that heapajunk
        arund.

"Okay, you're drunk, you don't mean that."

Damn rite iamdurnk! But it's chrue. YOUR UH DWEEEEB.

"Why are you talking like a robot?"

THIS IS MY ROBOT VOOOOICE.

"Stop! When can I come get you?"

U kin come get me ritenow ifuwanna.

"I thought the party was supposed to go until ten."

Nobuddy shoed up.

"Oh. Well now I feel bad for not going."

Iss okay. Yore comta get me now. All be... bl. b.. lub.

"Lady Love Lumps?"

...

"Are you there?"

Ah threwd up aginn.

"I'll be there in a few. Don't drink anything else."

Okee dohkee. Grgle grgle.

"What are you doing?"

Girglinne the wine.

"I said don't drink anything else!"

Am not dirnkin, am girglinne!

"Well, don't swallow."

Hee hee hee hee!

"Oh God."

I AM UH RowBOOOOwT.

"See you soon rowboat."

ship shift

Commander!

"Ah, right on time!"

I got it.

"Where is it?"

This. Right here?

"That's just a rock!"

It's the time machine!

"I figured you finally started to feel some sense of embarrassment about
    your... tightness."

They're called tights, but that's better than spats.

"Oh no, I still call them spats, I was just referring to the way they just
    wrap themselves right up around your–"

Forget it, let's get going. Is your crew ready?

"Of course. We've spent the last eighteen minutes preparing."

I thought I gave you thirty-five!

"Hey, blame my Lieutenant. I was ready as soon as you left. So tell me,
    are you sure that's a time machine?"

Yes, I just used it to come back from dinosaur times.

"Dinosaur times? But the greatest inventor in history was a cave man!"

Turns out that was a false lead... I actually taught that particular
    caveman everything he knows.

"What'd you waste your time doing that for?"

Well, I taught him, but not yet.

"I... you make my head hurt."

It wasn't a total waste though, because he led me to the real greatest
    inventor in history. A dinosaur.

"That's ridiculous! They didn't even have opposable thumbs, how could
    they invent anything?"

They use telepathy. It's pretty cool, actually.

"They use telepathy on a rock to travel through time."

Pretty much.

"Far out. And I know far out."

Yeah. Shall we?

"Now is as good a time as any. Hit it."

And... There we go.

"Nothing happened."

Look outside.

"Holy crap! Is that Earth?"

Should be.

"What a smooth ride. Nothing like going in and out of hyperspace."

Yeah, nice isn't it?

"Where is this alien threat?"

The other side of the country.

"Why didn't you transport us right on top of them?"

We need the dinosaur's help.

"But you could have just brought him with you..."

He's already here. Look on the lawn.

"Well I'll be damned, a real live dinosaur. Let's get him up here."

son of a hitch

"Oh hey doggy, what are you doing out here?"

Get back in the car.

"Whoa, what? How are you talking?"

Don't worry about that, get in the car and let me in.

"Wait a minute... are you an alien?"

What? No! I'm a super intelligent dog. Let me in the car and drive.

"Okay. But don't pee on the seat or anything."

Who do you think you're talking to?

"A ragged old dog."

I've been walking for days, buddy. Give me a bath and you'll see who's
        the ragged one.

"I'm not taking a bath with a talking dog, that's kind of weird."

No, you're not in the bath, just I am... Never mind.

"Where did you come from?"

Don't worry about that, worry about driving.

"Hey, I just quit my job and I'm headed home, I don't feel like going
        anywhere else."

There's a dinosaur I need to find.

"Wow, dogs really do like bones, huh?"

This dinosaur is alive.

"What? How... oh never mind, I'll roll with it."

Good, I didn't feel like explaining it to you anyway.

"So why do we need to find this dinosaur?"

I have to tell him something important.

"This doesn't have to do with the aliens, does it?"

If you want to call them that, sure.

"Where can we find him?"

He's at the White House right now, but...

"That's like a thousand miles away!"

But, soon he'll be in town.

"Well that's great news."

Where the UFO is.

"That's not great news."

So that's where we must go and wait.

"How do you know all of this?"

I told you, I'm super intelligent. In fact, I'm probably the smartest
mammal on the planet.

"Sure, why not."

Mock me if you will, but things are about to get rough.

"Ha ha, say that again."

Things are about to get rough.

"What was that last word again?"

Rough?

"Again?"

Rough! Rough!

"Ha ha ha, that's great. When we get there, where should I bark the car?
Heh heh."

You are a miserable human.

"Just do you know, if things start to get hairy, you're on your own."

You know what, just let me out as soon as we arrive. I only need you for
the ride anyway, my paws are killing me.

"Why didn't you catch a ride with someone earlier?"

I thought I could make it in time on foot.

"Smartest mammal huh..."

It's overconfidence, not stupidity! So what if I'm a proud dog?

"Pride killed the wildebeest."

That's not a... what?

"You know, a lion pride. They kill wildebeest all the time. Pride killed the wildebeest."

I don't know how you humans are even in charge of this planet. How much longer until we arrive?

"Five or ten minutes."

If we could spend the remainder of this journey in silence, that would be great. And by silence I mean lacking any further stupidity coming from your mouth.

"You're kind of a bi–"

Ah ah ah, silence.

"–tch."

slowly drifting

Whew, it took quite a while plus a ton of limes, but the ship is finally almost clean.

"No kidding, I'm dying for some of that spaghetti and meatballs."

I have to admit, spaghetti would really hit the spot right now.

"All we have left is the port stabilizer fin!"

Piece of cake.

"Mmm. I wonder if there will be cake for dessert?"

My stomach is already growling, stop talking about the food for five minute so we can finish.

"Alright, sorry. Just a squeeze of lime juice on the ol' wash rag and–"

What the?

"Where did the ship go?"

Oh my God, they hyper jumped without us!

"We would have heard the engines spin up though..."

You're right, I didn't hear a thing.

"Just freakin' great."

Hey... how much oxygen do we have?

"Something like four hours."

That's a relief, I'm sure they'll realize they forgot us and come back.

"Er... four hours total. We've been out here for three and a half."

What? Oh God, we're gonna die...

"Don't panic."

Alright, we'll just stay calm and hope for the best.

"The worst thing about this whole situation is..."

That we're going to die?

"That we're not going to get any spaghetti and meatballs."

Ugh.

"I loooooove me some– Hey! What did you just throw at me?"

I threw a lime.

"The limes, of course! We won't have to go hungry after all!"

You idiot! We'll suffocate long before we starve. How are we supposed
to get the limes into our helmets to eat anyway?

"Oh. So... this is it then."

Yeah.

"I never imagined it would end like this."

Me neither.

"I thought I would die with meatballs in my belly."

I never got a chance to say this before but...

"Yeah?"

We've really gotten to know each other these last couple years, and I
feel like...

"Just let it out. Nothing to hide now."

I feel like you're my sou– The ship is back!

"Thank God, we will have our spaghetti!"

What the... it's filthy again!

"Bullshit!"

moonsters

Hey naked man.

"Bigfoot?"

You got it.

"I thought you were a myth!"

And I thought people wore clothes. I imagine we're both a bit surprised
at the moment.

"You can say that again."

What are you doin' naked?

"I have no–aroooo!"

Ah, I've heard that before.

"You have?"

You are a werewolf, my friend.

"I knew it."

Welcome to the monster club.

"What are you doing out here on the highway?"

Oh, I was headed North when it hit me.

"You had an idea?"

No. Some jackass hit me with their van. Seriously, people need to keep
their eyes on the road.

"Oh man, are you alright?"

A little bloody, but I heal fast. I was laying there for a second, and THEN
it hit me.

"You got hit by the van again?!"

No, I got an idea. It would be a whole lot easier to go where I'm going if
I had some wheels to get me there. So I chased after 'em.

"I take it you didn't catch up?"

Oh I did. The fools stopped to see if I was okay. They probably thought
I was a deer or something.

"What did you do?"

I chased after 'em, but my leg hadn't quite healed yet so they got back
in their car and drove away. I scared 'em pretty good though. It
was fun.

"That's crazy. I'm just an accountant but that sounds like a blast."

You're not an accountant anymore. Stick with me. So what are you doing all covered in blood?

"Oh, I think I was eating a carib–arooooo!"

Killer! Was there any left?

"Judging from how full my stomach feels... I don't think so."

Too bad. What are you doing now?

"Waiting for an ambulance, I guess."

Hey, me too!

"I thought you healed quickly."

Well, after the van got away I got another idea when I saw that call box
    down the way...

"Yeah?"

Steal an ambulance.

"Woah, that's pretty major! Some random van is one thing, but an am-
    bulance?"

Hey it has wheels and it goes fast, that's all I need.

"So where exactly are you going?"

The North Pole.

"What's there?"

Santa's Workshop.

"Don't be ridiculous!"

I'm serious. Santa has returned and summoned all the snowmen.

"Like Frosty?"

Not men literally made of snow. Abominable snowmen. Yetis.
    Bigfoots.

"Don't you mean Bigfeet?"

No, that sounds stupid. Bigfoots. It's our preferred plural. Anyway, you
    want to come with me?

"What's going to happen there?"

Not sure. This hasn't happened since... Well, I don't think it has ever
    happened before. But my people have been taught about it for
    centuries. Prepared for it. It's part of why we've had to keep our
    existence secret from humans.

"This sounds a lot like some sort of sleeper army."

That's one way to put it. You're kind of one of us now, you'll never fit
    in with human society. Why not just tag along?

"Alright, but do I have to help steal the ambulance?"

It'll make it a lot easier.

"I don't have to... kill anyone, do I?"

I'll take care of that. You just... do your wolf thing and distract them.

"Do my wolf thing?"

Yeah. You don't think you can only transform when the moon is full do
        you?

"Well it's full right now and I–"

Exactly, the moon is full and you're a naked man sitting on the side of
        the road. It's linked to emotion and your mind. Just let your most
        primal urges take hold and, well...

"Hmm, I think I could do that especially since I keep how-roooooo!"

Don't fight it, just let the wolf come out.

"Grrrrrr!"

There you go! Don't get all angry about it though. Yeah, you like that
        don't you? Good boy!

"Grrrrrr!"

Ha, I'm just kidding. I won't pet you any more. Just know I can crush
        your skull with one hand when you're like this.

"Awrr."

Kidding! It would take both hands. Now get ready, I think that the
        ambulance I hear. Just stand out in the road and get their
        attention, they'll stop, and that's when I strike.

"Bark!"

Let's do this.

"Arooooooo!"

Ah, so you're the dinosaur that made this possible?

"I don't know what you're talking about."

You invented the time machine over there.

"That's just a rock. If I invented a time machine, why would I have
     spent 65 million years frozen in ice to get here?"

Really? Well... I was told you were supposed to be able to help us defeat
     the aliens.

"I vaguely remember something about that from my youth, I've been
     racking my brain, but it just isn't coming to me."

Tell me what you do know.

"Just that I've seen that alien craft before, and as far as I know it killed
     off my species. I figured they managed to guide a meteor into
     Earth."

Hmm... That doesn't help much at all. I guess we could blow up any
     meteors that they hurl our way, but that seems a bit too simple.
     Are you sure there isn't anything else?

"That's it."

Well, let's think like the aliens for a minute. Obviously they have some
     kind of time travel capability if they came here and back to the
     dinosaurs.

"Right."

They have some very advanced technology.

"Do you think they might be using some kind of weapon I'm not
     familiar with?"

Maybe something I'm not even familiar with. I know! They must have
     grasers!

"What did you say?"

Grasers. With an 's' apparently, although I thought that was pretty
     obvious being plural and all.

"I've heard that word before, graser."

Grasers. With an s.

"I remember now... the aliens threatened us with a graser! Tell me, what
     is a graser?"

Some kind of super powered laser. Can destroy planets and stars I guess.

We have a couple...

"Yes?"

But they're not installed. I didn't think we would need them yet.

"And the ship doesn't have any mounted weapons?"

We have torpedo bays, but to be honest with you, I dumped all of our ammunition to make room for horse feed.

"What?"

Let's not get into that.

"You have to get those grasers installed immediately. It's our only chance!"

I'm on it. And by that I mean my Lieutenant is on it.

para-normal-medics

So we're looking for a naked guy, huh?

"Apparently. Says here the call came from the call box up ahead. Slow up a bit."

Hey, what's that?

"It looks like a wolf."

I wonder why our siren isn't scaring it off.

"Uh... he's staring right at us. Turn off the lights!"

Why?

"If he sit perfectly still, maybe he'll go away."

It's walking this way!

"Quiet, it will hear you!"

It probably smells us.

"You're right, quick use this."

Oof, oh my God, what is that?

"Body spray deodorant. To mask our smell!"

I can't... breathe...

"No don't open your window!"

I need fresh air, that stuff is– AHHH!

"Bigfoot!"

Help, he's going to pull me out the window!

"Start the engine!"

And do what?!

"And drive! Maybe we can lose him!"

He has a death grip on my arm, he'll rip it right off, are you crazy!?

"Here, spray!"

Take that!

"Let's get out of h–"

AAAAIIIEEEEE! The wolf is coming in through the windshield!

"Come on, we gotta get out of here!"

What?

"We're better off running away, we'll come back for the ambulance. Hurry!"

You better know what you're talking about.

"Quick, down into that gully!"

That's more like a ditch.

"What's the difference?"

I think it's a matter of size.

"No, I mean, who cares what it is, just climb down!"

Fine. Whew, I think we lost them.

"I'm not sure they were even following us."

Hold on, I'm going to take a look.

"Be careful."

Huh, no sign of them.

"You sure?"

Yeah, let's head back.

"Alright. Man, I didn't know you scream like a girl."

I'm a high screamer. It's perfectly normal.

"Did your momma tell you that?"

As a matter of fact she did. Hey, we stopped the ambulance right here, didn't we?

"Yeah, I'm pretty sure..."

So where is it?

"Beats me."

Damn it, they must have stolen it.

"No freakin' way. Bigfoot and a wolf stealing an ambulance?"

It's the only thing that makes sense...

"Whoa whoa whoa, what are you doing?"

I'm calling the hospital to tell them abou–

"Do you have any idea how much they're going to make fun of us? No
way. We're getting our ambulance back."

Are you serious?

"We better start walking."

dawn

Hey, didn't you hear your alarm clock?

"Just five more minutes."

We have a species to destroy!

"Five mor... snrrrrrr."

Wake up!

"I'm up! I'm up. I'm uhhh.... snrrrr."

You asked for it.

"AHHHHH! COLD COLD COLD COLD!"

Get up, it's almost time!

"It's almost time? It's almost time! Why didn't you tell me?"

I've been telling you for the last... never mind.

"To the bridge!"

To the... Hey!

"Snrrrr... huh what?"

Try to stay awake!

"I'm fine, I'll be fine. Maybe I'll be fine. So sleepy."

Let's go, one foot in front of the other...

"Alright already, I'm not a baby. Let's see what we have here..."

Unfortunately most of the systems are still down so we can't
maneuver... but we can fry pretty much the entire planet right
from here using the graser.

"Fantastic. What is that?"

Probably one of those puny jet fighters the humans have been trying to
send after us all night.

"Ha, stupid humans. Wait, it's getting bigger."

It's not getting bigger, it's getting closer!

"Oh crap, they aren't supposed to have any aircraft that big!"

Large craft warning.

"Shut up and prepare the grasers!"

It will take at least 5 more minutes to...

"What's that, what are they doing?"

Is that... They must have grasers too!

"Cripes, they have two aimed directly at us! Get us out of here!"

I told you, all the systems are down and our grasers aren't ready yet!

"What can we do?"

There is one mobility system still operating but we'll have to call this mission off if we use it.

"Whatever it takes, anything beats being vaporized!"

Here, just push this button as soon as I'm gone.

"What? Where are you going?"

I'm staying behind. They have to know this isn't the end of this.

"But I need you!"

You never needed me. All you ever needed was right in there.

"Aw. That was beautiful. You're making me cry."

Wipe away those tears and push the button. Goodbye.

"Sigh. Here goes nothing."

left behind

Wow, it worked! Vaporized!

"All in a day's work, Spats."

My name is George.

"I know. I heard the Commander calling you Spats earlier and thought it fit perfectly, especially with those..."

These are tights, not spats!

"Oh they're spats alright."

Ugh. So grasers. Pretty badass.

"Indeed, but ultimately evil in the wrong hands."

So what now?

"I don't know, but... hey, wait a minute..."

What?

"Look down there. Is that what I think it is?"

Here, hand me those binoculars... Yeah, that's one of the aliens!

"It must have teleported off the ship before we fired the graser.

Give me your time machine."

Hey! That's mine!

"You got the big time machine from me, didn't you?"

Well, yeah...

"Then consider it a fair trade. Tell the Commander you can take his ship
    back to his time now."

You're not going with us?

"I need to have a word with that alien. After that... who knows? It was
    nice meeting you, Spats."

muck

Great work Lieutenant.

"It was nothing."

Nothing? If you hadn't ordered those grasers, none of this would have
    been possible!

"You would have thought of something."

Nope, we would have been royally screwed.

"Well, I went over your head by ordering them. I apologize for that."

Look at me. Don't you ever apologize for being the best damn
    Lieutenant a Commander could ever ask for.

"Yes sir, thank you for the compliment. But, there's a slight problem."

What is it?

"Firing the grasers kind of drained our battery. It'll take a few minutes
    to recharge."

That's quite the design flaw.

"We didn't have time to properly reconfigure our energy systems."

Fine, we have literally all the time we want anyway.

"That's not the only thing."

Oh?

"We're kind of falling."

Don't get sappy on my Lieutenant. I may have gotten a bit emotion-
    al there for a second, but I don't feel that way about you. Not
    anymore anyway, maybe back in the–

"What? No, we are literally falling out of the sky. Without the battery
    charged we can't stay aloft."

We've never had that problem when our battery was drained before!

"We've never maintained an altitude this low before. Usually we're in
        orbit when we charge the battery."

What are you trying to say?

"We're going down."

Crap.

"Temporarily."

Not so bad.

"Into a lake."

Oh man...

"My thoughts exactly. We have about two seconds before impact."

Oof!

"Oof!"

Should we be worried? Will this cause any damage?

"No, not at all. However the water is kind of murky."

Ah I see... But so what? I'm not afraid of murk.

"It's just that we may need to spend more manpower cleaning the ship
        before our official mission."

Is it really that murky?

"Muddy as a guppy. See, it's starting to rise past the window there."

Oh yeah, I see what you're talking about. That is not going to be fun to
        clean.

"Not at all."

It was worth it though. We saved the world after all. Plus cleaning builds
        character. That's what the Earth Navy is all about. Swabbing
        decks and building character. That and blowing stuff up.

"Yes sir."

What's that sound?

"I don't hear anything."

It was a sort of squeaking. Never mind. Hey, we don't need the battery
        to use that time travel rock thing do we?

"Actually, we don't need any power for that at all."

There we go, just tell Spats to take us back to a minute after we left.

"Yes sir."

And grab me another cola with a slice of lime while you're at it.

"I still haven't located the limes. Is just plain cola okay?"

Ugh... Fine, it'll have to do. Not too much ice. But not too little either.
Two and a half cubes.

"You got it."

Good man.

messenger

OUCH!

"You have some explaining to do."

Take your foot off of me!

"I know what you did."

We only blew up a water tower...

"Not that, I mean 65 million years ago."

I uh...

"You killed off my species!"

The dinosaurs? We haven't even done that yet!

"Yet?"

Yes, that was our next mission.

"What? That can't be, I just saw your ship vaporized by–"

Ha! You thought you destroyed our ship?

"Of course, I saw it with my own eyes."

Right before you fired your graser, my ship jumped through time. It
jumped to your time in fact!

"What's the meaning of all this?"

Revenge.

"I'll show you revenge!"

Go ahead, crush me. This isn't even my real body!

"What are you talking about?"

There's a button on the side of my head. Press it and see.

"I don't see a button."

It's right there.

"I can't press that, it's too small!"

Use the tip of your claw.

"I guess... oh man, I'm just so clumsy with these."

Watch it.

"You know I tried typing earlier and I just felt like one of those women with fake nails... Okay. There... What?!"

Yeah, that's right. It was us all along!

"You're just a little mouse!"

You dinosaur douche bags made our life a living Hell with your holier than though attitude. I'm glad to hear our next mission was a success! Ha ha ha!

"Impossible! How did you... But... Huh?"

We hitched a ride to the future on the pant leg of your flamboyant friend, and spent years plotting our rise to power!

"Surely you couldn't have done this all on your own."

You and the humans haven't seen the last of us!

"Who helped you? Who is behind this?"

Not talkin'.

"I will tear you limb from limb before popping you in my mouth like popcorn chicken."

You don't have the dexterity for that.

"Oh yeah? How's this for dexterity?"

Ow ow ow, my tail! Okay, it was Santa.

"Santa?"

Yes, Santa!

"Claus?"

Yes, he set this all up. He gave us the space ship, the time machine, everything! Now please let go of my tail!

"Where is he?"

Where do you think?

"The North Pole. Of course."

Can you put me down?

"Sure, right after I crush this..."

No! My body!

"I never want to see you again."

Oh no, don't flick me–aiiieeeeeeeeeeee!

"Good riddance."

passenger

"Hey!"

Who's there?

"Finally! I've been waiting for you."

Don't tell me, the dogs have a grudge against me too?

"No, I'm here to help! The aliens aren't the real threat."

I know, the real threat is Santa Claus.

"You already knew?"

That mouse just told me.

"What mouse?"

The mouse in the alien suit.

"Whoa, really? The aliens are mice? I didn't see that coming."

I kind of had a feeling. Damned vermin...

"That's harsh."

You know, I always tried to be nice to the mice. All I said back then
was 'hey, need a boost?' when they were trying to reach some
berries. Sure, I may have thrown in a 'pipsqueak' now and then,
but I was just trying to be funny.

"Don't beat yourself up. We have work to do."

What do you mean 'we'?

"We're going to the North Pole. Together. It's the only way to defeat
Santa."

I don't know, how are we supposed to do that? He killed my entire
species like it was nothing.

"He's unprepared. The elves have been living for centuries like
children. The time is right to strike and strike hard while he's
still getting all of this minions in line."

How do you know all this?

"I'm the smartest thing on this entire planet, and besides, do you have
any other choice but to trust me?"

I don't know. Small furry mammals aren't on my good side lately.

"I'm not small. I'm two feet from paws to withers!"

Eh... That's a bit of an exaggeration, don't you think?

"Shut up, my brain is the size of a Buick, that's all that matters."

Well, not literally the size of–

"No, of course not literally, a brain that big would crush my show dog frame like a fly."

Show dog? Nah, I don't think so.

"If I hadn't been locked up in a lab all my life would have won all kinds of awards."

Ha, maybe in the mutt category.

"There is no mutt category!"

Guess you wouldn't win any awards, then.

"That's it, as soon as we're done saving the world, I'm going to enter the National Dog Show! You'll see who's laughing then!"

You wanna bet?

"Yeah, if I win, you give me that time machine."

Fine, but if I win, you go back in time with me to defeat those aliens... er, mice once and for all!

"It's on! Let's go kick some Santa ass so I can get to grooming."

You'll need all the time you can get. Hop on.

shop talk

Bring me my hat.

"Yes, Master Claus."

Are preparations complete?

"Not quite."

What have you elves been doing all this time?

"Making toys."

I told you, toys are second priority! It's our cover, not our goal.

"But it makes the children so happy."

Forget the children, humans young and old have done nothing but trash this planet. They're worse than the dinosaurs were!

"Understood. We'll get started right away."

Are there ANY weapons ready?

"Not many. And what we do have is in cold storage."

Ho ho ho. I love winter puns.

"That wasn't a pun."

Sure it was. Well bring me what you can.

"Are you sure? They're kind of... outdated."

I'll make it work. Right now my only worry is anyone who's smart
  enough to figure out I've returned, but stupid enough to come
  here and try to be a hero!

"About that..."

Yes?

"There have been rumors that he's back."

That who is back?

"You know. Jesus."

My arch nemesis! So the prophecies were true.

"Yes, it looks like you two really are two sides of the same coin."

Damn the coin! I've been victorious before, and I'll do it again! This
  Jesus clown is nothing but a thorn in my side.

"More like a crown of thorns."

WINTER puns. I like WINTER puns.

"Sorry."

Turn on the weapon factory and get things churning.

"Everything in the factory?"

Everything.

"But that would require..."

Shut down the toy division. We'll never need those facilities again.

"As you wish."

Thanks Pal.

"Aw, I didn't think you thought of me as a friend."

What? No! I thought that was your name!

"Oh... No, my name is Paul."

Ah, I was close. Sorry, it's been a while you know.

"Don't worry about it."

Thanks Paul.

"No problem Nick."

That's Master Claus, or Santa Claus, or Master Santa Claus to you.
  Maybe even MC Santa if I'm in the right mood... but I can call
  you by your first name, not the other way around. Got it.

"Sorry Master Claus. I'll be going now."

Well, your brother still isn't talking.

"He uses sign language so..."

We know he's faking it!

"Easy, what did the table do to you?"

This is how this'll work. You're gonna give me answers. REAL answers.
True ones. Then maybe, just maybe, I'll go easy on ya.

"I told you everything I know."

Oh yeah? Well let's start again. From the beginning. I'll grill you again
and again if I have to. Where were you the night of the crime?

"You mean tonight."

Yeah, tonight of the crime.

"Like I said before we were driving around in the mountains after
grocery shopping."

Driving around on the very same highway where one could find **this**?

"What is that?"

It's the call box your victim called 9-1-1 from after being struck by a
vehicle. YOUR vehicle.

"You have no proof!"

You're startin' to feel it, huh. The pressure. The guilt. Getting hot under
the collar.

"Only because you turned up the thermostat when you walked in."

I have my methods.

"You have nothing on me, and I'll never admit to anything."

Our forensics team has all the proof they need to put you away.

"I'm telling you, I don't know how that got there. My mom must have
hit a deer earlier or something."

Oh yeah, that's right. Your 'mom.' How convenient. If she's your
mother, why did she report her van stolen earlier this evening?

"I don't know! She forgets things all the time!"

Mm-hmm. Your so-called 'family' sure has a very convenient memory.

"I'm serious about this! She has a hard time remembering things!"

Ah ha! So you weren't serious about everything else!

"I, er, no, that's not what I said!"

Your list of offenses is a mile long, kiddo.

"Don't call me that."

Give me one reason I shouldn't lock you up.

"I didn't do anything wrong."

Oh, of course, no problem.

"Really?"

No! Your only alibi is your stupid brother, so you're not going anywhere until I get some answers!

"Don't call him stupid!"

Er, I meant dumb, since he can't talk.

"I've never heard that before."

I've had enough of your impudence. If you're not going to– Hold on.

"Where are you going? ...Hello?"

Hey.

"What was that about?"

You're free to go.

"See, I told you I didn't do anything!"

Sorry for getting so fired up. The hair sample wasn't human.

"What was it?"

We don't know. It's an unidentified forensics object. The guys searched the rest of the van and all they found was a case of custard pies and a very poorly folded map. Guess you were telling the truth about going to the grocery store too.

"Wait, we HAD pie already? Er, I mean, of course there were pies."

On top of all that, we contacted your mom to let her know we have her car and...

"And?"

She admitted she forgot you and your brother were going shopping.

"Ha."

Don't be so smug. Your van is still impounded.

"What?"

You were speeding and your headlights weren't up to code. Plus you were pretty much a pain in the ass.

"That's not fair!"

You're lucky I don't make you stay here overnight!

"Hello?"

Hi Pete, God speaking.

"Where've you been all night?"

I'm kind of trapped.

"I know how you feel. There are so many souls to process and not enough time."

No, literally trapped. Imprisoned in some kind of... I don't even know what this is.

"What should I do?"

There's nothing you can do. But, I'm going to need you to run Heaven.

"What?"

It's easy, I just let my assistant do all the hard stuff.

"I'M your assistant!"

Oh then you're all set then.

"I'm NOT all set, I'm swamped as it is without having to do all your God stuff."

What's taking you so long?

"It's that light bulb guy. Ever since we looked into making an exception for him, everyone's been trying to find their own loophole."

Hey, you're the one that came to me about that one. If it makes it any easier just let everyone in and I'll sort it out later.

"Hello?"

Hey, comrade, Satan here.

"Ugh, what do you need now?"

I need a favor or two.

"Of course. All you ask for is favors but I never get anything in return."

What are you talking about? You aren't suffering like everyone, are you?

"No, I guess not."

Good. So, first favor. I need you to run Hell for a little while.

"What?"

It's easy. It's pretty much what you're doing already.

"I figured as much."

So you're all set then. Great.

"Hey, since I've been working so hard... when you get back can I go on vacation?"

Hmm... I don't know about that.

"Come on, I've been working my butt off ever since I died while changing a damn light bulb. You were sympathetic at first. Remember?"

Oh yeah, I forgot about that. You know what, you have been working hard. You deserve it. Why not take your vacation right now?

"Really? Are you sure?"
Yeah, I shouldn't be gone for
        more than a couple days...
        I hope.
"Great, that's a huge load off my
        shoulders."
Place needs a little shaking up
        anyway.
"It should be fine."
The angels can manage it.
"See you soon?"
Hope so.
"Bye."

"Really? are you sure?"
The souls will just suffer a little
        less for a while. No wor-
        ries.
"Thanks. That means a lot. I
        mean it."
Hey, I'm a good guy sometimes
        you know.
"Yeah. You are."
Enjoy your vacation, comrade.
"I will."
See you soon.
"Bye."

suparrival

"So this is Santa's Workshop, eh?"
Nothing like I imagined.
"It's somewhat terrifying."
You ready Rapido?
"Ready."
You ready Chuy?
"Uh..."
Where's Chuy?
"I don't know."
And where's Lady Love Lumps?
"I think she's off vomiting somewhere."
Just great. Well we can't do anything without them.
"This place scares the crap out of me."
Wait, is that...
"Chuy! He's going in by himself! We should go after him."
Now hold on, he's the son of God. I think he can handle himself.
"Really?"
Plus you had a point. That place is scary as hell.
"Yeah, I'm sure he'll be just fine. We should probably, you know... stick
        around and watch."
Like sentry duty?

"Let's call it that, sounds important."

Works for me. Is it just me or is it as cold as a polar bear's nose out
    here?

"Just you, Wham. You should have brought a better coat."

You're in your tights! How aren't you freezing?

"Temperature is merely the average speed of molecules in a given area.
    Since I can control the vibration of my molecules at will I never
    need a coat. Not even at the North Pole."

That's pretty awesome.

"It gets the ladies hot, that's for sure. Come here, let's warm you up."

Uh... no thanks. Not after that last comment.

"Do you want to die of hypothermia?"

Maybe if we got Lady Love Lumps over here...

"Don't make this weird."

It already is weird.

"Shhhh, shhh... there, there."

Petting my head isn't helping.

free dumb

Let's get out of here. You don't have to keep signing, we're not in trou-
    ble anymore.

"Sorry, I was in the moment."

I thought I told you to learn actual sign language for these situations.

"I figured you just wanted me to play dumb. Easy if I don't know what
    I'm doing."

Well you pulled it off. Everyone thought you were pretty stupid. So the
    van was impounded.

"Yeah, I thought that's what they told me, but that cop has a killer mus-
    tache so it was hard to read his lips."

Why didn't you just listen to him?

"I was really getting into it."

You're such an idiot.

"Did you hear about the pie?"

Yeah! How did we miss that? We wouldn't even be in this mess if I had
    known we already had the pie we needed!

"You must have thrown your coat on top of them or something."

I wasn't wearing a coat. You're the one always wearing coats, trying to look all hip and cool while you sit in the van. You know nobody's going to see you, why do you bother?

"Look, I'm wearing my coat now, and looking fine I might add. Have been this whole time, so it couldn't have been my fault."

What's done is done anyway. We need to go get the van or Mom is going to rip us a new one. She's probably already fuming about us being arrested.

"You mean YOU'RE going to go get the van. I've been to an impound lot before. Shady as Hell and that was during the day. You were the one speeding, and the one who hit the Bigfoot. You should go."

First off, Bigfoot doesn't exist. What we hit–

"YOU hit."

–had to be a bear or something. And second of all, you're going with me. End of story.

"I refuse."

Where did you get those handcuffs?

"I borrowed them."

Very funny, where's the key?

"Don't know. Guess you'll have to come back for me."

I hate you.

"Don't let the impound dogs bite."

second fiddles

Hello.

"Hey, is Satan there?"

No.

"May I leave a message?"

No.

"This is the right number, isn't it?"

Yes.

"Can I leave a message so he can get back to me?"

He's not here. And no, you can't leave a message. Don't call again.

"He hung up! How rude."

I said don't call again.

"Is this the light bulb guy?"

Who's asking?

"St. Peter."

You son of a bitch!

"Whoa, whoa, whoa, this is a friendly call. Sorry about what happened
        but I understand you have a pretty sweet deal down there."

I guess.

"Sometimes I get a bit of pleasure telling souls they didn't make it in to
        heaven, knowing they'll be punished for all eternity..."

Uh...

"But to actually get to do the punishing? That's gotta be a treat."

No, it's Hell. It's just as much Hell as it is for anyone else down there.

"You're exaggerating. Wait, what do you mean down there? Aren't you
        in Hell?"

I'm on vacation! Leave me alone!

"No wonder! If you're there, who's running Hell?"

No one I guess.

"This is why I called you. Heaven is over-run with murders, thieves,
        rapists... fans of vampire novels. It's Hell up here!"

That's not my problem.

"You have to have some kind of idea of how to control them."

Why did you let them in anyway?

"God told me to let everyone in until he got back."

God's gone too? What's going on?

"I don't know."

Well just close the gates on 'em.

"I can't. They propped them open with a stick."

A stick?

"A really hot stick."

Excuse my blasphemy, but good God, what kind of wimp are you?

"I'm not a wimp. I don't have any oven mitts."

So much for my next suggestion then.

"What's that?"

Well, I pour lighter fluid on souls to punish them. If you did the same they'd fall into line.

"That sounds even more dangerous than the stick."

There is the danger of blow back, but just pay attention to what direction the wind is blowing and you'll be fine.

"I don't think that's going to happen."

Didn't think so. Sorry Peter. Sounds like you're just going to have to tough it out until God and Satan get back.

"Where are they anyway?"

No idea. His calendar has swimming scheduled for this evening.

"God's calendar too!"

You don't think they're really...

"Oh God, no, no, God no, that's... No."

I don't know why my mind even went there.

"I'm gonna go and drink until I forget that image forever."

Wow, yeah, me too. Sorry about that.

"I guess I deserve it for not trying harder to get you into heaven."

Don't worry about it. I'm sitting on the beach sipping a mojito. Extra lime. Loving it.

"I just might come join you. I'm not getting anything done here."

Eh, I think that would kind of ruin the mood.

"Just a suggestion."

It was a bad suggestion.

"I'll go now."

That's probably best.

impound

Excuse me.

"Yes?"

I'm here to get my van.

"Ah, right. I've been expecting you."

You have a little uh...

"Hmm?"

White stuff. On your mouth.

"Oh, thanks."

Wait a second. Is that custard?

"Uh..."

You were just eating pie, weren't you?

"Maybe."

That's my pie!

"No, this is a different pie."

So you're saying all of the pie I had in my van will be there when I get
        it back.

"No. It was confiscated."

Why?

"Evidence."

I was proven innocent!

"It can't be unconfiscated. Sorry. If it makes you feel any better, it was
        delicious."

So you did eat it!

"What are you gonna do about it?"

I'm gonna... with a... and the... just get me my van.

"That's what I thought. One of the guys will have your van pulled around
        in a minute."

You're not even going to apologize?

"For what?"

Eating my pie!

"I did."

Nope.

"Just a minute ago."

You gave me an 'if it makes you feel any better.'

"That counts as an apology."

Apologies begin with something like 'I deeply regret' or 'I'm so very sorry' not 'if it makes you feel any better.'

"Sure they do. People say it all the time when they're sorry."

So you admit that you're sorry.

"No, I admit that I apologized. I never said I was sorry."

But you implied it.

"So?"

So why not just say it? How hard is it to just say the words?

"Fine. I'm sorry."

That's better.

"I'm sorry I didn't wipe my mouth before you got here so I wouldn't have had to listen to you whine for the last five minutes."

Oh I hope you liked that pie, you son of a–

"Here comes your van now."

Is it safe to go in the gate?

"Of course. Why wouldn't it be?"

Dogs.

"This is an impound. Not a pound."

Guard dogs.

"What kind of cartoons have you been watching? We don't have guard dogs."

I figured there would be...

"Pay up and get out of here."

How much?

"Two hundred."

Dollars? That's highway robbery!

"Actually, a large percentage of traffic fines go towards funding the maintenance of state highways."

Go find a pot hole and fill it.

christmas presence

It's over, Claus.

"I've been expecting you, Jesus."

I go by Chuy now. Chuy Christo.

"Nice outfit, but don't you think those mukluks will slow you down?"

I don't need elf shoes to outmaneuver you, fat man.

"Ho ho whooo do you think you're talking to?"

They walrus who stole my holiday, that's who!

"Walrus!? How dare you!"

What are you gonna do about it?

"You don't even want to know, but afterwards I'm going to be having a
        Merry Christmas indeed!"

Christmas is MY DAY! Yaaaaaaahhhh!

"Easy, Chuy Cristo. Let's take this outside away from all of this
        valuable equipment. You wouldn't want there to be a toy
        shortage would you? The children would be heart broken."

Screw the children! This is about you and me.

"I tried to ask nicely, but if you're not going to step outside I'm going to
        have to take you out myself."

Bring it on!

"Ho ho HIYAH!"

switch which

"This place was easier to find than I thought."

I wish that guy hadn't taken all the pies. This would be perfect. Just imagine the Eradicator getting a face full of pie.

"Wearing his mask and everything."

Classic. You're coming in with me this time, right?

"Hell yeah, get to see the inside of the Eradicator's secret hideout? Could be pretty damn neat."

But remember, we're on the job, not sight seeing.

"Got it."

Let's go. What are you doing?

"I'm tip toeing."

Stop it.

"I thought that's how you avoid detection. On the tippy toes."

Not at all.

"Tippy toes, tippy tippy toes."

No wonder you stay in the van, everything you know about burglary you learned from cartoons.

"And those Ocean movies."

Just walk like a normal person.

"Alright."

Like a normal person! Stop scuffing your feet!

"This is how I normally walk."

You are hardly a normal person. Walk abnormally so you stop scuffing.

"Can do."

Oh for crying out loud, what are you doing now?

"John Cleese's silly walk."

Are you trying to get us caught?

"You said to walk abnormally."

I meant slightly! Forget it, if your scuffing wakes anyone up it's the last of our worries anyway.

"But I was really enjoying the silly walk."

I bet you were. What are you doing now?

"My wrist hurts."

That's what you get for handcuffing yourself to a chair.

"It was worth it."

There weren't even any dogs at the impound.

"What? What kind of second-rate place are they running?"

The kind that eats pie they find in people's vans.

"That's messed up. Dogs were bred to guard places like that."

And what about places like this?

"I don't see any doggy toys laying around so we should be okay."

I think this is the door. Like I hoped, the security panel is deactivated...
        hand me the tool kit.

"The tool kit? I thought you grabbed it."

No, that's your job.

"How was I supposed to know? This is only the second time I've gotten
        out of the van. I didn't see it in the van anyway. Did you forget
        it at home?"

Crap, I must have.

"Don't worry, we can improvise."

What are you doing? No don't!

"Hyah! Oh, it was unlocked."

That's weird... I don't know about this. This seems like a trap.

"We've come this far already. Turn on the light."

What? We can't turn on the lights, we're burglars. We work under the
        cover of darkness.

"I want to see what this place looks like and I don't have a flashlight."

I don't have one either.

"Really? How do you ever pull off a burglary."

Today has been a rare exception. Fine, turn on the lights if you want.

"Here we go... Maybe not. Hmm, this switch is broken."

Maybe the power went out.

"Wait, there's another switch next to it. Doesn't work either."

Get out of the– What the Hell? There are hundreds of switches here!

"Try them all!"

There are way too many, and none of them work!

"There must be some kind of secret combination of switch positions that
        activates the lights..."

Or maybe the power is out like I said. Wait, do you hear that?

"Sirens. You don't think they're for us?"

We gotta get outta here!

"He had a security system after all!"

Come on, run faster!

"This is how I run."

You're silly walking again!

"Silly running, thank you very much."

Get in the van.

climax!

Looks good to the South.

"Looks good to the South too."

What about over there to the South?

"Nothing to report to the South. How's Lady Love Lumps doing?"

She's passed out in the back seat of the Wham-Mobile.

"Why did you even bring her?"

Eh, I dunno. I kinda like her.

"Pfft. She's contributed nothing to this operation

In fact she's been a distraction more than anything."

A pretty hot distraction.

"Eh, maybe a seven."

You should see her without the parka.

"Hey, what the Hell was that?"

Jesus!

"Chuy just got thrown through that wall!"

That must be Santa!

"What gave it away? The beard or the hat?"

Shut up. Oh man, they're really going at it. Should we go help?

"No way, I can't take a blow like that! Is Santa weilding a mace?"

Oh damn! That's gotta hurt!

"Chuy's got some fight in him, that's for sure."

Hey, there's an ambulance pulling up.

"I didn't know there was a hospital up here."

Hold the phone; is that a wolf getting out of the driver's seat?

"Not only that, Bigfoot's getting out too!"

Are they here to help Chuy?

"I don't know, they're running towards... oh no, no, they're not helping
        Chuy at all!"

Oh man! This is better than pro wrestling.

"I think maybe now we should go and help."

Hold up, what's that coming over the ridge?

"A dinosaur? What's going on here!?"

Not only that, but there's a dog riding it!

"We need to get in there before that thing eats Chuy."

The dog just tackled the wolf!

"Yeah dog! You're my dog, dog!"

The dinosaur is all over Bigfoot!

"Bigfoot's running for it!"

Uh oh, the wolf has the dog pinned.

"You can do it dog! Fight back!"

Oh no, oh no!

"Gross!"

Is that what I think... Oh gross!

"Did that dinosaur just sneeze all over the wolf?"

Disgusting!

"It worked though, that wolf is runnin' with his tail between his legs."

But look, Santa's got Chuy in the corner!

"Where did he get a Halberd?"

What the Hell is a Halberd?

"It's an ax on a long staff, known for its use by Swiss armies in the 14th
        and 15th centuries."

Damn, Santa's old school. OH MY GOD!

"CHUY! NOOOO!"

I don't think he can come back from that.

"I've never seen so much blood..."

It's over. The world is doomed.

"Hey look!"

The dog ain't givin' up!

"Yeah! Sick it to him, dog! Tear that ankle up!"

He's distracted, and OHHHH!

"OHHHHH!"

That was AWESOME!

"I didn't know a dinosaur's mouth was that big!"

Swallowed WHOLE.

"Damn."

Uh oh, it looks like Santa does not go down easy.

"He's about to puke. Get out of the way dog!"

What's the dog doing?

"CPR?"

He has some kind of device in his mouth.

"Is that a bomb?"

Take cover!

"Uh... Did it explode yet?"

I didn't hear anything.

"Neither did I. I was expecting the ground to shake or something."

I'm afraid to look.

"Me too."

We'll look at the same time, okay?

"Okay. Phew... Alright. Ready?"

Ready.

"And go!"

What do you see?

"I don't know. I'm too scared to open my eyes. What do you see?"

I can't bear opening my eyes either.

"Fine, I'm going to look. What the Hell?"

What?

"Open your eyes."

Where did they go?

"They're gone."

I can see that.

"Huh."

Well... I guess the day is saved then.

"Imagine that."

Job well done, Rapido.

"Same to you, Wham."

blackened

Who goes there?

"You're going to have to come with me."

I don't think so! Back up!

"Did you see anything unusual in the sky tonight?"

Daggone right I did!

"I thought so. Please come with me."

I'm not goin' with you! You're probably one a'dem!

"The aliens are gone."

Horse spit! Get outta my house before I shoot ya!

"I just want to talk."

What's with the get up? Goin' to a funeral?

"No, this is–"

Wrong, you're goin' to YOUR funeral!

"Lower your weapon, you don't want to shoot me."

You bet your britches I wanna shoot ye. No one barges into my home
      uninvited, specially not someone wearin' sunglasses in the mid-
      dle of the night!

"Alright then, I'll take them off."

Goodness gracious almighty...

"You will come with me now."

Of course... Your eyes, they're so...

"Where is your wife?"

My who? Beautiful...

"Your wife. She saw the phenomenon too, yes?"

Those ey– what am I doin'? Get the Hell outta here! You ain't redactin'
      me and you ain't redactin' my wife!

"Ow my arm!"

That was jis' a warnin' shot! Imagine how that'll feel in yer face!

"Okay, don't shoot. You win."

Back up real slow. No funny bis'niss.

"I'm leaving. You can put down your gun, but know this. You haven't
      seen the last of me."

You ain't seen the last of me either, pal.

Pete, what's going on here?

"Where have you been?"

I'd rather not talk about it. Explain all of this!

"You said I should just let everyone in."

There's no way this many souls died in the short time I was gone.

"Well... Pretty much every soul in Hell escaped and came here."

Chuy Cristo! How could you let this happen?

"They overpowered me and propped the gates open with that."

This?

"Don't touch it, it's really hot!"

You're such a wimp, this is hardly even room temperature.

"You almost gave me a heart attack. So what can we do about this?"

It looks like all the sinners have already corrupted everyone. I can hardly tell the difference between them. Sex, drugs, and rock 'n roll
everywhere in sight.

"Not to mention the bad language."

There's no way we're going to sort this out. We'll have to start from
scratch.

"You mean..."

That's right, send them all to Hell. Only newly deceased souls will be
considered for entry.

"That doesn't seem fair. Not fair at all."

Even if they deserved to be here in the first place, they blew it. As far as
I can tell, there isn't an innocent soul up here. Except for you,
maybe.

"Thanks, I appreciate that."

Wait a minute, are you drunk?

"Maybe."

You can tell me.

"But then you'd send me to Hell too."

For drinking? Don't be ridiculous.

"Oh good. Then yeap. I'm pretty drunk."

You're a very civilized and sober drunk. Well done. Alright, you may
want to stand back for this.

"For what?"

HwaaaaGHAAAAARAAAA!!!!! That should do it.

"Whoa. That was incredible."

That was nothin'. You should have seen when I let there be light.

collision

"Drive faster!"

I'm going as fast as I can!

"I can't go back to the joint. Don't let them take me!"

Stop freaking out, we're going to be fine.

"Yeah, we'll be fine if you drive faster."

The headlight's still broken, we might crash into something again.

"We'll see about that."

Hey, stay on your side!

"We're doing things my way now."

Your way is smashing my foot!

"Pedal to the metal, baby!"

Let go of the steering wheel!

"You let go!"

Watch out!

"AHHHH!"

AHHHH!

"Oof. Are you okay?"

My head is killing me.

"What happened?"

We crashed into an... ambulance?

"That's convenient."

I think they're in worse shape than we are.

"Is that Bigfoot?"

Enough with the Bigfoot business...

"No, I'm serious."

Well I'll be damned. That is Bigfoot.

"I told you we hit Bigfoot! Twice!"

And a naked guy. Ew.

"Let's get out of here."

You can say that again.

"Let's get out of here."

I hate you.

"I can't wait to get home to some hot chocolate."

I wouldn't count on that.

"What?"

It was on the grocery list.

"Damn it, why does everything bad have to happen to us? Do you think
        we could stop somewhere on the way?"

Are you crazy?

"Crazy for hot chocolate."

full as hell

"Hello?"

Satan again. How's your vacation going?

"Great, I'm kind of tipsy right now."

Fantastic. Glad you're enjoying yourself.

"Is something wrong?"

Quite the opposite.

"Why are you calling me then? Are you back in Hell?"

Yes, I have returned. I must say whatever you did before you left...
        well done.

"I'm not sure I know what you're talking about."

Every single deceased soul is now in Hell! I don't know how you pulled
        it off, but I'm very pleased with your work.

"I uh... thanks."

I want you to go ahead and take off an additional week. But be well
        rested and ready for action when you get back. I have plans for
        you.

"Like a promotion?"

You could call it that. Take care, comrade.

"Wow, thanks!"

ambulare

What luck!

"Is that our ambulance?"

It sure is. I told you we'd find it if we kept walking. Come on!

"I can't run. My feet are killing me."

Don't be a wimp.

"Ow ow ow ow ow ow."

Why are you stopping?

"Leg cramp."

Do I have to carry you?

"No, I'm okay, just slow down a bit."

Alright, but you better be ready to have my back.

"I have my walking stick."

It's just a stick.

"That's what walking sticks are made of! Either way, packs a wallop."

Have your stick ready then.

"Walking stick."

What happened here?

"Clearly there was a wreck. Look! Bigfoot!"

And a naked guy in the driver's seat. Ew.

"Oh man, I wonder if that wolf from earlier was..."

There's no such thing as werewolves! Looks like they're out cold.

"And the ambulance seems like it will still run."

Help me drag these guys out of here.

"We can't just leave them here. We're paramedics. We have a code."

Screw the code, do you want to find out what these freaks will do to us
        when they wake up?

"True. I'll grab this end."

And heave!

"Ho!"

Heave!

"Ho!"

Watch it, watch it, watch it!

"He's so heavy, I can't keep my bala–"

Ooooh. Ouch. I don't think his leg is supposed to bend that way.

"Uh... there."

I don't think just straightening it out will help, the damage is done.

"They were in a car wreck, I don't think it will notice the difference."

Nothing we can do about it now. Help me with the naked guy.

"Nuh uh, you're on your own with that one."

Why not? He's practically dead. We touch practically dead skin all day.

"This feels dirty."

Grab him under the arms and pull that way. I'll get his feet.

"Fine, I got him, you can... Ah!"

Jeez, he's all slippery. What the hell?

"Get him off me!"

Ha ha ha! Serves you right.

"Come on! Whatever this goop he's covered in is getting all over me."

There. Better?

"Not at all. I don't even want to know what this stuff is. Get in."

What? No, you're driving.

"The driver's seat is covered in goop!"

Exactly. No sense in me getting covered in it too. In fact...

"Hey, I'm not a towel!"

This stuff is gross, I don't want it on my hands.

"I don't want it anywhere!"

Come on, let's get out of here.

"Let me grab something from the back t– Crap, Bigfoot just moved!"

Hurry up! Get in and drive!

"Wow, that was close."

Lucky though, eh?

"Easy for you to say. You're not covered in goop."

Maybe you'll turn into a werewolf now?

"Shut up."

knock knock

Hello?

"Get outta here! I'll shoot ya, alien scum sack!"

Whoa, I'm just trying to find my way home. I got lost and was hoping
for directions.

"Yer voice sounds familiar. Do I know you?"

Hey... yeah! I talked to you on the phone earlier!

"What's the secret knock?"

Shoot, uh...   Knock knock kno-knock knockknock knock kno-kno-
knock kno-knockknock.

"You rushed it there at the end, but good enough. Come on in."

Thank God, I've been driving around in circles for the last hour.

"Don't thank God, thank good ol' fashioned secret knocks."

Wow you really barricaded yourself in here didn't you?

"If you wouldn't mind, could you help me push this frig-rater back in
front of the door? Don't want another black barging in here."

Whoa whoa whoa, I had no idea you were like that!

"Oh sorry, I meant the aliens. One came in here wearing all black."

I thought the aliens were blown up.

"Nope, it's all a plot t'make us think we're safe. The aliens are still here.
He tried to obstruct me."

How did you know he was an alien.

"He took off his sunglasses and I could see it in his eyes. Like looking
into the emptiness of space. It was mesmerizin'."

Wow. Is your wife okay?

"Aw shoot, I don't have a wife."

But you said...

"Listen, in times like this sympathy is your biggest weapon. Next
biggest is surprise. Next to that, a well maintained shotgun."

You made it all up then?

"Just the wife. Everything else was abs'lutely true."

Wow, I don't know how to feel about that...

"Thanks to me, you're alive and your not gonna be adducted."

Really close that time.

"All Hell is about to break loose, we stick together and we'll make it

through this.."
Well I have nothing to lose. I'm in.
"Let's get you a shotgun."

afterbath

Hey, wake up.
"What happened?"
We were in an accident.
"My head is killing me."
We have to get out of here before someone finds us.
"Where's the ambulance?"
We must have been blown clear of the wreck?
"Out of sight? That's ridiculous."
Forget about it, we have other things to worry about. I think I see a car
    coming!"
"Into the forest!"
Ow, ow, ow, my leg.
"Push through it, we just need to get far enough in to hide and... do you
    hear that?"
No, what are you talking about?
"That high pitched whine... Kind like, weeeege-weeeege-weeeege."
Oh great, yeah now I do. Now I can't **not** hear it. So annoying.
"Sorry. I wonder what it is?"
It sounds like it's coming from over this way.
"Something's glowing."
Here, I'll give you a boost so you can see.
"Alright, on the count of three lift me up."
One... two–
"On **my** count."
Why can't I count?
"I'm the one getting boosted."
But I'm doing all the work, I should call it.
"It's like a rocket launch. I need to be ready."
Exactly, it's like a rocket launch. The astronauts don't do the count-
    down, that's mission control's job. You just sit back and wait.

"Ugh, whatever."

Boosting and... one... two... three!

"Ahhh!"

Are you alright?

"I didn't want you to throw me over!"

Sorry, my hands slipped. Whatever your covered in is slick as Hell.

"Dinosaur snot."

What?

"I'm covered in dinosaur snot, okay?"

Gross!

"Hey, you have to see this. Some kind of pool."

A spring?

"Doesn't look like water... and it smells fruity. Come see for yourself."

Hold on I need to find a strong enough branch to get started and...

"It tastes fruity too... kinda like limes."

Oof!

"Hmmm..."

Oh I'm okay, don't even worry about me. My leg wasn't already hurting
        like Hell or anything.

"You said you heal fast, you'll get over it."

I may heal fast but it still hurts, jerk. Wow, this is really something.

"I can't pry my eyes from it's beauty."

Wait, look at the reflection!

"What about it?"

That's not the forest we're seeing!

"Oh my, you're right! What IS that?"

Some kind of city... do you think we should?

"Should what?"

You know... Jump in.

"Are you crazy? We'll probably drown. We don't even know what this
        stuff is!"

The cops are probably hot on our trail by now, and you already drank
        some, what's the harm?

"Okay, I need to wash off this snot anyway. Here goes nothin'."

What a night.

"You've got that right."

It makes you think, you know?

"Yeap."

What does it really mean to be a hero?

"Who's to say?"

Does it mean having super powers like my super strength or your super
      speed and Lady Love Lumps' uh... whatever she does?

"Maybe."

Or does it mean standing up for your beliefs in the face of adversity?

"A little of that, too."

Protecting the innocent? Or giving the voiceless a voice?

"They each have their merits."

Or maybe it means sacrificing yourself for the good of mankind.

"Poor Chuy Cristo. I'll miss him."

I don't think it's any of those things.

"Oh yeah?"

No, being a hero means wearing spats with pride.

"You do know spats are shoe accessories, not tights, don't you?"

I've heard it both ways. Who knows what adventure awaits us on the
      other side of tomorrow?

"We'll have to wait and see."

So what now?

"I guess we could just go back home. No need for us to get frostbite
      while yakkin' away. Speaking of yakking, did you check on
      Lady Love Lumps?"

She's fine. The back seat is rather accommodating, she's probably sleep-
      ing like a baby.

"The Wham Mobile has more than two seats?"

Of course.

"You said I had to run up here on my own because you didn't have
      enough room!"

Right, Lady Love Lumps was sleeping across the backseat, and Chuy
      already called shotgun.

"I don't know why you brought her, she was useless."

So were we.

"At least we can tell the tale to the masses. She's been unconscious this entire time!"

Come on, she's Lady Love Lumps. The glue that holds together the Crime Brigade!

"How many time do I have to tell you? That name is terrible!"

It's a great name and you know it!

"Why couldn't we just go by our old band name?"

Rapid Whammy Love?

"Yeah man, that's pure power in name form."

But that excludes Chuy.

"That's okay, he's dead."

Way to be blunt. Hey, now what if we go all out and get the band back together?

"What? That's not what I meant."

Yeah! One phone call will get us a gig TONIGHT.

"I haven't played in years, I don't think I could—"

Badoobadooba...

"Wha woow, reeoowwwww manamanaoowww!"

You still got it!

"Imagine how that'd sound on a guitar! Alright, I'm in. Do you think Lady Love Lumps is up for it?"

Oh, she's up for anything. If you know what I mean.

"You are such a.... Hold on, what about drums? There's no way Little Whammy will join us."

You can beat box, right?

"Who can't?"

Well there we go.

"Brilliant."

I'll get you the deets on the gig.

"The what on the what?"

The deets.

"Uh..."

Details, come on.

"Oh, right. Do you think we should practice first?"

Nah, you heard how awesome we were just then, this will be magic. Don't want to waste the magic on an empty rehearsal space.

"Alright then, let's get goin'."

What are you doing?

"Riding shotgun."

You can't run back?

"I don't want to. Plus we could work out the set list on the drive down."

You'll get home faster if you run.

"I don't want to run!"

I strongly suggest you run.

"What's the problem? There's plenty of space now, my legs are tired and— oh I see, you were hoping to get lucky with the lady, weren't you?"

Maybe.

"You scoundrel."

So you'll run back?

"Yeah, fine."

See you in the green room!

"Green room it up!"

That's not a thing.

"I'm making it a thing. Say it."

No.

"SAY IT."

Green room it up.

"Hello there, I'm looking to buy a new vehicle."

Sure, we just got the new Mini in.

"What are you trying to say?"

I was just...

"I'm a leprechaun, okay? Go on, get 'em out."

Get what out?

"The short jokes. Just get them out of your system so we can get down to business."

Please, let's just forget all that and move on. Have a look at this great new model we got in today. It has all the newest features. Seats, steering wheel, tires... The works.

"No, that's garbage. I want an SUV. Something with size, power, what the french call OOMPH!"

Ah, I see. Compensation?

"Excuse me!? Would you mind repeating yourself?"

Oh, I'm sorry, I meant... how are you looking to pay? It greatly impacts the pricing and finances. We want to pick the vehicle that's best fit for you.

"You will not tell me what vehicles I will fit in!"

I mean financial fit!

"Yeah, I'm sure of it... Anyway, money is no object. I'll be paying in gold coins."

I'm not sure we take gold coins...

"Sure you do! Everyone takes gold! It's better than cash, plus it's shiny and tastes so good..."

Ew, I'm not going to take gold coins that have been in your mouth.

"All money has been in far worse places than inside leprechaun mouths.

In fact, leprechaun mouths are even cleaner than dog mouths!"

I don't think that's true.

"Scientific fact from the BOLS."

Bulls?

"Board of Leprechaun Sciences."

I think that study may be a bit biased.

"Listen here, I have gold that I'm willing to give you today, and in return all I'm asking for is an answers-to-no-one kick ass SUV. Now what do I have to do to get one of your fine vehicles today?"

I suppose I could ask my supervisor if I can—

"You'll take my gold and give me an SUV! Don't go running off to your supervisor any time you wet your pants a little bit. Man up and make this sale, or I'll turn you into a stack of potatoes!"

You wouldn't dare.

"I've done it to people I like more for less."

You're going to have to show me the gold. Usually we have to run a credit check, but obviously...

"Sure. Here's a coin. There are hundreds more where that came from."

I can't just take your word for it.

"Well, here's the thing... I can only access my pot of gold when there's a rainbow for it to be at the end of."

Hey, here's a question for you... if there's a double rainbow, does your gold supply double?

"No, don't be ridiculous!"

It's a perfectly valid question!

"You can't just go out and find a pot of gold at the end of the rainbow, the leprechaun who owns the gold has to be present. Obviously, I can't be be at the end of both rainbows at the same time."

That's too complicated.

"It's not important. What's important is that you sell me that SUV over there right now."

I told you, I have to see all the money before we go any further.

"It's not raining, how am I supposed to do that?"

There has to be some other way.

"Hmm... Is there a hose around here?"

Like a radiator hose?

"What? No! A garden hose or something."

We don't have a garden here at the dealership.

"A garden hose doesn't have to be used in a garden... What is wrong
with you? I mean any kind of hose that sprays water."

Like a radiator hose.

"No! Surely you guys wash these cars somehow."

Ohhhh, you mean a washing hose.

"That's not a thing..."

Yeah, we have a washing hose around back.

"Yeah, fine, okay, a washing hose, whatever. Take me to it, we can make
our own rainbow."

Whoa, really?

"Yes."

How does that work?

"Well the droplets of water in the air, when you have the sun at your
back, bounces back at your eyes, and depending on the position
... you know what, just look it up online."

Hmmm...

"Hand me the hose, dummy."

Oh, wow! So pretty! And look, a pot of gold just like you said!

"Yes, just like I said. Now, can we get this sale on paper now or
what?"

So shiny...

"Hey, listen to me!"

Where'd it go?

"I've shown that I have the gold to buy that SUV, so let's go inside and
take care of the paperwork."

You made it disappear! Like magic. You're some kind of witch aren't
you?

"I'm a leprechaun, not a witch!"

I know, but leprechauns aren't magic, are they?

"I just conjured up my pot of gold using a garden—"

Washing hose.

"Sigh. Using a washing hose. Of course leprechauns are magical."

Do it again!

"I'll do it again after we sign that paperwork!"

Awesome! So you wanted this model over here?

"Yes, it's perfect."

More like imperfect.

"What's wrong with it?"

Mileage is terrible, the ride is bumpy, the rear view mirrors are slightly too small. What you want is this puppy over here.

"But it's not green."

You can get it in green.

"But that one over there is already green."

We have a green one in the back lot. This is just the floor model.

"I see... Alright, I'll take it."

Wait, don't you want to know why this one is so much better than the other one?

"It has better mileage, a smoother ride, and bigger rear view mirrors."

Exactly, how did you know?

"Had a feeling. Great, so I'll take it."

But wait! Why settle for this ravenous beast when you could go hybrid, plus built in LCD screens in the back of every seat.

"But I'll be driving."

Do you have children?

"No."

Plan on having children?

"Leprechauns can't have children. We're immortal so reproduction would just cause an over abundance of leprechauns, and we can't have that can we?"

I suppose not... but how about road trips with your bros?

"True. Let's do it. Give me the works."

But wait, why settle for—

"Just give me your best SUV and stop giving me the runaround!"

The Experimenter it is.

"Uh, what?"

The car industry has been running out of synonyms and ex- names so... I assure you, it's the best sports utility vehicle on the market.

"What's a sports utility vehicle?"

SUV. That's what SUV stands for.

"Hmm I see, I did not know that. Learn something new every day. The Experimenter it is, but this better not be some weird sex thing."

No sexual exploits will come from this vehicle. Unless that's you want. There's a button on the left side of the dash for that.

"I don't think I'll be—"

It has a picture of boobs on it. Or maybe it's balls... There aren't nipples, so it could go either way.

"Maybe it's a butt?"

Of course! The booty call button. Let's go do some paperwork.

hot chocolate

Mrs. Johnson?

"Yes, may I help you?"

I'm from the police department. I spoke to you earlier about your sons.

"You don't look like cop... Cops don't wear suits."

I'm a detective.

"Oh, of course. Come on in, detective."

Thank you. I couldn't help but notice your van isn't in the driveway.

"The boys haven't come back home yet."

Is this typical behavior?

"It's not unusual... Are they in trouble?"

No, nothing like that. I just thought I'd stop by and check in with you in case you've heard anything.

"I see. I haven't heard from them, but I'm sure if they were in trouble they would give me a call. Would you like a hot chocolate?"

No that's quite alright, thank you.

"Are you sure? It's delicious."

That's okay.

"I insist."

Please, don't go to the trouble...

"It's no trouble. Wait here, it'll take just a moment."

Have your boys been displaying any unusual behavior lately?

"What's that?"

Unusual behavior.

"I can't hear you, you'll have to speak up."

HAVE YOUR BOYS BEEN DISPLAYING—

"Here, fresh cup of hot chocolate. Careful, wouldn't want you to burn your mouth."

Oh wow, that... that's like liquid Heaven.

"Told ya."

Mmm, could I get the recipe for this?

"Never!"

Sorry, I didn't mean to...

"It's alright, I just get very protective about my hot chocolate. I learned the recipe from my husband, you could say it's his legacy."

Oh, can I meet him?

"No, no... He ah..."

Need a tissue?

"Thank you. He went on an expedition to Antarctica years ago.

A hot chocolate expedition?

"What?"

Sorry, go on.

"He never came back. The company he worked for denies he was even an employee."

Very interesting...

"The boys were still in grade school back then... They took it real hard. Started making trouble around the neighborhood."

They were trouble makers?

"Yes they were. Still are. Afraid they haven't changed. I just let them be though. They never do anything that does anyone harm."

So they don't share much with you about their exploits?

"I'm not bothered as long they bring home everything on my grocery list. Their business is their business."

I think they may have been involved in a hit and run accident. They were in two accidents, actually.

"Oh my! Are they okay?"

Haven't been able to find them.

"That's a good thing, right?"

In so much as they're still alive if they're still able to drive around...
They're probably just scared, laying low. I was wondering if
you have heard from them, maybe they mentioned encountering
anything out of the ordinary?

"They haven't called me. They never call."

Not even if they come across, say, a wild animal in the road?

"Like a raccoon?"

Maybe something larger, like a deer.

"You know what, they texted me late last night before they were arrested. It didn't make any sense, then again none of their slang
makes sense to me."

Can you show me the message?

"Sure, here you go. It says... Hit bigfoot, headlight broken. Sorry."

What's not to understand about that?

"Thought it was some kind of sex act, figured they meant to send it to
one of their lady friends."

You've been very helpful, I'll be in touch.

"That's it? What am I supposed to do now?"

Do nothing. I was never here. Again, amazing hot chocolate.

unicon

"Welcome fellow unicorns. Thank you for attending this conference,
I— Oh, there's only one of you."

Hey.

"Well this is awkward."

Little bit.

"I prepared this big rallying speech and everything."

I'm not really in the mood for that.

"Hm."

Are we really the last two unicorns?

"Nah, there must be at least a couple who stayed home sick."

I hope so, because if we're the last two...

"What?"

No offense, but I'm not all that attracted to you.

"Oh yeah? Look who's talking. You should be called an uglicorn."

You want to say that to my face?

"I just did! Uglicorn!"

I will stab you. Hard.

"Why don't you come over here and try it?"

Hold on just a second.

"What's the matter? Chicken?"

No, I... I can't go down stairs.

"What the... I'm coming up there to kick your ass."

Fine! Try it!

"Oh. It's kind of crowded up here. Can't really..."

Yeah, this is uncomfortable. And you smell real bad.

"Me? I smell bad? No way, you smell way worse."

You're probably just used to your own smell, but trust me, it's terrible.

"You're probably just used to YOUR own smell! Get out of here, you're
        stinking up the place."

I told you, I can't go down stairs...

"Well neither can I!"

This is just great. Hey, I think I know where all the other unicorns might
        be.

"Yeah?"

They must be stuck on a second floor somewhere.

"Oh thank God. There was no way I was going to procreate with you."

Bite me!

"Don't mind if I do!"

Ouch! You're going to pay for that!

"Ow ow ow ow, stop it!"

Say uncle!

"Never!"

Say it!

"Owwwwwww, heeyah!"

Ouch! Enough is enough! We should work together and find our fellow
        unicorns. We have to make sure we're not stuck together.

"Fair enough. Truce. But, how are we going to get down from here?"

I have an idea.

"Ow! I said truce, and two seconds later you push me off the stage... Oh hey, good thinking!"

Now push that pillar over so it knocks me off.

"Are you sure? That looks like it might hurt."

You can't push me off yourself, because you'd have to come up here to do it, then you'll be stuck and then I won't be able to push you off without coming up here myself and... You get the idea.

"Okay, but you can't be mad at me if it hurts."

It's fine. I'm ready.

"Stop making that face."

I can't. It's my imminent pain face.

"It's really unattractive."

Push the pillar over already!

"Unflattering."

PUSH IT!

"Downright repug—"

Oof!

"—nant. How was that?"

Oh that wasn't bad at all. I was so riled up by your insults that I was more surprised than anything.

"You're welcome."

Let's go find our brethren.

"Could you pop this on your head while we're out?"

What's this?

"A paper bag. I already made the eye holes for you."

I hate you so much.

poolside

"Whoa, that was intense."

Check it out, you're all clean now.

"Hell yeah! I was not fond of the dinosaur snot."

And you're naked.

"I've been naked this whole time."

But it's daytime here... wherever here is. Seeing you naked is a whole different experience in sunlight.

"What am I supposed to do?"

Cover up or something.

"Do you see any pants around here?"

No, but we can't go in the city with your private parts flapping around willy nilly.

"How'd you know that's it Willy Nilly? Oh wow, that is quite a city, it's so shiny."

Yeah, it's breathtaking. You're ignoring the issue, we need to get you some pants, man.

"Let's see, there are some trees over there."

Leaves aren't going to cut it.

"Leaf cuts would hurt so bad."

That's not what I meant.

"Once I got a paper cut right on my—"

That's not what I meant! Oh look, somebody dropped a satchel.

"Don't look at me, I went behind a tree before we jumped into the pool."

A bag, they dropped a bag. Who ever used 'satchel' to describe a poo?

"You seem like the kind who would."

Anyway, you can use the satchel. You can cut holes in it and wear it like a diaper.

"That's barbaric!"

It's either that or somehow get a bunch of leaves to stick together as pants.

"Sap would do the trick."

Sap?

"Like maple syrup. It's sticky right?"

These aren't maple trees.

"Well it doesn't have to be maple syrup, it could be aspen syrup or pine syrup, or any syrup."

Palm syrup?

"Don't be gross."

I think it'd be easier just to make a satchel diaper.

"I will not be seen wearing a diaper, how degrading."

Think of it as a leather speedo. You know, like what olympic swimming gold medalists wear. But leather.

"Hmm... Like the James Dean of olympic swimming gold medalists."

Exactly.

"I can live with that. Hand it over."

Oh, there's stuff inside.

"Of course there is, why would anyone have a bag and not put anything inside? What do we have, gold coins? Rubies? Diamonds? Gold coins encrusted with rubies and diamonds?"

It's an entertainment book.

"Oh, like a book of naughty pictures?"

That would be a gentleman's entertainment book. No, it's a book of coupons.

"Those are such a rip off. You buy them from your neighbor's kid for thirty bucks, and you end up using maybe one coupon before the whole book expires. Lame."

It's not so lame if you find one for free!

"Good point. When do the coupons expire?"

August 31st, 5314.

"Man, we have three thousand years to use them!"

That doesn't seem right... Did we travel to the future?

"Maybe, those crystal towers seem like pretty advanced technology. Super futuristic. We have to find out what the date is today, these coupons might already be expired!"

Put on your diaper and we'll get going.

"Leather speedo! We agreed it was a leather speedo!"

Put on your leather speedo.

"Do you have a knife? Gotta cut the leg holes."

I don't have any pockets, how could I have a knife?

"Oh, maybe there's a knife in the bag. What's this?"

Looks like a rock.

"Surely it has to be more than just a rock. Why would someone just put
    a rock in their bag?"

Maybe that's why they left it here. Figured, why the Hell am I carrying
    this bag around when all I have in it is this rock?

"A rock and an expired entertainment book."

That has yet to be verified.

"Well that's junk... oh here, a pair of scissors. And.... Alright there we
    go! Perfect!"

I've never seen a better leather dia—

"Speedo. Leather speedo."

I've never seen a better leather speedo. Let's head into the city then!

"I'd kind of prefer if I went in alone. I'm not sure people will be willing
    to lend me pants if I'm accompanied by a wookiee."

Excuse me? I ain't no wookiee, bud.

"Yeah, I know, but most people would... Look, for all we know, people
    here in the future are just as scared of bigfoot as in the past. I'll
    go in and find myself some actual clothes. Though I must admit
    I look pretty damn sexy in this speedo..."

You werc saying?

"Er, and I'll get you some kind of disguise. "

Fine, my leg still hurts pretty bad anyway, I need some more time to
    heal.

"Give me the entertainment book in case there are coupons for clothing
    outlets or costume shops."

The blue section.

"What?"

The blue section of the entertainment book is retail stores, so that's
    where you'll find those coupons.

"Gotcha. Oh yeah, right there in the blue section. Perfect. Let's hope
    these aren't expired."

I'll see you later then?

"I'll be back in a couple hours."

See you then. Er, hold on...

"Whoa whoa whoa, watch where you're pawing."

Your tag was sticking out in the back.

"Oh, thanks."

new blood

Where am I?

"You're in my lair, don't you remember?"

What... Oh, OH! Get away from me!

"Take it easy, I'm not going to hurt you."

You tricked me into giving you all my blood!

"You're a bleeder, what was I supposed to do?"

Not bite me in the first place! How am I still alive?

"I felt bad that I tricked you into letting me drink all your blood..."

Ha, so you did trick me!

"Yeah, well, I decided the least I could do is keep you from dying."

Mhmm... What's the catch?

"You're now a vampire!"

I knew it! You jerk, this had to have been your plan all along!

"Yes, my plan was to trick some idiot into becoming a vampire that I'd have to be responsible for until one of us dies. That's exactly what I was looking for when I went down for a nap."

It makes more sense than you accidentally leaving your door unlocked so that just about any old vampire hunter could come in here and drive a stake through your heart.

"You think you deserve to call yourself a vampire hunter? You didn't even drive the stake through the correct side of my chest. By the way, even though it didn't kill me, it still stings quite a bit. I'll never forgive you for that."

You're the one that's unforgiven! How could you do this to me? Here I was hoping to become the world's greatest vampire hunter, and you go and turn me into a vampire.

"Face it, you were going to suck. Now you'll just suck in a much more productive way. Shh! Did you hear that?"

Hear what?

"Footsteps... a mile out. Sounds like the rawhide boots of Arnie Freeman, world's most notorious vampire hunter."

Oh my God, he's my idol! How can you tell it's him?

"Vampires have heightened senses of... everything. Hearing, smelling,
seeing, tasting, touching, wheeling."

What the hell is wheeling?

"We'll get into that later. For now, we have to get the Hell out of here."

You're not strong enough to take on Arnie Freeman?

"Not when I have you dragging me down. It's for your own good, follow me."

That's a fight I would pay to see in person. Where are we going? These
are some smelly caves.

"You'll get used to it, that's just your senses adjusting to their new sen-
sitivity."

No, I think it would smell bad in here even if I was a human. Did you
have cabbage for lunch or something? Whew, it stinks.

"If I have gas it's from eating your inferior blood. Stop sniffing, we
don't have much time."

You're so bossy.

"You don't understand. If anything bad happens to a vampire within
their first ten years their maker is held responsible. If you die,
I'll be taken to vampirc court."

That's a long time.

"Usually I'd say ten years is nothing compared to the thousand years
I've been around, but with you I have a feeling it will feel like
an eternity."

Gee, thanks.

"Here, help me move this panel."

You mean the rock?

"It's a panel."

Looks like a big rock to me.

"Come on kid, just help me move it."

Fine. On three?

"Just start pushing, we don't have time for this."

Woah, that was easier than I thought. That must be the superhuman vampire strength!

"Nope, the panel is just made of plywood and papier mache. Not gonna do a damn thing to stop Arnie, so we have to seal it up."

I could have sworn that was rock... I guess it was a panel after all.

"I'll take that as an apology, and a compliment."

Oh, you made that?

"Of course, what else am I going to do down here, mine for gold or something?"

That would make you a whole lot more money than making papier mache panels that look like rock...

"Not everything is about money. Roll this disc in front of the panel."

Holy Hell, this thing weighs a ton.

"Two tons to be exact. Believe me, you wouldn't be able to budge it as a human. Make sure the edges are lined up with those girders."

Like this?

"Perfect. Now shield your eyes."

What are you doing?

"Welding it shut."

How will we get back into your lair?

"Don't worry, I have a plasma cutter in here too."

Alright, so what next, where are we going?

"We're staying right here."

What do you mean?

"This is the only way in and out of this room. It's what you could call a panic room. Back when I was human, we called it Henry."

What if he finds us? We'll never be able to get out if he's just sitting out their waiting for us to come out. What if he's in this room already?

"Calm down, he'll never find us, but just to be safe we need to be as quiet as possible."

Fine by me.

special task

You're the elevator operator, right? Or is it elevator attendant?

"Well, operator is kind of feminine since it conjures the image of the old time telephone operators... You know, gossipy ladies sitting at the switchboards patching through calls and such. However the word attendant is just as feminine. You've got flight attendants, and the lady school teachers who take attendance. I guess what I'm trying to say is that either title is fine."

Elevator guy it is.

"That's good. Masculine. Guy... I should use that."

Have a seat elevator guy.

"Sure. What can I do for you sir?"

You're a valuable employee, and I trust you with my life every day.

"I do my best."

Well your best isn't good enough!

"Oh God, please don't fire me!"

What? Oh I'm sorry, that came out the wrong way. I want you to do even better! That's why I have a special task for you.

"Oh?"

Of course, you'll get a very healthy bonus.

"I like bonuses. I've never received one before, but I'd love to start."

Before we proceed, as far as anyone outside of this room knows, we never spoke. Understood?

"Uh..."

Understood?

"Yeah, okay. Not a word."

Great. I knew you were the man for the job. Have you ever used one of these before?

"A backpack?"

Oh good, you're familiar. Inside this backpack is a... well, don't look inside the backpack. Have you ever seen one of these?

"Another backpack?"

Fantastic, you're a sharp young man.

"Don't look inside that backpack either?"

You're catching on. And now, have you ever seen one of these?

"That's another backpack."

Yes indeed. I really did pick the right person for this.

"And I shouldn't look inside that one either?"

No, this one you do want to look inside. It has all the instructions, maps, passports and money you'll need to pull off the operation.

"What's the operation?"

It's all in this backpack. From now on, if I need to contact you I'll use the code phrase 'operation backpack.' Can you remember that?

"It'll be tough, but I think I can manage."

What do you mean it will be tough, you have three backpacks and it's called operation backpa— oh, you're being funny. Ha! I love a good sense of humor statement. Read the materials, you'll know what to do from there.

"Sounds good."

What are you doing?

"I'm reading what to do next. How am I supposed to get to Guam?"

Don't ask me, consult your instructions!

"Let's see here... oh. Where are the escape pods?"

Right, I forgot I need to help with this first part. The escape pods are right this way. I'm letting you use one of my personal escape pods, quite the honor if I say so myself.

"How many escape pods do you have?"

Six.

"Why do you need six?"

In case something really bad happens.

"But you're only one person."

Backups. If the launch mechanism fails on this first one, I can just pry the door open and give the next pod a try. Fairly conventional CEO escape set up. Anyway, after you seal the door just press that button there that says 'eject'.

"Are you sure that isn't the button to eject from the escape pod?"

That... I'm not sure. I've never actually used one of these pods before.

"What about this button that says 'launch'?"

That's the lunch button. Drops in a fresh submarine sandwich, a bag of chips and a bottle of cola with a twist of lime. You know, in case you're unable to pry open the door and have to sit there for a while waiting for someone to get you out, you've gotta have some kind of sustenance.

"Makes sense. So what do I press to get to Guam?"

I was pretty sure it was the eject button... but it might be that one.

"The button that says 'escape'?"

Yeah, that might be it.

"Well, it's on the computer keyboard, so I'm not sure it's that kind of escape."

Oh, the computer interface, of course. Pull up the help screen.

"Alright."

Type in 'escape pod'.

"30,000 articles."

Do we have time to read that many?

"Nope. We should use more specific search terms."

Right, of course. Type in 'escape pod escape'.

"30,000 articles."

Shoot, I thought we had it that time. Did you put it in quotes? Oh, yeah see, you didn't use quotes.

"Okay, same thing with quotes... Zero results."

Damn. We need to think of something more specific than 'escape pod', but less specific than 'escape pod escape'. Hmmm...

"I'm going to try the eject button to see what happens. Stand back."

Give me a wave if it works!

"I'm pressing the button now."

Great! Is it working?

"Hmm."

What happened?

"It's a video tape. It came out of this slot. The label says: How To Launch Your Escape Pod."

Perfect, I knew we'd figure it out! I think you've got this under control, report back to me as soon as you've completed... you know what, this is all in your instructions, I'll leave you to it. Good luck.

powers that be

Hello, St. Peter?

"Nope, God here."

Oh fantastic! So you made it home alright.

"Couldn't be better, Heaven's the most peaceful it's been in centuries."

I'm glad that you're back in the hot seat, so to speak. Though really, it's me who is in the hot seat, right? Right?

"Right. Listen Luke, I have a feeling something hasn't gone as well as we would have liked."

I thought you said things were going great?

"For now, yes. It's Santa."

Christ.

"No, Santa."

He's dead, I thought.

"Not so much dead as incapacitated."

I see... So what should we do?

"I'm going to resurrect Jesus."

I thought you already did that. Twice.

"Santa cut his head off..."

So you've proven that he's absolutely worthless.

"I wouldn't say that..."

Worthless against Santa, anyway.

"Do you have a better plan?"

I don't know. I haven't done all that much since I got that new assistant. He's really good at my job.

"Ah, delegation, you're finally catching on. St. Peter has been doing all of my work for years, except for signing 8x10's for fans."

Can't he do that too? Your signature's easy to forge, I do it all the—

"What did you say?"

Nothing, what are we going to do about Santa?

"I'm sending Jesus. Whatever you want to try is your business."

Hm, I guess I should bring my assistant back from vacation.

"You let your assistant take vacations? Damn, you're a nice boss."

snow lumps

Oh Gerald!

"Shh!"

Why so upset, Gerald?

"Stop saying my real name, we're in costume!"

But Captain Wham is so... impersonal.

"Listen, we have to get back down South before I freeze to death."

Hold me!

"I'm already holding you and frankly my arms are starting to hurt."

You're so romantic.

"Oh God, your breath stinks of alcohol vomit."

Where are we anyway?

"The North Pole."

What?!

"We were going to fight Santa alongside Jesus and Rapido, but then you
          went off somewhere to puke while Santa got eaten by a dinosaur
          and then exploded by a dog with a bomb, I think."

No really, why are we at the North Pole?

"Forget it."

It's funny, I know it's snowing and everything, but I don't really feel all
          that cold.

"Why do you think I'm holding you?"

But your arms are like icicles.

"You're warming me up, Love Lumps!"

I do still feel quite a bit of alcohol in my veins.

"Yeah, that's why."

Oh crap, what time is it?

"That depends."

On what?

"On where we stand. See now, it's 1 in the afternoon. And over here...
          it's 10 at night."

I don't like your North Pole humor. What time is it back home?

"About 11 in the morning."

Crap! I was supposed to be at work two hours ago! You have to get me
          there immediately!

"Easy, I'm sure no one is freaking out because their shoulders are tense."

That's exactly why most people freak out! Tension is the source of all conflict.

"There there."

What are you trying to do?

"Rubbing your shoulders so you'll calm down."

You're doing it all wrong! Here, put your thumb here, and grip... yeah that's it. Ohhh yeah.

"Huh, imagine that."

Hey, stop it! I have to get to work, seriously.

"About that, Rapido and I talked and we decided we're getting the band back together."

Rapid Whammy Love? Really?

"Yeah, in fact I already have a gig lined up for us tonight! So forget about work, we've got some rockin' to do."

I suppose if we hurry I'll have time to practice before the concert.

"Ehhh, practice is for Bachelor of Music students, we'll be fine! Come on, the Wham Mobile is a short hike that way."

Why'd you park so far away?

"Have you heard my monster of an engine? We had to park far away so we could sneak up on the Clause."

You don't really call him that.

"I do now."

Could you carry me?

"To the car? Or in theory?"

To the car.

"If I was able carry you, we would be back home already. I've been waiting all this time for you to wake up."

Oof, I feel like throwing up, I think I'm going to— BLLLRRRGHHH!

"All over my pants! Get up, we're leaving before this puke freezes into my tights."

Drive back over here and get me, I need a nap.

"You can't nap in the middle of a snow bank!

Nap nap nap...

"Ugh, I give up. I'll be back for you in a minute."

below the waist

Hello there, I'm looking for some—

"Clothes."

Yes.

"Obviously. Come with me. Let's get you out of that dreadful diaper."

It's not a diaper, it's a leather speedo.

"A whato?"

You know, a speedo... oh right, you don't know.

"Listen, I don't know how people dress where you come from, or what
       kind of fancy tailors named speedo you have, but I assure you,
       everything you will find here at Jimbeau's is the finest in all the
       land."

This is quite the store you have here.

"Here, this would suit you perfectly."

That's a... what is that?

"Ha, what a joker! Try it on."

Er...

"Put your arm through there, and your opposite leg there. It's like you've
       never worn one before!"

I haven't.

"Quit with the jokes. Now, do you have er... problems?"

What kind of problems?

"You know... sphincter control."

What?

"Because of the diaper."

It's not a diaper! It's a leather speedo... no, it isn't even that, it's just a
       bag I found and cut leg holes in because I was naked.

"Why were you naked? You're not a sex deviant are you? This city is
       not fond of sex deviants."

But you're okay with grown men wearing nothing but leather diapers.

"Not when it means I can make a sale."

Alright then.

"So you assure me you're not a sex deviant?"

I am not a sex deviant.

"Promise?"

I promise. I just need clothes so I'm not walking around in a leather bag. It's starting to chafe.

"Alright, we shall proceed. How does that fit?"

Uh... it fits well I guess. I'm not really sure how it's supposed to fit.

"Hmm, it looks a little loose around the hips. Here."

Whoa! What are you doing?

"I'm adjusting your hips, relax. Sometimes it's just the way you stand that will make this particular garment breathe too much."

I have to walk around in this, I can't be worried about standing exactly the right way.

"How else do you suggest keeping it snug around your hips?"

I don't know, a belt maybe?

"You can't wear a belt with this, are you mad?"

Why not?

"It would throw off the entire ensemble."

How is this an ensemble? I have a single piece of cloth draped around me.

"Exactly. Simplicity and elegance."

Uh...

"You wouldn't want anyone else to think you're a sex deviant, right?"

Of course not.

"Then simplicity and elegance is the way to go."

The leather diaper was pretty simple.

"But not elegant at all!"

Can I just get a pair of pants and a shirt? This is just too much trouble.

"Look around you at this magnificent store."

I wouldn't say magnificent...

"It's magnificent! Does this look like the kind of place that would cater to the hum drum masses who do nothing but wear drab, blah, boring pants and shirts?"

Not all pants and shirts are drab, blah, or boring.

"Ha! As if you know fashion. Give me that back."

I'm not sure I know how to take it off.

"Just... look, step through that part, and twist the... yeah, like that."

Ow ow ow!

"What?"

It's constricting around my...

"Oh dear, let go of that part. Shake your hips a little."

Oof... That's better.

"Now take that part and swing it over your shoulder."

Alright...

"Your other shoulder."

How can this possibly be a real article of clothing.

"Those who belong in them become accustomed."

What a pain in the ass.

"Now move your leg in a circle."

Like this?

"A little higher, you have to let the fabric unwind naturally."

It wasn't nearly this complicated to put on.

"Stop complaining, you're almost done."

I wasn't complaining, I was just pointing out that—

"Hop."

Hop?

"Yes, like a chobit."

What the hell is a chobit?

"Ha! Again with the jokes. How can you not know what a chobit is? It's only the most common animal in the country. In fact, it's our national animal."

Oh... is it like a rabbit?

"What's a rabbit?"

Never mind. Okay, now what?

"You want to grab that corner there, and pull out at an angle."

Okay, this should be it...

"Steeper angle."

And I just pull?

"Really hard."

Oof!

"See, it wasn't that difficult was it?"

It could have been worse. Can you direct me to a store where I might find some regular pants and a shirt?

"I know of no place."

Are you just being snobbish, or do pants and shirts really not exist here?

"Snobbish."

Great, thanks jerk.

"Now wait a second, I didn't mean to offend you. You seem nice enough... I might have something similar to pants.

Great, let's have it.

"It's tucked away behind... yes, here it is."

These aren't similar to pants, they ARE pants!

"Shh, not so loud. You can never refer to these as pants, the reputation of my boutique is at stake! Here, hand me your diaper and slip those on."

It's a speedo. Satchel. Whatever. Here.

"Those leg coverings look fabulous."

You think so? They fit great!

"I have an eye for that kind of thing."

How much do I owe you?

"That'll be four pieces of silver."

I don't have any silver... would you be willing to trade for the bag?

"The bag that's been encasing your sweaty privates? I don't think so."

Oh wait, I might have a coupon! There's a coupon book in my satchel.

"I'm not touching anything that's been in there!"

Give me that... yeah, right here, 50% off one item.

"Fine, that'll be three pieces of silver."

Half of four is two!

"Half of two is one."

And half of one is one half! I don't understand what we're doing.

"You're buying two leg coverings, this coupon is only good for 50% off of one item. So, you get half off the cost of one leg covering."

That's outrageous! Who only buys one leg covering?

"There are many pirates who frequent my boutique. Peg legs require no no coverings, but I do have a wide selection of custom peg leg skins. Would you like to have a look?"

No, I just want to be on my way with my lower body properly covered.

"Fine, I'll be willing to trade the leg coverings for the satchel and coupon book."

The whole coupon book?

"You can keep the skiing section, I'll tear it out..."

I don't ski.

"You're kidding! You have to try it, great fun."

Forget it, keep the whole book. Are we square?

"That'll do, enjoy your leg coverings!"

Thanks.

"Wait a second... What's this in the side pocket?"

I don't know, I thought I checked all the pockets.

"Oh my..."

What?

"This stone!"

Oh, that's just a rock I found in there.

"This isn't just a rock! This is the most enchanted stone in all the land! I can't take this from you."

I, uh, what?

"It's very important that you protect this stone with your life!"

Doesn't look that special to me. There isn't even any writing on it.

"Trust me. Now go, you've wasted enough time here!"

What are you talking about?

"The stone will guide you on your way. Listen to it... with your heart."

I'm confused.

"Go!"

the ones that got away

"Welcome to the Whammy Bar, what can I get ya?"

I'll have a vodka tonic.

"Coming right up."

Hey, aren't you...

"Little Whammy, in the flesh."

That's crazy, I didn't know you were a bartender!

"Decided to go solo a while back. Tired of being overshadowed by that middle-aged has been."

I hear ya. Man, what a day.

"Oh, you're one of those."

One of who?

"A talker. Alright, let me have it. Talk my ear off so I can get back to cleaning these glasses."

Oh, no, feel free to clean all the glasses you need to clean while I speak my mind.

"Thanks. Some people don't like the squeaking."

Ah yes, the squeaking. One of many tell tale signs a vampire is near.

"A vampire?"

In bat form, of course. They use the squeaks to see in the dark, so to speak. It's a form of sonar. Echo location, they call it.

"What did you say about a vampire?"

Two of them. Outwitted me. DAMN THEM!

"Whoa, careful, you might crack the bar in two."

Into what?

"In two pieces."

Ah, right.

"So you're a vampire hunter then."

Best damn vampire hunter in the country.

"But vampires don't exist."

Don't you ever say that! They prey on the ignorant, the unbelieving, the weak! The moment you show any skepticism, they come for you next!

"Fine, but if you're the best vampire hunter in the country, how did these two get away?"

It's a long story.

"I've got nothing else to do but clean these glasses."

And refill my drink.

"And refill your drink. That was fast."

Don't you judge me. I'll drink at whatever pace I find pleasing, thank you very much.

"I wasn't judging, it was just a... never mind. Tell me your story."

I wasn't always the best vampire hunter. Far from it. Back in the day I was a schmuck with a sharp stick and an order of garlic bread sticks. God knows if I had encountered a real vampire back then, I wouldn't be here sat on this bar stool before you today.

"So what happened?"

I discovered a man called Sam Winston. Inspirational speaker, his books and audio tapes changed my life. Soon after letting Sam Winston into my life I was accepted into Vampire Hunter University.

"Oh, that's fantastic."

Online degree. Legitimate, I assure you.

"I wouldn't doubt it."

But things were rough. I graduated into some tough economic times, my friend. Tough economic times indeed.

"So what'd you do?"

I did what any man would do in my situation. Turned to bounty hunting. The exact same skills applied, but all I had to do was trade in my stakes for a tranquilizer gun.

"Wow, that's remarkable."

The vamp population has been growing steadily over the past five years. Mostly sultry teenage girls begging vampires to bite them, I imagine. It wasn't before long that I noticed a good portion of my bounties had the telltale signs of being vampires. My past training kicked in immediately, and I've been dropping vamps left and right ever since.

"I'm impressed, although... I don't see what any of that has to do with the two vampires that got away from you tonight."

Oh right, of course. So there I was, approaching the vampire domicile on foot.

"Is that usual?"

Always. They can hear a combustion engine from ten miles out. Pour me another drink, please. So there I was, approaching the vampire domicile on foot.

"There you go. So you walk a whole ten miles every time you approach a vampire domicile?"

Well, I don't walk the entire time, I always run the last mile.

"That seems a bit odd, wouldn't you want to be more quiet the closer you get?"

No, not at all. No matter what a vampire will hear you from a mile out.

"So you can run a mile faster than you could drive ten miles?"

What do you mean?

"No matter what, the vampire will hear you coming from a mile away on foot, so if you can run 20 miles per hour..."

That sounds about right.

"Then you'll travel that last mile in three minutes. If you're driving a car, the vampire will hear you from ten miles out. So, if you're driving 60 miles per hour..."

Very rarely is 60 miles per hour possible, residential speed limits.

"Okay, so even if you could go 60 miles per hour, that would take you six minutes to travel those last ten miles. Alright, going on foot does make sense."

I could have told you that.

"I apologize. Please continue."

Alright. So there I was, approaching the vampire domicile on foot.

"What kind of shoes?"

What now?

"What kind of shoes do you wear?"

These beauties.

"Those... are those flip flops?"

I prefer calling them slip slaps.

"No wonder they can hear you from a mile away."

You would think so, but check this out.

"Wow, a lap around the bar and I didn't hear a thing."

I would call them hush puppies if that wasn't already a brand of shoe.

"Now that's impressive, but you can sprint in those?"

These increase my speed by four percent.

"I didn't think flip flops were capable of that."

Quite the feat.

"Yes, your feet are looking pretty good too."

What?

"What?"

Anyway... So there I was, approaching the vampire domicile on foot.

"Just one more question."

Yes?

"Where did you get them?"

The vampires?

"Your flip flops. You have me sold, I want a pair as soon as possible."

Actually, I make them myself.

"Get out of here, custom hand made flip flops!"

Yeah, just a small business on the side.

"Well sign me up!"

Pretty long wait list, but you can sign up at Arnie's Slip Slaps.

"Dot com?"

AOL keyword. Just type it in and it will take you right to the site.

"Great, I'll order a pair when I get home."

Could you give me another—

"Refill comin' right up. Now back to your story."

Alright, here we go. So there I was approaching the vampire domicile
        on— Hey is that...

"Hm?"

Oh my God, that's Sam Winston sitting at that table!

"Sam who?"

Sam Winston! Sitting at that table! Sam Winston!

"Sam... Oh, right, the guy who changed your life."

What are the odds? Excuse me, I have to talk to him.

"I'll keep your tab open."

eradivacation

"Excuse me, you're sitting on my towel."

I don't know what you're talking about.

"The towel you're sitting on belongs to me."

This is a public beach.

"That doesn't mean it's a public towel!"

Prove that it's yours.

"Look, it says 'The Eradicator' in epic villain font, and there's a picture of my face."

How do I know you're not just a fan trying to steal my Eroticator towel? You could have bought that mask at any adult book store.

"It's The Eradicator, not Eroticator, and these masks would be found at a comic book store, not an adult book store, which you would know if you were an actual fan. Therefore, you can not be the owner of that Eradicator beach towel!"

Fine, it isn't my towel. It's pretty lame that you own a beach towel with your own name and face on it.

"I get them for free. I had to cut a few corners on my expenses for this vacation due to recent events."

Ah, that explains the cheap sunblock.

"It inexpensive, but it's quality! It's affordable because they don't waste money on advertising."

You should try some of my stuff. Here.

"SPF 7,000? What the..."

Lather some of this on and you're good for a week. Assuming you don't go swimming or take a shower...

"Where do you even get something like this?"

Oh, it's almost a requirement where I come from.

"And where do you come from?"

Ah... I probably shouldn't say any more.

"Wherever it is, I don't think I'd like to visit. Sounds a bit Hellish if you ask me."

You may not have a choice.

"What?"

I work in Hell. I'm Satan's assistant.

"So you're some kind of demon?"

No, just a regular person with a sweet job in Hell. Other than the need for SPF 7,000 lotion. Go ahead and try it.

"If it's good enough for Hell, I guess it wouldn't hurt to try a bit on my nose."

But... your mask.

"Ha! I almost just put sunblock on my mask, how silly of me. This mask is the ultimate sunblock."

You could put some on your shoulders, also a very vulnerable area of the body.

"Good thinking."

So what brings you to Guam?

"Y'know, just getting away from all the stress back home. Local hot shots always on my back about this and that. How about you?"

My boss gave me some time off for a job well done.

"Nice! What did you do?"

Well, we obtained all the souls from Heaven.

"What? All the angels and stuff went to Hell?"

Exactly. Don't tell anyone, but I'm not even sure how it happened! I'll take the credit though, why the Hell not?

"That's bonkers. Oh, sorry, I have to take this call."

Oh that's fine, my phone just started ringing too.

"Hmm..."

What are you kidding me?

"Hmm..."

I've only been here for like an hour!

"Hmm..."

Fine, I'll get there as soon as I can.

"Well, my house just got broken into. Yet again."

And my boss needs me back in Hell.

"What a bummer. Guess we're both packing up."

Yeah. What hotel are you staying at?

"The Fifth Season, just over there. Great view."

That's where I'm staying too!

"How about that. It looks like the next flight that'll get me home is in two hours. I better hurry."

Would you mind if I took a look at that?

"Oh, sure."

The flight I need to take is in two hours too.

"Flight 2?"

That's the one.

"Me too. Guess we can share a cab to the airport."

Sounds like a plan. I'll meet you in the lobby, I've gotta try to get my money back since I only checked in a few minutes ago...

"Good luck, the guy at the front desk is a jerk."

back in black

Are you in there Officer Wilson?

"Bug off!"

Calm down, I just want to ask you a few questions.

"Don't expect me to fall for your tricks this time."

Every single... how many times do I have to explain to you, I'm not in the business of dealing harm.

"Forgive me if I don't trust you, but last time..."

Give me five minutes and I'll be on my way.

"Have you forgotten what happened last time?"

I give you my word; this will be nothing like last time. I'm not even carrying a lighter.

"Just give me a minute, alright?"

Kinda need you to hurry up, you're not the only one I need to talk to.

"Leave me alone if you're in such a hurry!"

My superiors wouldn't be too happy with me if I didn't get the answers I came for.

"Not my problem."

Oh I'll make it your problem. What's taking you so long?

"Pants... I can't find my pants."

Quit screwing around and get out here.

"Really, I can't find a single pair of pants anywhere!"

Slip on a towel for all I care.

"The towels are missing too. I don't understand..."

Understand this: I'm growing very impatient and if you're not out here in thirty seconds, regardless of your decency, I'm breaking down this door!

"Very interesting…"

What?

"Until now, everything we've been saying has been an acrostic of the alphabet."

You noticed that too? I'll be damned, that was pretty neat. Why'd you have to go and ruin it?

"Saying something that starts with an X would have felt too forced."

Good point. What a shame. Have you found your pants yet?

"Been wearing them this whole time."

What the… get your ass out here!

"Fine, sorry. I just wanted to keep the acrostic thing going… What can I do for you?"

I understand you spoke with a UFO witness last night.

"That crazy old man with a shotgun? I wouldn't say so much 'spoke with' as 'shot at by'. Holy crap, what happened to your arm?"

You're not the only one that crazy son of a bitch laid fire to.

"He shot my hat."

I feel for you, I really do.

"I wasn't trying to… here, come in, we have to take care of your arm before you get an infection."

No need, I just have a couple more questions for you and I'll get out of your hair.

"You're dripping blood all over my welcome mat."

Sorry. Could I borrow a towel?

"I told you, all my towels are missing."

I thought you said that to keep the acrostic going?

"I started that sentence with 'the,' I could have said just about anything. Nope, every single towel is gone. Some kind of pervert probably broke in here and took them, you think?"

I don't know, you're the police officer.

"It was definitely one of those towel-sniffing freaks."

I'll stand in the grass.

"Is it safe out there? There's been some crazy stuff going on."

You don't have to come out if you don't want to.

"I'll stay right here if you don't mind."

I don't.

"Great."

So, tell me about all this 'crazy stuff.'

"Well, you know, the alien invasion."

No need to worry about that, the aliens are long gone.

"How can you be sure?"

I'm sure. Was there anything other than the aliens?

"Well I got shot in the hat."

Other than that.

"Pulled over a couple of teens in a van."

I know exactly who you're talking about.

"You do? Well, the front end was all busted up. Had to let them go, lack
      of solid evidence. But..."

But?

"The evidence we did get, a few strands of hair, was very strange."

An unidentified forensics object.

"Exactly. Definitely wasn't human and didn't match any known animals
      in the area."

You've been a tremendous help, thank you officer.

"There's more. I don't know if it's relevant but there was an incident
      involving an ambulance."

That's where I'm headed next.

"Really? Is all of this connected somehow?"

Unfortunately.

"Hold on, I'm coming with you."

That's not a good idea.

"Eight years experience on the force here. Plus, however many years of
      whatever it is you do. We're going to solve this mystery!"

It's not so much a mystery as a...

"I want to call it a mystery."

Fine. Get in the car.

"Look at us, you're in black and I'm in blue! We should call ourselves black and blue!"

This is going to be a long day.

respawn

"What the Hell, Dad?"

You will not use profanities alongside my name.

"I said Dad."

Which is short for Holy Father.

"What the Holy Hell, Father?"

That's bett... wait a second.

"Enough of the preaching, I want to know why I got taken down like a
punk. I thought I was supposed to be the ultimate bad ass super
hero or something."

I was hoping for that, but unfortunately I can't create anything more
powerful than my own creator.

"You're kidding me. Santa is your creator?"

Indeed.

"And when were you planning on telling me?"

I was afraid it would ruin your confidence in battle.

"Well I ended up dead. Again. Thanks."

You made it back to Heaven didn't you?

"I figured that was a given."

Oh, not at all. If you hadn't realized that you missed the garbage can
when throwing away the price tags from your mukluks you'd be
burning right now.

"People can go to Hell for littering?!"

It's true. Some clown thought it would be fitting to leave that one out of
the commandments, along with seventy nine other no-nos. He's
largely to blame for our general low population here in Heaven.
Ironically, the 90th commandment was 'though shalt not omit
commandments.'

"He must not have read all of them first."

I did only give him a couple minutes to write it all down. Not my fault
he brought a hammer and chisel instead of a pen and paper.

"Now wait a minute, so back when I suffered for the sins of all mankind,
most of those sins were things like littering?"

Pretty much.

"That's so stu—"

Thou shalt not call things stupid.

"Hm. So this Santa situation..."

Yes, about that... He's not quite dead, and I need you to go back and finish him off.

"No way! I'm not about to go marching off to my death yet again."

Technically, you won't be alive this time.

"What?"

You'll just be inhabiting a body temporarily.

"I've never had to do that before."

And hopefully you'll never have to again. Once you're back, you need to find your brother.

"I have a brother?"

Well, in as much as he is also my son. You've never met him because he was born long before you, and has yet to die... The name is Bertram.

"What a stup—"

Thou shalt not call things stupid!

"Sorry. So my brother is immortal?"

I didn't originally intend for it, but yes, he's proven to be one tough cookie to crumble. Once you find him, he'll know what to do to stop Santa.

"So one son of God isn't strong enough to defeat Santa, so two should do the trick?"

I sure hope so, there isn't a third one... that I know of, if you know what I mean. Eh?

"I get it."

By the way, how good are you at sailing?

"Why do you ask?"

Oooooh!

"How many times do I have to tell you? You need more warble!"

Not that kind of ooooh! Look at the TV!

"Sam Winston, motivational speaker. So what?"

He's my favorite!

"You have a favorite motivational speaker?"

Of course. Don't you?

"Motivational speaking is for dummies."

That's one of his books! It details how anyone can be a motivational
      speaker if they put their mind to it. It's his most motivational
      book to date!

"You're crazy."

I wouldn't be half the man I am today if it weren't for Sam Winston's
      books and tapes.

"You're a ghost."

Exactly.

"You're dead."

Yeah.

"How can you be any worse than that?"

I could be all alone. I've befriended a pretty girl, haven't I?

"Stop it. You're making me blush. But that didn't have anything to do
      with Sam Winston. We're friends because I'm a nice person, not
      because of some self help mumbo jumbo."

Or was I?

"Of course not. How could you possibly have been given the advice to
      act the way you do. You're just about the worst ghost ever."

It's time I was honest with you. Here.

"What's this? 'Be a Terrible Ghost to Get the Ladies' by Sam Winston.
      This can't be real."

Nope, look inside.

"Hmm... Wait, you've done all of these things!"

Yeah.

"Including 'call the girl pretty even if she isn't' here on page ten! I'm
      not really pretty?"

Of course you are.

"The next page says to say 'of course you are' if ever questioned about page ten."

He really does think of everything...

"This is a really specific book. How could you use this crap on me?"

I'm sorry pooky.

"Ah ha! Page 21, 'call her pooky.' So unoriginal!"

That's a lame pet name, isn't it? It sounds too much like spooky.

"But I call you spookums..."

That's unique though!

"Wait, this book is about how to get the ladies."

Yeah.

"Plural. As in more than one. As in more than me. Who is she?!"

Whoa whoa whoa, you're reading too much into this.

"Page fifty three, the more ladies you woo, the more boobs you boo."

Please stop reading.

"You've been lying all along! Not only about this book, but about the other boobs you boo!"

Yours are the only boobs for me, boo! Oh hey, boo makes way more sense than pookie...

"Don't change the subject! Tell me who she is, I'll rip her hair out!"

I swear, there is no one else in my lif— er, afterlife but you!

"Prove it to me."

How?

"We're going to see this Sam Winston jerk, and you're going to tell him that what he said is wrong."

But calling you 'pretty' worked.

"Not that part. Keep calling me pretty. I mean his entire section that encourages ghosts to lie and cheat to their life partner!"

Afterlife partner.

"I'm not dead."

It's a mixed relationship.

"Shut up and put your shoes on. We're going to the Plaza to have a word with big shot Winston."

I don't wear shoes.

"I said shut up!"

tummy ache

Wow, my stomach does not feel good...

"I bet. Did you even chew?"

Didn't have time... Plus I was afraid I would get Santa blubber stuck
	between my teeth. Hey, where are we?

"North Pole."

But it's quite pleasant here. And this is a city park.

"In the future. Global warming. Shift of the Earth's axis. All that fun
	stuff."

Ah, I see. What are we doing in the future?

"Using the time machine stone is all I could think of! You had just eaten
	a fat elf, I panicked."

Well, take us back.

"Why? We saved the world, you're from dinosaur times, and I don't
	have any friends. Let's make the most of it here."

I mean back to dinosaur times, ugh... I have to do something about my
	stomach. How far in the future are we?

"Dunno, the rock doesn't have a digital display."

What about the analog display?

"It's a rock!"

Give that to— ouch!

"Do you have appendicitis?"

No.

"Ulcer?"

No! I just ate a fat elf!

"Oh yeah. We should get you to a doctor to remove him? Or a vet?"

As much as it hurts, I think he's trapped. We can't let him get out, or the
	whole universe is doomed.

"We should make sure it stays that way. Maybe we can reinforce your
	stomach somehow?"

There has to be some kind of cybernetics company around here. Do you
	have a phone book?

"Does it look like I have a phone book?"

I thought you had on one of those saddle things.

"What saddle things?"

The ones the helper dogs wear. With medicine and stuff in the pockets.

"A phone book isn't medicine."

It is if you have to call a doctor.

"All you need for that is a business card."

Do you have any business cards in your saddle thing?

"I'm not wearing a saddle thing!"

We should get you a saddle thing.

"Why do you need a cybernetics company?"

I think they can help me keep Santa contained with cyborg implants.

"Cyborg implants? I want some of those!"

What do you need cyborg implants for?

"I don't know... It only seems fair."

I suppose so. We should get there as soon as possible. This is getting really uncomfortable.

"I think I'll get a laser paw!"

What would you do with a laser paw?

"Write CD's."

You can use a CD burner for that. And how are you going to spin the discs?

"CD tray paw!"

That's ridiculous. If you're going to get cyborg implants, at least get something that's useful. Or find a better use for a laser paw, like... precision cutting.

"What do I need precision cutting for? I could just bite whatever needs cutting."

You can't bite *everything*.

"That's it! I'll get a mechanical jaw, like that movie with the shark. That way we can have biting contests!"

You're thinking of the James Bond villain.

"No, the shark in that movie was a robot."

Well yes, they had an animatronic shark made, but it is meant to portray an actual shark on film.

"But it's really a robot shark."

Behind the scenes, yes.

"So that's what I meant, I want a mechanical jaw like that behind the scenes robot shark."

I think you're better off asking for jaws like Jaws.

"Yes! That's the movie!"

No, not the movie Jaws, the big tall guy from The Spy Who Loved
    Me.

"You mean Moonraker?"

He was in both.

"Oh, oh! I want a laser paw like in Moonraker!"

There weren't any laser paws in Moonraker, just a laser gun.

"Right, I want my laser paw to be like the laser gun in Moonraker!"

So you want a laser paw and mechanical jaws.

"And a CD tray paw."

It's either the jaws or the paws, you can't have both.

"Why not?"

I'm just getting one implant. If we're keeping things fair, you should
    only get one too.

"How about you get more?"

I don't need more.

"Come on... think about it."

There's nothing to think about. My implants are for business only.

"That's what she said."

Can we find the cybernetics company already?

"Fine, but I'm getting both the paws and jaws. I don't care what you say.
    If you want it to be fair, then you better think of something new
    you want."

I have always wanted to fly...

"Oh! I want to fly!"

No! You already chose your implants!

"Okay, but you have to give me rides."

If it will get you to shut up and find this place...

"Great. I have a feeling there's one this way."

How do you know?

"I can smell it. Follow my nose!"

"Whew, I'm sure glad we got a seat, aren't you?"

I guess so.

"And no sitting next to a smelly homeless guy."

He's right over there and can still hear you.

"Eh, he's used to it. Aren't you smelly homeless guy? He's nodding."

I think that's just a nervous twitch.

"I'd be twitchy too if I smelled that bad. So what are you doing with so many shopping bags this early in the morning?"

I'd rather not talk about it.

"Oh, something personal. I get ya."

Not personal at all. I just don't want to talk about it.

"Alright, then let's see..."

I don't want to talk about anything else either.

"Why not?"

I don't want to talk about it.

"Heh heh, you're funny."

I'm not trying to be funny! Forget it.

"Hey, why's the train slowing down?"

Don't know. Maybe they'll make an announcement.

"Shhh! They're making an announcement!"

That's what I was—

"Shhh!"

…

"I can't... can you understand them?"

Nope.

"That intercom sounds like how that homeless guy smells."

Okay, now he is actually nodding.

"Told you he wasn't offended. Oh great, now we're completely stopped. Maybe someone peed on the third rail and got electrocuted and passed out across the tracks and we just barely stopped in time before running him over and splattering his guts all over the place."

I'm pretty sure that isn't what happened.

"Is it raining?"

How about that.

"I don't see any clouds."

I've seen it rain without clouds before.

"That's impossible, that would be like baby ducks popping up out of nowhere."

What?

"You know, baby ducks. Popping up out of nowhere."

How is that anything like rain without clouds?

"They're not hatching from eggs, like how rain comes from clouds."

I'm sure there's a better analogy than that.

"Fine, let's hear it if you're such an expert."

Okay, let's see... Rain without clouds is like if it were snowing. Without clouds. But not as cold.

"Perfect! I knew there was a reason I like you."

You like me?

"Duh! Why do you think I wanted to sit next to you?"

So that you wouldn't have to sit next to the smelly homeless guy.

"That too. Hey, do you think the rain has something to do with the train being stopped?"

I've ridden the train in the rain plenty of times.

"But have you ever ridden the the train in the rain without clouds?"

Not that I can remember.

"Well there you go, that must be it. Oh, shh!"

I wasn't talking.

"Shh! I'm trying to listen to the announcement..."

…

"…"

I don't—

"Shh!"

…

"Okay, still can't understand the guy. Hey what's that over there?"

Oh that's the water tower, you didn't know that?

"Guess I didn't recognize it knocked over spewing water all over the— hey, that's where the rain is coming from!"

Makes sense.

"Looks like it fell onto the tracks. That must be why we're stopped."

That satisfyingly explains our situation.

"Hey smelly homeless guy, hop outside real quick. Free shower!"

pint size

Whoa, are you a bigfoot?

"Yes, what's it to you small fry?"

Do NOT call me small fry!

"Oh sorry, your kind are sensitive about being called short, huh?"

It's not that, it's just that taters are very important to my people.

"I see. You're a... lamborghini, right?"

Leprechaun.

"Damn, I knew it started with an L. Where did you come from?"

I came through the pool, just like you.

"Oh. Were you following us?"

Nothing like that, I just popped over to visit the fair. What a waste of
          time, bastards wouldn't let me on the roller coaster... But at least
          I got a new car.

"Oh, is that it over there?"

That's a pumpkin. My new SUV is over there.

"Ah, very nice."

So there's more than one of you?

"Well not more of me, per se. I came through with my friend. He's not
          a bigfoot. He's naked."

In that case, I'll give you two some privacy.

"It's not like that! He left to get some pants."

What are you guys doing here anyway?

"We came across this shimmering pool in the woods, he was covered in
          dinosaur mucus, and the cops were after us, so why not?"

Sounds like you had a hell of a night. You look like you could use a pint
          of stout. Come on back to my place, it's just through the woods
          this way.

"I won't fit in there. Your entire house only comes up to my waist."

I didn't even think of that. Have a seat on that stump over there and I'll
          be right out with your drink.

"Great, thanks. The trees here sure are different... I don't know what it is about them."

That's because they're magic. Everything here is.

"Like hocus pocus abacadabra magic?"

I said magic, not parlour tricks. Here's your drink.

"This is hardly a pint."

It's a leprechaun pint. What, you expect me to be able to fit full pint
     glasses in my cupboards?

"You could've let me know that you were offering a leprechaun pint."

I'll pour you a second, don't worry about it.

"It's basically a shot of beer. Who drinks shots of beer?"

They have shots of beer at that one restaurant.

"Yeah, but you get multiple shots so you can try all of their beers."

I get so drunk there.

"I'll never get drunk at this rate."

So when's your friend coming back?

"I don't know, as soon as he finds some pants."

That could be a while. Nobody takes money from the other side here,
     primarily because most of them don't even know the other side
     exists. That's why I trade in gold, it's good everywhere!

"He didn't have any money, he was naked."

And you didn't have any money?

"Look at me. I'm naked too."

I didn't even think of that... great, now all I can think about is the fact
     that you're naked.

"It's okay, I'm hairy so you can't see anything."

That doesn't help.

"Sorry."

Say, you're going to be waiting a while anyway... How about you come
     with me into town? Maybe we'll find your friend, and we can
     pick you up a pair of pants.

"Should you be driving in your condition?"

So you should drive? You drank just as much as me.

"Yeah, but I weigh about 50 times as much as you. I'm hardly more
     buzzed than I am after using mouthwash."

Mouthwash gets me PLASTERED.

"Lucky. So are there any weird traffic rules here I should know about?"

Nah, most people use bicycles, horses and large dogs. Just don't run over anyone and we'll be fine.

checking out

Checking out?

"That's what I just said."

Just checking.

"Out."

What?

"Checking out."

I know, you've said that three times now.

"You said I was just checking. I'm not just checking, I'm checking OUT."

I meant I was double checking.

"No, I'm here by myself."

Double checking that you were checking out.

"Yes, I'm checking out."

I know.

"Then why did you have to double check?"

I wasn't double checking just then, I was explaining that I had double checked a moment ago.

"Alright... just as long as we're clear on everything."

Here's your check.

"What now?"

Your check.

"You already checked that I want to check out."

No, your bill. Here's your bill.

"Oh, I see. Hold on, I only just checked in an hour ago, why am I being charged for a full night?"

Let me check on that.

"Now listen here..."

Ah yes, I see what you mean. Unfortunately, all cancellations have to be made 24 hours before check in.

"I'm not canceling, I'm checking out."

Since you've already been in the room that counts for the night's stay.

"I haven't even gone up to the room yet!"

I have no way of knowing if you're telling the truth.

"Why would I lie about something so stupid?"

To get out of paying your bill.

"Good point."

Will you be paying by check?

"Not this again."

We also accept traveler's cheques.

"Oh, you mean method of payment."

Check.

"What?"

Affirmative.

"This is so... I'm in a hurry and have a plane to catch. I'll just pay for
    the night. Here."

We don't accept korunas.

"What? You asked me if I was paying by Czech!"

st one

"You there!"

Are you talking to me?

"Yes you, the one in the pants."

What's up?

"Please, come inside. You're here for a reason. I can sense it."

That's right, I was here to get some pants.

"Not here here. HERE here. This universe!"

That's... yeah, I came here through some kind of shimmering pool.

"Exactly as I saw in my visions! But something is different about you...
    There's a reason you were naked..."

Yes! I'm a—

"Shh, don't tell me. You're... a werepig!"

Really? You go to werepig first?

"Oh sorry, I meant werewolf. Right?"

Yeah. Well maybe. I didn't really have a look in a mirror so I might have
    been a fox or something.

"No no, you're definitely a wolf. I can feel it. I can really... feel it. Do
  you work out?"

Please don't touch me like that.

"Ahh, such a privilege. I never thought I'd encounter a real werewolf.
  What's that you're holding?"

Oh this? This is nothing. Some stone I guess. I found it after I came
  through the pool.

"That's the stone of immensity! You're the chosen one! You are the
  Saint of Immensity! Here, let me see it..."

You're not going to steal it from me, are you?

"You can trust me. I'm merely a fortune teller, my interests lay only in
  setting fate on it's path. Oh wow, that smells like..."

It was in my leather speedo.

"Go wash it off. There's a washing basin in the back."

Do you have a cleaning brush or anything?

"You can use this."

Oh gross!

"You've never used a cat's paw to clean dishes?"

No, why would anyone do that?

"They use their paws to clean their faces, so the paw must be a perfect
  cleaning instrument."

I guess I don't have any other choice... Is this the soap here?

"That's the liquified stomach of the Highland Yark."

What's a Highland Yark?

"It's like a yak, but bigger and gassier."

Wait, you're grossed out by something that's rubbed up in my crack, but
  you have a jar of liquified yark stomach on your sink?

"Yark stomach. It has very special properties that help make my work
  possible. Ultra pasteurized. It's hardly like it's a Yark stomach
  anymore. You could even drink it if you like."

I would not like.

"It's great for impotence."

I'm not impotent!

"You might be some day. Here's the soap."

So you know about where I come from?

"Of course, I'm from there too."

You don't say.

"Years ago, when I started studying to become a fortune teller, I found
        out that there are portals all over the place that connect the two
        worlds. I figured the best place to really polish my craft would
        be in this land of magic. I've been going back and forth ever
        since. Make boatloads of cash over there."

So how do I fit into all of this? What the hell is a stone of immensity?

"It's one of the most important objects in the world. Some say it has
        the power to destroy. Others say it has the power to bring world
        peace. Perhaps both are true. All I know is that the person who
        possesses it is the chosen one."

Chosen to do what?

"To save the world! I thought I just said that."

Do you have any idea what being the chosen one entails? Should I go on
        a quest or something?

"Yeah, do that. Here, this will help you."

What is it?

"This is a magic scepter."

What does it do?

"Magic."

Like... Card tricks?

"Yes."

Neat. You know, I kind of feel something welling up inside of me.

"Oh yes!"

I'm a hero, here to hear the call of destiny!

"What's destiny saying?"

Treasure. And maidens.

"I'm a maiden!"

Eh.... Technically. Excuse me, I must go. Destiny calls, and I hear it!

"Promise me you'll come back for me!"

You make me uncomfortable. So, which way do I go for adventure?

"A dragon lives in that mountain over there. Good place to start."

And so I start! Farewell.

"Hello?"

Who's goes there? Spindly Pete, is that you?

"I'm Jesus."

Stop messing around, I know that's you, good old Spindly Pete! I thought you died in the battle!

"I did, er HE did... I'm just using his body for a while."

Good one Pete. I'm glad you survived, I'm getting a bit sick of being around First Mate Gilbert. Still thinks he's a bird.

"What?"

Never mind that, the important thing is that you're here, alive and well! Oh, what's... oh gross.

"Sorry. Great going Dad, sending me into a decomposing body..."

You're not talking like you usually do, Pete.

"That's because I'm not Pete, I'm Jesus."

What kind of name is that? I thought you were the creative one, Pete. You've had far better pranks, but I don't need to remind you of that, do I?

"I'm not pulling a prank, Pete is really dead, and I'm a different person named Jesus who is using Pete's body temporarily."

Alright, if you're not really Pete, then what did we have for dinner last night?

"I don't know."

That settles it, Pete would have known that. I guess you're telling the truth. What kind of mission are you on?

"A mission from God."

Can you be a bit more specific?

"I'm here to find someone named Bertram."

What did you say?

"I said I'm here to—"

I heard what you said! How dare you! Come on my ship and then demand I take you on a suicide mission! I should slit your throat right here.

"Wait wait wait! I don't need you to take me there, I just need to know where he is. I can get there myself."

Ha, what are you going to do, fly? We're in the middle of the ocean!

"You let me worry about that. Hey, where's the rest of your crew?"

Uh... They're all dead. Except for my first mate! He's down below repairing the hull. Hey wait a second, you can help fix my ship!

"No way, I'm no carpent... Oh wait, yes I am."

Perfect! Help me rebuild the hull and I'll tell you where Teufelberg is.

"Is that where Bertram lives?"

Maybe... Damn it.

"That's all I needed to know. I've got it from here."

No, don't jump! These are shark infested waters!

"Watch me."

You're 180 pounds of chum, they'll be on you like ants on a leaf!

"Where I'm going, I don't need to swim."

I'll be damned, he's walking on water.

pair of medics

Whoa, hold on, I need to pull over.

"What? If we miss another call we'll be fired."

If there was ever an industry that understands emergencies...

"Alright, but be qui—"

Horfghhh!

"Oh come on, it's bad enough that there's goop all over the place."

HORRRFFGHH!

"What the Hell?! Aim out the window! Ugh, what in the world did you eat? This is... sticky."

I don't... I think it's the goop. All my muscles are stiffening up and yeaarrrgh!!!

"Holy crap, you're turning into a werewolf after all! That's so cool!"

I need... I need... unnngh!

"Hold on! I'll get you strapped on to the gurney in the back. Good thing we're in an ambulance, right? Ha ha... Hang in there buddy. And CLEAR!"

HNPH!

"CLEAR"

HNPPHH STOP DOING THAT, MY HEART HASN'T STOPPED.

"Yes it has, you don't have a pulse... but—"

How am I sitting up talking?

"All your vitals tell me you're dead."

I don't feel dead. I just feel... hungry. For you...

"What!? No get away from me!"

Just one bite! One little bite...

"Ow, my leg!"

Hmm, that doesn't taste very good.

"Of course it doesn't, IT'S MY LEG! Stop right now or I'll stab you with this sca— HORFGH!"

Uh oh, what's happening?

"Ugh, I think... whatever happened to you is about to— HORRFFGH."

I'm so sorry, I didn't mean to— here, lay down!

"I don't want to die!"

Clearly it's too late, and it acts fast. Just think about puppies. It will be over in no time.

"Thanks for not taking advantage of the situation and eating me."

I'm sorry for trying to eat you in the first place, I don't know what came over me...

"I think maybe UNGH since you're dead and UNNNGH you have an appetite for human flesh UUUNNNNGH we might be turning into UUNGH—"

Zombies!

"..."

You were about to say zombies, right?

"..."

Hey, wake up. Don't fool around! Oh God... But I was fine so you should be fine too. No! I'm so sorry! Nooooo!

"Oh hey."

You're alive! Sort of.

"Let's go get some grub!"

Sounds good to me! Hm. The engine won't start.

"Push in the clutch all the way."

I did that.

"And turn the key."

I know how to do it! It's not working. We'll have to go on foot.

"We could hitchhike..."

And eat the kind soul that stops to give us a lift!

"Hell yeah!"

This is way better than being a paramedic.

don't jump

Hey, is that them?

"Where?"

Up there at the top of the tower.

"Oh yeah! Hey guys! What are you doing up there?"

I can't tell if they're yelling back down at us, or just yelling at each
      other. Hold on, that guy is climbing over the ledge.

"They're stuck up there."

Jump! It's the only way you can get down!

"NO! DON'T JUMP!"

How else are they going to get down?

"If they jump, they'll die. And if they die, we're stuck together as the
      last two unicorns in the world."

DON'T JUMP!

"Crap, I don't think they can hear us. He's still trying to climb over the
      ledge. We're going to have to go up there and tell them."

Hold on, we can't do that.

"It's the only way."

But then we'll be stuck up there too, and for all we know they're all just
      as ugly as you.

"You mean just as ugly as you! What, was your mother a donkey or
      something?"

Donkeycorns are majestic animals.

"That makes you a mulicorn! It all makes so much sense now."

At least I don't have a stupid face. Stupid face.

"Ass."

Proud of it.

"How are we going to get them down?"

Crane?

"A crane couldn't lift a unicorn. Plus they can't fly that high."

What are you talking about?

"There's no bird big enough to carry a unicorn."

A crane. The mechanical device. Not the bird.

"That makes a lot more sense. The problem is..."

Can we get a crane that's tall enough?

"You finished my sentence."

Yeah that was kind of uncomfortable.

"I don't know, I kind of felt something..."

Magical. Damn it, why am I doing this?

"Oh mulicorn, you beast."

Forget I said anything... we should find that crane.

"Here, finish this sentence..."

No, I refuse to.

"I have to know if this is fate, or just a coincidence."

There is no way that you are suddenly in love just because I finished a
        couple of—

"Sentences. Ooh! I got chills!"

I think it was fairly obvious that I was about to say—

"Sentences!"

Stop saying—

"Sentences!"

For crying out—

"Sentences! Oh, wait..."

Actually, I was going to say sentences that time too. Are we done now?

"Yeah, I think so. Whatever you'd like."

Stop rubbing against me and think of where we can get a crane.

"Maybe we just need a really big flying thing."

Like a hot air balloon?

"That would take too long to inflate."

A kite?

"That's... no."

A dragon!

"Where in the world are we going to get a... Oh yeah, there IS a dragon
        around here! Let's go get him."

They said it'll be about five minutes.

"That's pretty quick for cyborg implant surgery."

Well, everything does seem to be faster in the future.

"Hey, could you do me a favor?"

I suppose so.

"I'm trying to read this magazine but... well, can you turn the page for
        me?"

Why can't you?

"I don't have thumbs!"

Neither do I.

"Well this sucks."

Why don't you get cyborg thumbs?

"But then we won't be even and you'll start complaining again."

I'll get thumbs too.

"Are you sure?"

Yeah... I've always wanted thumbs.

"I don't know... thumbs are so weird. They kinda just stick out."

But then you can turn the page of your magazine.

"I'm not going to spend all kinds of money just so I can turn magazine
        pages. Hold on, how are we going to pay for all of this?"

Shh! Not so loud.

"What'd you do?"

I told the receptionist we could pay next week.

"But we can't raise that much money by next week."

We have a time machine, we'll be gone next week!

"Of course!"

Yeah, time travel is great.

"Not that, I just realized I can turn the pages with my tongue!"

There you go. Is that a tabloid publication?

"Not sure. I have no idea who these people are."

You can tell by context, though.

"Oh God!"

What is it? Did this week's most popular actress have a fling with last
        week's most popular actor?

"No... blech. That page was a perfume sample. That tastes so bad..."

I thought you would have smelled that coming.

"I did, but the whole magazine smells..."

Oh they're calling your name.

"My name isn't Byron."

Shh! I had to give them fake names because... I don't know your name.

"Well that's nice! Here I was thinking we were best friends, and you don't even know my name."

Sorry, it just never came up.

"Well I'm mad. I'm not talking to you."

Listen, I'll make it up to you later, but for now just go with it so we don't lose our appointments!

"Nope, I refuse."

Hold on, do you know MY name?

"That's not the point!"

You can't be mad at me for not knowing your name when you don't know mine either!

"Sure I do. It's uh..."

Yeah?

"Mmmm... Nnnn... Puh."

Give it up.

"Glerson. Manpuh Glerson."

Neither of those or names. They're starting to yell now, you should go.

"But it's not my name!"

Do you want a laser paw or not?

"Hmph... Yes, that's me! Byron the talking dog!"

motivatered

"It's really you!"

Yes.

"Sam Winston! In the flesh!"

That's right. May I help you?

"I'm a huge fan! I have all of your books and tapes. You changed my life!"

Thanks, glad you're a fan. Uh... why are you looking at me like that?

"Go on, say it."

Come on man, I don't...

"Please? It would make my day. My month. My year. It would make my decade. Seriously."

You know, it's really a whole stage persona thing, I don't like to do it outside of conferences.

"Please please please please please?"

Sorry.

"Pleeeeeeeeeeease?!"

Will you leave me alone if I say it for you?

"Yes."

Promise?

"Yes..."

Fine. Ahem. You done got motivatered!

"Oh my god oh my god oh my god!"

Sigh.

"Now let me get a video of us saying it together."

For crying out loud. The deal was that you would leave me alone if I said it, so scram!

"We never shook on it."

So?

"In your book 'How Not To Skin That Cat', page seventy six paragraph three, you say you should never get it on without a handshake."

I was talking about business propositions and high class prostitutes, not this... this, whatever this is.

"I always thought that you were a man of your word, ever since your book 'Man Up Your Words'. I guess I was mistaken."

Look, if it really means that much to you and it will make you happy...
      I'll do it. I would hate to lose such an obviously devoted fan.
"Oh yeah! Biggest fan right here!"
But after this, you'll move on your merry way, alright?
"I think you're forgetting something."
Ugh... Shake on it?
"You have yourself a deal, kind sir."
Sigh.
"Hell yeah, let's do this thing!"
Uh, why are you getting so close to me?
"Gotta get us both in frame. Come on, don't be shy!"
Please stop smooshing your cheek against mine.
"Sorry, this camera has a long focal length."
Just give me a little bit of room to breathe, why don't you?
"How's this?"
Little more room.
"Is this better?"
Yeah, you're still too close.
"How about..."
Do you really have to be in the video with me?
"Of course I do, we were going to say it together. No one would believe
      that I was here with you in person if I'm not in the video."
You could just pan over to me.
"You're right! That's genius! This is why you're Sam Winston and I'm
      just plain old Arnie Freeman. Any other suggestions?"
If we're going to do this, it's worth doing right. You were planning to
      upload this to the internet, weren't you?
"Er... no..."
Don't lie.
"Oh! 'Don't lie!' The title of chapter three in 'Put Meat on the Skeletons
      in Your Closet', subtitle 'But in case you have to...' that's my
      third most favorite chapter in the book, although I thought the
      revisions you made in the fourth edition made it lose some of
      it's potency."
Actually one my assistant handles all of the rewrites for new additions.

"Oh man, you need a new assistant."

He's sitting right next to me.

"Oh hi. So yeah, to tell you the truth I was planning on posting the video on the web. I was hoping for a thousand views."

Unacceptable. What did I say at the top of side two tape three of 'Aim Higher'?

"Uh... was it 'aim higher'?"

Yes. Exactly. Your video will be at the top of charts because I'm going to make sure it's done right.

"This is such an honor, the one and only Sam Winston directing my internet video! Where do we start?"

Okay, what I'm going to have you do is start outside.

"Ooh! Getting fancy."

When I say action, you come in.

"I don't think I'll be able to hear you."

Trust me, you'll hear me. Positions!

"Oh man, this is so great!"

And ready...

"Ready!"

Wait for it.

"Waiting for it!"

So, as I was saying...

"Sam? Can I call you Sam? Did you say action?"

Ugh. No, not yet, just keep waiting.

"Will do."

donut

What a night.

"I can't believe we didn't get caught."

Well, we did get arrested...

"And released!"

True.

"Let's stop and get some hot chocolate."

Can't you wait? Mom's hot chocolate is way better than anything we
    can get at store.

"Except for—"

Dippy Donuts' Hot Chocobot!

"Best hot chocolate in the world."

I think there's one a couple blocks over this way... Wait a second, we
    can't go there. That place will be crawling with cops.

"We don't have to go inside, we'll use the drive through window!"

Genius. You're really starting to pull your weight.

"I'm just thirsty for some Dippy D's Hot Chocobot."

You have no idea how excited I am.

"I think I have a good idea of how excited you are."

Remember how Mom would ground us for weeks anytime we got hot
    chocolate somewhere else?

"Especially if we went to Dippy D's."

Let's see her ground us now! Ha!

"Do you think we should call her?"

That's kind of cruel.

"I mean to let her know we're okay."

Oh, sure. Give her a call.

"Get me a large. And a dozen Dippy D-Holes."

Why don't we get a Dippy D-Bag? It includes a dozen D-Holes.

"Are you going to eat the Drippy Dippies?"

Of course! Why would I suggest the Dippy D-Bag if I wasn't going to
    eat the Drippy Dippies?

"Just checking. Wouldn't want them to go to waste. Calling Mom. Re-
    member, large Chocobot."

Hot Chocobot.

"Of course HOT Chocobot, if I wanted COLD Chocobot I would— Oh
     hi Mom."

Er yes, we're ready to order.

"No, what? No I didn't say Chocobot, we were just talking about the
     Autobots. Yeah. Transformers. Optimus Prime and the gang."

We'll have two large Hot Chocobots and the Dippy D-Bag.

"No, you didn't hear him say Chocobot again. Dude, she totally heard
     you. So yeah, we're doing just fine, I know you were probably
     worried about us getting arrested and all last night."

No, TWO large Hot Chocobots.

"Yes, the Autobots are really hot! And large! Hey cut it out already."

Sorry, this guy isn't the brightest employee. No, sir, I wasn't talking
     about you. I was talking about the last place we were at. Get off
     the phone!

"Don't worry about us, we'll be home soon. What's that? Oh. I see. And
     you told him... alright then. No, no, there's nothing to be con-
     cerned about. I'm sure it was just one of those weird things that
     happen, you know?"

Yes, extra drippy on the Drippy Dippy's please.

"See you soon. Er— you too. No I'm not going to say it. You know I
     do, I don't have to say it every time I talk to you! Fine. Yes, he
     does too."

I what too?

"You know."

Oh yeah, yeah. You too, Mom

"Yes, he says he does too. Bye."

So what was that about?

"She wanted me to say—"

I mean before that.

"Oh right, I guess some detective came by the house, was asking a lot
     of questions."

Crap.

"I think we're fine. She showed him our text message and took off like
     he was on some kind of mission."

What text message?

"The one about bigfoot."

Did she say what the detective looked like?

"Just said he was wearing a black suit."

D-Bag!

"Oh you know him?"

No, the Dippy D-Bag is ready. Here, hold it.

"Woohoo!"

And here's our drinks. Thank you sir! Oh, sorry... Ma'am. It's just your voice is so deep over the intercom. And now in person. In fact, I'm still no entirely convinced that you aren't a man... I'm going to stop talking now. Thank you, have a nice day!

"This is like if you were in Heaven and everything was just amazing, but then you died again and went to Heaven's Heaven."

Isn't it?

"So that detective..."

He's no detective.

"What is he then?"

He's the worst thing that could possibly happen to us.

"That sounds slightly unpleasant."

For now, let's just enjoy our Chocobots.

lky

"How are ya? No, don't tell me my fortune, I know exactly where it is, haha ha ha... ha!"

Are you drunk again?

"Ah yes, indeed. My constitution is always especially vulnerable to the warming effects of a few pints of stout after a trip to the other side."

Short and stout, as they say.

"Shut your— BELCH."

Gesundheit. You didn't drive here, did you?

"I did! Well, I was driven. In my brand new SUV, I might add!"

They let you buy an SUV? Can you even see over the dashboard?

"That's a non-issue, m'lady! I have found myself a driver. Although I believe he's probably under the impression this is a one time deal, I am sure he will be under my employ for ages."

A driver, huh? He's not from the other side is he?

"He is! How did you know? Oh, oh course, you're a fortune teller! Don't
worry, I didn't bring him over, he was already here!"

Tell me more about this guy.

"Tall, spindly fellow. Naked."

Oh...

"Lots of hair. Very hairy. Almost completely covered in hair. But naked,
nonetheless. Do you have any pants that would fit a bigfoot?"

I'll see what I can find in the back. I did turn a giant into the newt the
other day... had to take his clothes with me.

"You mischievous woman, you. I love it!"

Here they are, will these do?

"They will do just fine, thank you! So my SUV, you'll never guess what
model I obtained from this fine car salesman. Sure, he was a bit
on the insensitive side at first, but once we got to know each
other he was quite helpful."

You got the Experimenter, didn't you?

"How did you know? Oh, right, again, fortune teller."

I'm good, what can I say?

"You know, there's a booty call button."

How does that work?

"I don't know, but maybe we can go find out!"

Oh stop it, you're making me...

"Wet!"

Shh, someone might hear!

"Er, I meant, wait!"

Oh.

"I just remembered, I'm supposed to help my driver find his friend."

Was he wearing only pants?

"Quite possibly! Originally he was naked, but then he fashioned a diaper
out of a bag so that he could come into the city to find pants."

I did meet a guy with pants a few minutes ago... I gave him my scepter.

"You didn't!"

I did.

"How could you?"

He had the Stone of Immensity. He's the one.

"Oh my, the Saint of Immensity! Where is he now?"

He set off on a quest to kill the dragon.

"No feckin' way!"

It's true.

"I have to go after him!"

Wait a second, I'm coming with you. Just gotta grab my overnight bag.

"Be quick, there's not a second to lose!"

Why do you have to go after him?

"I don't know. Sounds fun. I'm drunk, stop asking so many questions!"
Sorry.

"This'll be a long journey, are you sure you want to accompany me?"
Yes.

"There won't be a lot of bathroom stops."

I have a huge bladder.

"And there are lots of stairs."

Love 'em.

"Dangerous monsters."

The tastiest of meats. Hold on, you have an SUV. This trip will take a
half hour, forty five minutes tops. And what stairs? The dragon
lives in a mountain.

"I was trying to get you to change your mind."

I see how it's going to be. If you're going to act like this, I'm not going
with you!

"Good, I didn't want you to go!"

Then why did you ask me?

"I just wanted to try out the booty call button!"

Oh... Maybe we can try it out when we get back?

"Yeah, just maybe!"

Why are you still yelling?

"I'm drunk, I'm excited to try the booty call button, and I'm gonna go
watch a Saint slay a dragon!"

If that's not worthy of yelling, I don't know what is. Good luck!

"Luck is my business. My vanity plates don't say LKY for nothin'!"

stuck hiding

Do you think he's gone yet?

"Shh!"

Shh your shh! My whispering is far more quiet than your piercing shh!

"Okay, I won't shh you, but please shut your face. I have a feeling he's
   close. Real close."

What, more vampire senses?

"That and I'm a bit psychic at times."

What times would those be?

"The times where I think something is going to happen, and then it ends
   up happening."

This happens often?

"Nah, only sometimes."

So you're basically just guessing.

"Predicting! Like a psychic does."

Bullshitting like a psychic does.

"This is going to be the worst ten years of my life. If you're so confident
   he's gone, why don't you take a look through the peep hole?"

There's a peep hole that we could have been using this entire time?

"Maybe. Go ahead and have a look."

Alright, let's see... Looks like empty tunnels to me.

"Give it a minute. Watch for any shadows moving, he could be pressed
   up against the wall."

Hmm... I don't see any movement at all.

"No puffs of condensed moisture in the air?"

No puffs of condensed moisture in the air.

"I think he may have given up and left then."

It's about time. So let's get out of here.

"Remember, I have to cut all the welds. This is my favorite part."

Whoa, look out there.

"Sorry, I meant to say stand back."

Sure you did.

"Remember, I'll get in trouble if I hurt you."

You seem like the kind of guy who would lie, saying that I burnt myself
   while pulling a tray of freshly baked cupcakes out of the oven.

"Is that slang for something?"

Is what slang for something?

"Burnt yourself while pulling a tray of freshly baked cupcakes out of the oven."

How could that possible be slang for anything?

"You know. Double entendreuendo and such. Like dropping the kids off an oceanside cliff ledge, or roasting a hollow mallow."

What the hell are either of those phrases supposed to mean?

"Dropping the kids off an oceanside cliff ledge. You've never heard that before?"

I heard something like it maybe... It means going to take a pee, right?

"You're thinking of something else. No, dropping the kids off an oceanside cliff ledge is like... well, it basically means getting rid of whatever is causing you headaches. Example, a client at your marketing agency—"

I don't have a marketing agency.

"For the purposes of this example, pretend this is your real life."

Okay, so a client at my marketing agency does what?

"They bother you constantly for changes, revisions, updates, reupdates, anything they think of they call you up right that second and ask you to do it. You can't stand it anymore, so you drop the client and move on. You drop the kids off an oceanside cliff ledge."

Oh I see now, that does make a bit of morbid sense. What about that other thing you said?

"Roasting a hollow mallow?"

That's it.

"You know when you're really working hard on setting something up, but it ends up not having any substance inside? That's roasting a hollow mallow. It's like spending all this time roasting a marshmallow, then when taking a bite into it you realize that the marshmallow is hollow."

These situations are hardly in need of a less offensive versions.

"That would be a euphonium, not an entendreuendo."

You mean euphemism. Those were both euphemisms.

"Euphonium, ententreuendo, whatever."

Sigh. Are you going to cut these welds already? That cutter is burning up all the oxygen in here.

"Oh we don't need oxygen. We could be buried in a coffin for centuries, no problem."

That's pretty cool. Nonetheless, I'm getting a bit claustrophobic, let's get out of here.

"Claustrophobia and vampirism do not mix well. Sleeping in coffins and all."

Why do you have to sleep in a coffin? Can't you just sleep anywhere that's dark?

"Tradition, mostly. Helps with security, too."

Wouldn't it be harder to hear if someone was coming to stake you if you're inside a little box? I mean, that's how I was able to sneak up on you.

"And obviously that worked out well."

If I hadn't stabbed you on the wrong side, you'd be a goner right now.

"Ugh, anyway... stand back."

That torch works really well.

"Got it at Staples."

They sell that kind of thing?

"Oh, no. Just one of the guys I know who works there sells them out of the back of his van. Oh, watch it! Grab that fire extinguisher!"

What happened?

"Cut through to the papier mache. That'll go up in flames as if—"

It were made of paper.

"Hey watch where you spray that! It's— Great."

What?

"The cutter is all clogged up with powder now."

Just clean it out in the sink.

"There isn't a sink in here. We're vampires, there's no need for running water. We'll have to cut out by hand."

This will take forever!

"We have time."

Hey little buddy, what's happening?

"Oh hey, long time no see..."

Why are you standing out here? You look kind of anxious.

"I'm waiting for Sam Winston to say action! Did you hear that?"

Hear what?

"I thought I heard him say action. Damn, he's taking forever to get ready
    for this shot. So what brings you around these parts?"

There's a crime spree going down, and I'm hot on their trail.

"Sounds great, but I'm kind of in the middle of my own hunt."

More vampires? Come on man, I didn't take you under my wing so that
    you could end up being some Buffy wannabe.

"I'm good at it and it pays the bills."

You want to pay some bills? We'll go fifty fifty on this this bounty and
    you'll be set for years.

"Wow these guys must be dangerous."

Nah... Not so much dangerous as... Well they're not dangerous at all.
    They're wanted for attempted armed robbery of a grocery store
    in town.

"They sound like small fish."

This grocery store is loaded. Do you have any idea how much soda they
    have up in there?

"Well most grocery stores do..."

And limes!

"Ew, I hate limes."

Those suckers are expensive this time of year. They ship them in from
    South America via Africa.

"That seems kind of out of the way."

They're professionals, they must have their reasons. So are you in?

"I'm getting the feeling that Sam Winston was just trying to get rid of
    me... so I'll help you out."

Fantastic, just like the good old days!

"You're way more excited about this than I would have thought."

I missed you little buddy. Remember that time when we caught that one
    dude and you stripped down and ran through the lobby?

"Yeah that was the night we met."

I know I gave you a hard time back then, but you were kind of a bad ass. I could just sense your raw potential.

"I already said I'll help, you can stop sucking up."

I'm not sucking up. The truth is, I've had a bit of a drinking problem...

"I know."

Let me finish! I'm recovering and I'm in the making amends phase.

"Ah ha, so you didn't mean anything you said!"

Of course I meant it! I was too busy being drunk to ever tell you how I really felt. Right in here.

"That's your stomach."

Really? I thought that was where the heart... no wonder everyone I've shot seems to survive, I've been aiming in the wrong place.

"You would make a terrible vampire hunter."

That's fine by me. What do you say, are we cool?

"Yeah alright. Let's bag these guys so I can get back to my job."

High five.

"Uh..."

Let's try that again.

"You're drunk aren't you?"

Yeah...

"How did I learn anything from you..."

Come on, I parked by that tree over there.

"You're car is wrapped around that tree over there."

Maybe you should drive.

meet bob

Oh, hello. I wasn't expecting to see anyone up here.

"Like wise. The name's Bob."

Nice to meet you Bob, I'm the Saint of Immensity.

"Nice title. Got one of those special rocks, eh?"

Sure did.

"I'm lookin' to score one for myself. Legends say the dragon guards a
magical stone that can bend space and time, the Rock of Ages!"

Kind of like a time machine.

"Yes. So how about we team up? You slay the dragon while I steal the
Rock of Ages."

How am I supposed to do that?

"With your stone, of course!"

Uh...

"Surely it has to do something useful."

It might, I just have no idea how to use it.

"Let's see... it's the stone of immensity... so that must mean that it can
make you grow very large!"

Oh, that's pretty cool. Let's see if I can get it to work.

"Concentrate. Maybe."

I'm concentrating.

"Focus."

Same thing as concentrating.

"Sorry. I'll let you focus on concentrating."

... It doesn't seem to be doing anything.

"BOO!"

Ah! What was that for?

"I thought maybe it was like the hiccups."

That doesn't even make sense.

"Try using your wand."

This isn't a wand, it's a scepter.

"What's the difference."

Size? Also there's this gem thing on the end. Wands don't have that.

"I've seen a couple wands that do."

Fine, just the size thing then.

"If you were a giant, could you use it as a wand?"

I don't see why not. How do I use this?

"You don't know how to use the scepter either?"

A fortune teller lady gave it to me, no instruction manual or even a
       hands on training course. I could have asked, I suppose...

"I think you have to wave it around and say something in Latin."

Akemay emay igbay!

"Real Latin, not pig latin."

Uh... cre mihi magnus!

"I think that was close."

And nothing.

"I'm sure you'll figure it out when the time comes."

Hold on, how am I going to slay the dragon without any weapons?

"How did you get this far without them? This whole forest is crawling
       with monsters."

Monsters haven't bothered me. Actually it's been kind of a pleasant
       stroll. Maybe they left me alone because I'm a werewolf?

"How about that? You should be fine then. Until you go up to slay him,
       the dragon won't even suspect a thing. As long as we're as quiet
       as possible, I doubt he'll wake up anyway."

Sounds like a piece of cake.

"I'd like to think so."

You go first.

"No way, you go first!"

If we keep arguing, we're sure to wake him up.

"Fine, but only if you're right behind me."

Well, maybe a few steps behind you, don't want to risk giving you a flat
       tire. You seem like the type that would let out a yelp in the event
       of a flat tire.

What are you talking about?"

Your general demeanor gives me that impression.

"I mean what's a flat tire?"

Oh, it's when you're walking behind someone and step on the heel of
       their shoe, and their shoe either partially or fully comes off when
       they go to take their next step.

"That's not very nice. Why would you do that?"

It's not always on purpose, I was saying if I walked behind you too
   closely, I might accidentally give you a flat tire.

"I think you would do it on purpose."

I promise I won't.

"Hmm. Okay, I'll go in first."

Great.

carry on

Place your bags on the conveyor belt.

"Sure. I'm headed home from a vacation to Guam!"

How wonderful. Place your shoes on the conveyor.

"No problem. Perfect vacationing shoes."

I get it, you were on vacation. Has anyone had access to your bags other
   than yourself.

"Ever?"

Since you packed them and came to the airport.

"I suppose the maid at the hotel could have accessed them, because you
   know, that's what I've been doing. Vacationing here in Guam.
   Just came from the hotel. Where there are maids..."

Just a yes or no will suffice. No need for theoretical suppositions.

"No, then. Although the maid, at the hotel I was staying at for my vacation here to Guam, could have had access, I am confident she did
   not put anything in or remove anything from my bags."

You seem nervous.

"What, me? Nah... ha ha... Me nervous? Of course not, I just spent time
   vacationing here in Guam. I'm totally relaxed. Not nervous. Not
   nervous at all."

Really nervous.

"I'm uh... a nervous flier! That's it. I'm so scared of flying, I get nervous
   just thinking about it."

Why are you wearing an elevator operator's uniform?

"Costume party! Yeah, that's it. The costume party went late, and I didn't
   have any time to change before heading here to the airport. You
   know, so I could fly home from my vacation here in Guam."

Sure. I'm going to have to search your bags.

"Uh...Okay."

Let's see here... This is a whole lot of electronics.

"Wow, it sure is! Er, I mean... Yes. There is."

This isn't the first time you've seen what's in these bags, is it?

"Of course not, like I said, I've been here—"

Vacationing in Guam. Got it. What are you doing with all of these electronics? Surely, one man needs only so many cell phones, media players and e-book readers.

"Uh... hand me that book over there real quick."

Which one?

"The one that says instructions."

Okay...

"Just a sec... hmm... I am an electronics salesman and I was here on business demonstrating mobile technology to clients here in Guam. Yep."

I thought you said you were here on vacation.

"Did I say vacation? I meant business! What a silly mistake for me to make."

Whatever. The chemical swipe didn't indicate anything, and there's no rule that you can't have a ton of cell phones. Just make sure you turn them off before your flight. You're free to go. Carry on.

"Thank you for being so nice!"

Don't push it.

apologies to the ghoul friend

"Mister Sam Winston, I need a word with you!"

What now... oh, hello beautiful.

"Cut the crap! You're giving terrible advice to people, ghosts specifically!"

What are you... Oh, that book?

"Yes. THAT book. Who do you think you are?"

Sam Winston!

"Yeah, Sam Winston. Biggest jerk in the world. Tell him what you did because of him!"

Uh, what?

"I'm not talking to you, I'm talking to my ghost friend. Go ahead, tell him."

I don't... you think there's an actual ghost here?

"Yes, he's right here beside me! Apparently you're invisible to everyone but me."

Uh...

"Don't 'uh' me, you know very well ghosts exist. Why else would you write a book for them?"

That's a joke. Like writing a dating guide for cats... I wrote one of those too. It's part of a series. Ghosts aren't real.

"Tell that to him!"

Well if he's standing—

"Floating."

If he's floating right there, then he heard me.

"You're need to apologize for giving terrible advice."

Even if he's real, he ended up with you, didn't he?

"Yes."

So it worked.

"That's fine and dandy for him, but what about me? He's been lying this entire time!"

You're okay being in a relationship with a ghost, but you're not okay with that ghost lying?

"My mother used to say that lying is the first step on a downward spiral that ends with murder-suicide on a sandy beach."

At least it would happen in a nice location. And he's already dead, so at
        most it would be a murder or suicide, not both.

"Stop justifying your terrible book and apologize!"

Fine, I'm sorry that your ghost boyfriend took the advice I gave in a
        book that was never meant to be taken seriously because ghosts
        don't exist.

"Just because you start with 'I'm sorry' doesn't make it an apology!"

Sure it does. I'm sorry you don't think so.

"Stop it! You look up to this guy? Are happy you met him now?"

What are... oh right, you're talking to him.

"No I'm not going to ask for his autograph!"

Here, you can have my autograph, you have a really weird way of going
        about asking for one.

"I don't want your autograph!"

It's okay, I understand. You want to be memorable. Theatrics and all.
        Happens all the time.

"No, there's really a ghost with me, he's right here!"

Fine, what's his name?

"Oh, good question. What's your name?"

You didn't even know his name?

"I didn't think to ask. His name is... Johnson. Ray Johnson."

And how did hc dic?

"Ahuh. He's trying to remember. It's kind of hazy."

I'm sure it is.

"You were what? Uh. He was eaten by a dinosaur."

You've got to be kidding me. Take your autograph and get out of here.

"He was in Antarctica on an expedition when he found a dinosaur fro-
        zen in ice. He thawed him out, they shared some hot chocolate,
        and then the dinosaur ate him. Wow, really? Really, he says."

Adding more ridiculous details doesn't make it any more believable.

"He says that truth is stranger than fiction."

Please leave me alone before I call the bartender over.

"That little guy?"

That little guy is Little Whammy, former sidekick to Captain Wham.
        Guy could kick the hell out a telephone pole.

"Why would anyone do that?"

Just a gauge of strength. Like ripping a phone book in half.

"Ripping a phone book in half is impossible."

Right. That's why I said Little Whammy can kick the hell out of a telephone pole. Totally possible.

"What does that even mean? Does it break in half ?"

Disintegrates into a pile of splinters. One single kick does the trick. Pow.
Splinters all over. It's like watching a six month old Christmas
tree strapped to the top of a van go under a too-low overpass.
Pow.

"I see. Pow."

So if you know what's good for you, you'll let me be, and we all can get
back to enjoying our drinks.

"I wouldn't want to get disintegrated into a pile of splinters."

Damn right you wouldn't.

beach bump

Spindly Pete! I thought you were away on a voyage!

"I'm not Spindly Pete, I'm Jesus."

Ha, good one. Give me a fist bump!

"Er... ah, here."

Ow!

"What?"

Why did you punch me?

"Is that... what is a fist bump?"

Well it isn't punching me in the face!

"Worry. I misunderstood."

You're one weird guy sometimes. Did you just come up off the beach?

"Yeah."

I don't see your ship.

"I came alone."

No rowboat either?

"I walked."

What? Oof, you smell ripe. Surely you mean you swam. You smell like
rotten fish. But... you're bone dry. Huh.

"I'm decomposing and can walk on water. Like I told you, I'm Jesus."

I don't what that is. Come with me, let's get you a bite to eat.

"I'm not hungry, thanks... whatever your name is."

How could you forget my name? Spindly Pete! I'm disappointed in you! It's me! Palatino Phil!

"Why do they call you that?"

Oh come on, Spindly. It's my favorite font! If you ask me to make a sign, write an essay, or even just jot down a phone message, you bet your buns I'll be writing in Palatino font!

"That's kind of strange."

Sometimes I'll mix it up, I'll bold it up. Maybe italicize. Every now and then a strikethrough when I make a mistake. I use a calligraphy pen, y'know. No erasing mistakes. Strikethrough and move on.

"Look, that's all well and good and it's been great chatting, but all I need to know is how to get to Teufelberg."

You're not... No, say it ain't so Spindly Pete!

"Yes, I'm looking for Bertram! Why is everyone so afraid of him?"

I need to go. Good luck with that.

"Hold on, I don't know where I'm going. Can you at least point in the general direction?"

See that tall, dark wedge of black rock piercing the sky over there?

"Yeah."

That's Teufelberg. That's all I'm saying. You were never here. Get out of here, you suicidal maniac.

"Wow, these people really aren't fond of Bertram."

black and blue

"Wow, this is a really nice car."

Stop saying that every five minutes.

"I can't help it. Look at all this chrome. And carbon fiber. And whatever that material over there is."

It's a top secret material.

"Awesome. Okay, what does this button do?"

It activates that button over there.

"And then what does that button do?"

It deactivates the first button.

"So then... they both basically do nothing."

No, they're very important. They're existential.

"Hmm."

Makes you think, doesn't it?

"I'm thinking alright."

You see, parts of my car run on what you might call alien technology.

"I might call it that?"

For simplicity's sake.

"I see."

Current human technology relies on electricity or chemical combustion, but this alien technology is powered by thought.

"That's very interesting. So we're zooming down the road due to the energy of our thoughts?"

Ha, oh no, not at all. We haven't been able to reverse engineer anything that advanced. For now, all we've gotten it to do is control the radio. Go ahead, think of your favorite genre.

"Alright... Hey, that's cool! The exact song I was thinking of, even!"

Now try thinking about left or right.

"Hmm..."

Left. Or right.

"Whoa! Did I just change the balance?"

Sure did. You can do the same thing with the fade. But here's the real challenge... change the bass and treble levels.

"At the same time?"

That's why it's a challenge.

"Alright, I can do this."

Don't put your fingers on your temples like that.

"I thought it would help. I've seen it on TV."

Don't believe anything you see on TV.

"And concentrating..."

Okay, too much bass. Way too much bass. My head is rattling.

"Uh..."

No, not MORE bass, turn it back down!

"I can't concentrate with all of this thumping!"

Quick, push that button!

"Okay."

And now that one.

"Alright."

Then turn that knob two full rotations.

"Clockwise or counter clockwise?"

Uh... either. Now, pull that lever over there.

"Got it."

And stomp on that small panel.

"How hard?"

Very hard. No pussyfooting around, this is important.

"And done. Whew, the music stopped."

That was a close one. You follow directions well.

"That's what they teach us at the academy."

I really don't give you cops all proper props.

"No worries. We say some mean stuff about you, so it all evens out."

Aw, what? That's not nice... what kind of mean stuff?

"Just making fun of how you always wear sunglasses. And that hat. And
       a tie. Your like one of the Blues Brothers."

The John Goodman movie?

"That was the sequel."

Same concept, right? Hello, there's the ambulance... Look's like it's had
       a rough night.

"Where are the paramedics?"

According to my notes... The paramedics came out this way to check up
       on a bloodied naked man.

"Maybe the bloodied naked man killed them?"

Not likely. Here, come with me to have a look.

"What are we looking for, exactly?"

Ah, here we go. Unidentified forensics object.

"Hmm... hey, these match the hairs from those kids' van! Do you think they're the ones that..."

Oh no, I'm sure they're not capable of that... The paramedics are still close, I can sense it.

"Man, this ambulance really took a beating. Looks like it won't even run anymore. The paramedics can't be far if they're on foot, right?"

Ri— get back in the car immediately!

"Why, what's— OH SHIT."

Get in, get in, get in!

"Ow, this one has the grip of a gorilla!"

Kick him!

"Hyah!"

Not like a soccer ball, like in that one movie where that Scottish dude who played a Greek king. You know, with the bottomless pit and slow motion.

"Oh yeah, I remember that one. THIS. IS. SPORTS BRA!"

Well I can't complain with results. Get in the car!

"I don't know how to operate this handle!"

Pull UP. Pull UP then OUT!

"I can't, it's not..."

Ugh, I'll open it for you from the inside!

"Thank you! I'm good, go go go!"

Holy Charles Grodin, what in the world...

"I think those were zombies."

What the Hell are zombies doing here?

"They were wearing EMT uniforms... must have been the paramedics from the ambulance."

This situation is worse than I thought. We have to find those damn kids in the van.

"No, Bob, NOOOO!"

What? Who else is in here?

"Er..."

You!

"Why did I have to yell..."

Explain yourself, pitiful human!

"I'm sorry mister dragon, I was just passing through. Look, I don't even
        have any weapons."

I suppose you have a point. Wait, you have a magic scepter. And what's
        that in your other hand?

"Walking stick and a skipping stone. Couldn't be more harmless."

Hmm... You're lying.

"What?"

You have ten seconds to tell me who you really are and your purpose, or
        else I will eat you like I did your lime tasting friend. Ten.

"Oh that guy? We weren't friends, we were just—"

Nine.

"You're not really going to eat me, I'm not even..."

Eight.

"I mean, I probably taste even worse than Bob did."

Seven.

"Okay, fine. I didn't want to have to do this but..."

Six.

"UNNNNGH!"

Five.

"Damn it, nothing. Really?"

Four.

"Stand down dragon. I am the Saint of Immensity, and all should fear
        me and my sacred Stone of Immensity!"

Ha ha ha! Are you serious? Poor, pathetic little thing. You obviously
        don't even know how to use the powers you wield.

"Sure I do! All I have to do is wave this like so and—

Gulp. Hmm, he actually tasted pretty good. Wish I had chewed to get
        more of that flavor...

recovery

"Ah, you're awake. Stay calm and don't try to move, all the stitches still need some time to heal over."

Huh, where am I?

"You're in one of the recovery rooms at Fountain Lake Cybernetics."

Where's my friend, ah, Byron, the talking dog?

"Don't worry, he's in the next room doing fine. He hasn't woken up quite yet."

So the implants... They went well?

"Yours were a bit tricky. Your stomach is full of all kinds of interesting stuff..."

You didn't let anything out, did you?

"No, don't worry. We followed your wishes to keep everything that is in your stomach contained within your stomach."

Great.

"See, we built the implant around your stomach, like you might do with papier mache around a balloon. Then, we popped the balloon, your stomach, and pulled it out of your esophagus. And there you have it, cyborg stomach."

Well that sounds fantastic.

"Be careful when you belch. There's the possibility of the methane igniting as it passes through your esophagus."

Going the other way too?

"Far less likely, but anything is possible. Keep in mind that your cyborg stomach is self healing due to the nanotechnology used. There is the possibility that they will someday replace more and more of your body, especially your skin."

So I'll have self healing metal body armor.

"Exactly. Virtually indestructible."

That's very cool. And how about the wings?

"Here, let me help you up out of bed so you can get a feel for them."

Ah thank you.

"Go ahead and flap them a bit. Not too hard, this is a small room."

Wow, not only are they awesome, but I can feel every inch of them. The literal wind beneath my wings.

"Just wait until you get outside."

Let's go right now!

"Our regulations require you to stay for observation for a minimum of an hour after surgery."

How long has it been?

"About 56 minutes... But you want to wait for your friend Byron to wake up, don't you?"

Who's Byron?

"That talking dog."

Oh, right, of course. I suppose I can wait. How did his implants go?

"Very well. Hand and paw replacements are a common procedure."

Has anyone ever asked for something as silly as a laser and a CD tray for paws?

"Quite a few actually. I install a laser and CD tray combination at least every other week."

Is it really that useful?

"No idea, I always try to talk them out of it. Trading dexterity, high fives, and all the other pleasures that hands and paws bring for an underpowered laser that reads discs and a tray to hold and spin those discs? Absolutely ridiculous."

Folks will be folks.

"And they're paying me loads of cash, so what do I care what stupid things they want on their hands. That reminds me, your address is 123 Fauxdress Boulevard, right?"

You go it.

"You can expect your bill in a few days."

Sounds great.

"Well, it's been an hour since you're surgery. You seem like you've made a full recovery, so feel free to head on over to Byron's room if you like. I'm sure he will be happy to see you."

Thanks, doctor.

"No, thank you Bertram."

vats misfortune

"What's happening?"

The pressure levels in the vats are rising.

"No! What could be causing this?"

Looks like a rise in temperature. It could be from that UFO that was
    threatening to destroy us!

"I'm sure the would target a dog food factory first."

I'm just saying, you saw what happened to that water tower. Maybe
    there was a residual effect. That water tower was only a couple
    blocks away.

"Enough theorizing, what can we do to fix it?"

I don't know if we can, the pressure is rising too fast.

"We'll have to vent the vats."

Vent the vats? But at these pressures that could be disastrous.

"And if we don't it could be even more disastrous! Damn, this week is
    not going well."

Obviously.

"Our test dog learns to talk and tricks me into letting him out, now this.
    What am I supposed to do?"

We should move this project to the far side of the lab, just in case.

"The hormone adjustment formula, good thinking. At least we won't
    have to start from scratch if these vats blow."

Alright, I'm going to start the valve release process.

"Our formulas are safe on the other side of the lab, we're good to go."

And releasing...

"Oh man, that's loud."

Uh oh.

"Uh oh? I can't afford any more uh oh's!"

The release valves, they must have deformed from the intense heat.
    They won't budge!

"Can we release them manually?"

They're really high up, and the only ladder we have is in the warehouse.
    We'll never get it in time!

"I guess this is the end."

It's been great working with you.

"Eh."

What?

"I didn't really enjoy our time here. I liked the cat food factory more."

Fair enough.

"That banging and hissing really is deafening."

It sure i— AGGGH!

"AAAAAAGH!"

sold out

I can't believe it, we sold out for tonight already. Not bad for a show that
was announced today.

"Are you kidding, this is Rapid Whammy Love, the greatest superhero
folk-punk-rock band in all of Gilpin County!"

Never heard of them.

"You're fired. Get out of here. Right now."

Are you serious?

"Dead serious."

Well screw you man, I work my ass off for you here, taking credit cards,
cutting up credit cards... other stuff too. I'm glad you fired me
because now I don't have to quit!

Whoa, whoa, whoa, I was just kidding. You do such a fantastic job
around here, and I appreciate you more than you'll ever know.

"Oh. Thanks. I was... I was kidding too."

What was that you said about cutting up credit cards?

"When a credit card is declined we're supposed to cut it up into tiny
pieces."

Are we in some kind of 80's comedy film? We don't do that here.

"I thought that was some kind of law? The smaller the pieces, the better.
Maximum shame, especially if the guy is on a date."

There aren't any laws that contain the words 'maximum shame.'

"There should be. Though, I don't think I could bring the maximum at
all times. I could maintain a solid 90% consistently."

I have no idea what you're talking about.

"Forget it. This concert could be what saves the venue!"

Damn right! I've been waiting for this day since the band broke up over three years ago. Granted, I've kept the venue unbooked just in case they needed somewhere to play if they decided to reunite on a whim... Had I been putting on shows all this time, we might be in better financial shape. But now we're back baby, yeah!

bros

"Bertram?"

Who dares call me by my name?

"Holy mother of me... You're Bertram?"

You know very well I am! Identify yourself!

"I'm Jesus! Your brother."

What are you talking about? I don't have a brother, especially not one that's a human!

"I'm not any human, I'm the son of God and so are you. Apparently."

Ha! God? I've been alive for millions and millions of years, and I've seen no evidence of such a thing.

"But isn't that proof itself? You're immortal! How could that be the work of anyone but God?"

Nanotechnology.

"What?"

I've lived this long because of nanotechnology! Every single part of me is a nearly indestructible yet very flexible alloy. Every scale, every blood vessel, every organ. It's wonderful.

"Where would you even get something like that?"

The future, of course! So why are you here making ridiculous claims of being my brother?

"Our Father sent me here."

So that's it.

"We're supposed to destroy Santa."

What?

"Fat, jolly elf. Actually pretty evil."

Oh my, you are the real deal. Santa is in my stomach. I ate him at the North Pole. He's the reason I had cyborg stomach implants!

"You ate him at the north pole? I don't remember a dragon there."

I was merely a dinosaur back then! Had these wings put on when I got the new stomach. And what about you? I don't remember a decomposing pirate being there...

"I was in my normal body wearing mukluks."

Oh yes, I remember the mukluks!

"You believe me now, right?"

Everything checks out.

"We need to figure out what to do to destroy Santa."

Hmm. God didn't tell you how to do that?

"He told me you would know how to stop him."

I've had him pretty well under control for millions of years now...

"Maybe you could drink some acid or something to dissolve him?"

Ow, that would hurt. A lot.

"I thought your entire body was indestructible?"

My body reconstructs itself really fast, but that doesn't mean stuff
    doesn't still hurt. And what if he's invulnerable to acid? Then
    we'd just be making a hole for him to escape out of.

"Damn. Do you have any ideas?"

Hot chocolate?

"What?"

I could go for some.

"How is that supposed to help?"

Helps me think. And it's delicious.

"Delicious... I've got it! Poisoned cookies and milk."

I don't follow.

"That's Santa's thing right? Eating cookies and milk children leave out
    for him on Christmas Eve."

No wonder he's so fat.

"Send down a plate of poison cookies and a glass of poison milk and he
    won't be able to resist."

Let's get baking!

detour

"So you saw an actual UFO."

Yeah that's right, a you foe.

"Were you scared?"

No I wasn't scared! I don't get scared, I get angry!

"What's that up ahead?"

Oh sweet marmalade, it's a couple of zombies!

"Looks like they took out that ambulance!"

Quick, take a left!

"Whew, that was a close."

I don't think they seen us.

"What is going on here? The world is falling apart!"

Must be the beginnin's of the pocky lips.

"The what?"

The pocky lips! The end of the world!

"Oh right, the apocalypse."

That's what I said!

"Oh what is this all about?"

What's this train doing here?

"Looks like it's stopped."

Sure ain't movin'. We could be sittin' here for hours.

"Holy crap, what was the sound?"

Splosion! Looks like the old dog food factory! Must be the aliens team-
      ing up with them zombies to destroy us all!

"We've gotta get out of here."

Look, there's a mansion up that way. That'd be a safe place.

"It seems kind of spooky."

At least it ain't splodin'!

"What should we tell them?"

Tell who?

"The people that live there?"

I dunno, that we got lost or something. If they resist, we'll just pull out
      our shotguns.

"We can't kill anyone!"

We're not gonna kill 'em, just let 'em know who's boss. Maybe shoot a vase or two. I love shootin' vases. 'Ping!' Very satisfactionary.

"I've never shot a vase before."

You'll love it! Get you in some good practice for when the aliens and
    zombies come for us.

belly

Ho ho who's there?

"Santa?"

Yes, what's it to you?

"You got really thin. I hardly recognized you."

There's not much to eat in a dinosaur's stomach!

"This is a dragon, not a dinosaur."

What?

"Where did you come from? Where's Bob?"

Who's Bob?

"The guy who got eaten right before me."

He's over there. Dead.

"What?"

Or asleep. I don't know, I'm no doctor. Who are you?

"I'm ah.. the Saint of Immensity! I guess... The last time we met I was
    a wolf, though."

Of course, back in the epic battle with Jesus! You're exactly who I was
    waiting for! You have the Stone with you, don't you?

"Let's see... Yes, got it."

Great, that's our ticket out of here!

"What does it do?"

It makes the user immense!

"That's what we thought, but I couldn't figure out how to work it."

It's simple, just cup it in your hands.

"Okay. Now what?"

And give it a good shake, like you're about to roll some dice.

"Six, twelve, or twenty-sided?"

Uh, twenty-sided, I guess.

"I can do that..."

Wait, not yet. Let's go over what we're going to do once you bust us out of here.

"Sure, of course."

Somewhere here in the dragon's lair is the Rock of Ages. I need you to find it and give it to me.

"Is that all?"

Yeah, then do whatever you want. Stomp a village or two, wade in the ocean...

"Hold on, will my pants grow too?"

What?

"I went to a lot of trouble to get these pants, I'd hate to rip them to shreds when I become immense."

Of course your pants will grow too!

"That's a relief."

Any other questions?

"Nope."

So we're clear on the plan?

"Yeah."

Alright, get ready, and...

"Hold on, how to I become small again?"

You shake the Stone again.

"Does the Stone get bigger with me?"

Of course it does, otherwise you would lose it too easily. Stop asking stupid questions!

"Sorry. I'm ready now."

And shake it!

"I need a beat!"

What?

"Beat box for me!"

Oh, uh... boom chicka tack geh boom chicka tack!

"Yeah, that's it!"

Boom. Boom. Ba doo doo boom, SHAKE IT! Boom chicka tack geh boom chicka ho ho ho!

tray tables up

"You were right, that guy at the front desk really was a pain."

I could have socked him right in the— Oh hey, put your tray table up.

"I'm trying to read my magazine!"

They just said for us to put our tray tables up because of the turbulence, aren't you listening?

"That's just a suggestion, there's no actual harm in having the tray table down, now is there?"

What if we crash? The tray table could impale you!

"If we crash we'll have a lot more to worry about than a tray table impaling anything. I mean, explosions, shards of glass and metal flying everywhere, blood spraying from all the severed limbs, people puking, severed limbs flinging into our laps, your girly screams causing my hearing loss. Need I go on?"

If you want to break the rules, go right ahead, but don't expect me to pull the tray table out of you.

"It's better to leave it in anyway, helps keep the bleeding to a minimum until you're able to seek medical attention."

You're thinking of arrows.

"Same concept."

Oof, that was quite the bump.

"It's just some clouds, perfectly normal for this kind of flight."

This kind of flight?

"Yeah, the kind that ends in a terrible crash."

Don't even joke about that.

"Who's joking?"

Shit, you knew this was going to happen, didn't you?

"I'm not saying another word."

How could you let me on this plane with you if you knew we were all going to die?

"Hey, keep it down, the other passengers might start freaking out."

They should be freaking out, these are their last moments on Earth!

"Technically we're not on Earth, we're thousands of feet in the air."

You know what I meant, smartass.

"Did you really expect things to go well hanging around with me?"

Well I figured there would be benefits.

"I am not going to make out with you!""

Not those kinds of benefits! I meant immortality, or divine protection or something like that. Tell me you can keep me from dying in this plane crash.

"I guess I could if I really wanted to..."

Come on, please please please?

"There are definitely some benefits to keeping you around up here."

On the airplane?

"On Earth. You're a supervillain, so you kill lots of people, right?"

Uhhh... Not that I can think of.

"How do you strike fear into the citizens if you don't kill anyone?"

Actually the townspeople are pretty nice to me. Just before I left for my vacation this nice guy from the hardware store hooked me up with this great security system. See, my old security computer locked me out and started beating me up just because I couldn't remember the unlock codes and—

"That's nice, but we have a deal to work out here. If you're going to stay alive you're going to have to help me out a little bit. I pretty much work on commission. As long as souls are coming in, I don't get grief from the big guy."

What are you trying to say?

"I need you to start killing people."

Innocent people? I wouldn't feel comfortable...

"Well, no. Truly innocent people will just end up going to Heaven and that doesn't help me at all. You have to kill people who have sinned."

Oh, so I would be like a serial killer that kills other serial killers.

"They don't have to have sinned that bad. And you don't want to risk becoming a serial killer that only kills serial killers who kill serial killers. We can work with the lesser sins, like littering and leaving dogs in the car without cracking the window."

Those are sins?

"Oh yeah. It's really hard to get into Heaven, man. Do you know what got me sent to Hell?"

Forgot to brush your teeth?

"Nope."

Ordered too many french fries and had to throw the ones you couldn't
      eat in the trash because they're just gross if you try to save and
      reheat them later.

"That is a damnable sin, but not one I was guilty of."

I give up.

"I knocked over the limbo stick."

What?

"There were a bunch of minor infractions that put me in limbo in the
      first place, but when push came to shove, I couldn't get under
      the damn stick."

That sounds terrible. If killing people is all I have to do to live forever,
      why the Hell not?

"Exactly."

So it's a deal?

"It's a deal, and just in time. Hold on, this might sting a little."

landing

"Wow, these clouds are unforgiving."

No kidding, and did you see that strange flash of light a minute ago?

"You saw that too? That's a rclicf, I thought I was hallucinating."

Don't worry, our instruments will get us through this. Thank God for
      tech— wait a second.

"What's wrong?"

Somebody didn't turn off their cell phone.

"Oh no..."

There's a laptop in standby mode as well. Strike me thrice and call me a
      Turkey, there are over a dozen mp3 players still on, and half of
      them are playing Bieber!

"What should we do?"

Pray.

"What about our instruments? I thought they could get us through any
      storm safely."

All of the plane's resources are being sucked up detecting everything

with an on/off switch, the flight computer is frozen! Oh come
    on, someone just turned on an electronic book reader. Do they
    have any idea what they're putting us through?

"We could try turning it off and back on again."

With this many electronic devices on board, we may not be able to turn
    the computer back on. The interference is just too much.

"So we'll have to—"

Yes.

"But--"

It's a risk I'm willing to take.

"In that case..."

What are you doing?

"I'm calling my wife."

Put that cell phone away!

"But we're already..."

Turn it off and stow it.

"You don't have to freak out."

Sorry, I've never done a manual landing, let alone in an emergency. I'm
    just a bit stressed out.

"Wait, you've never done a manual landing?"

That's what I said.

"But you're the pilot!"

I'm not proud of it.

"I'm stuck being second fiddle while a clown like you who has never
    even done a manual landing is in the driver's seat?"

Pilot's seat.

"Pilot's seat!"

Well, have you ever done a manual landing?

"No. But that's not the point!"

Hey, what's that in your backpack?

"My cell phone, I just put it there."

No, beneath that.

"Let's see..."

I hear something... It's like the faint sound of pop music intended
    primarily for tweens.

"Oh no."

You're kidding me, why would you bring a backpack full of electronics on an airplane?

"Someone must have swapped my bag!"

Those evil sons of bitches... I should have known, we're the victims of a terrorist attack!

"We have to get rid of it, we all could die!"

Quick, throw it out the door!

"But the doors swings inwards, the cabin pressure makes it impossible to open them at altitude."

Damn, you're right. Looks like we're going to have to take her down to crop dusting altitude. You ever do any low flying?

"No, have you?"

To be completely honest, this is the first time I've flown an airplane.

"Are you kidding me? I should so be the pilot."

My dad owns the company.

"Well I hope he goes bankrupt."

You take that back! Hey, wait a second.

"What?"

How fast are you at pressing buttons?

"I'm pretty fast. I'd say between moderate and very."

Quick, turn off all of the devices in the backpack!

"Manually?"

Manually!

"I've never turned off this many electronic devices manually before..."

You have to try, it's our only chance!

"How do you turn this off?"

What is it?

"MP3 player."

There isn't an on/off switch?

"No."

Try the stop button.

"Which one is that?"

The one with the square!

"Shouldn't it be an octagon?"

Maybe, but we can write the electronics industry about that later.

"It's not working!"

How long did you hold it down?

"You didn't say to hold it down!"

Who doesn't know to hold it down?

"That function isn't immediately obvious from its design!"

But it's a convention that is considered common knowledge in this age of media consumption!

"Don't you talk down to me."

Hand it to me, I'll do it.

"Fine, since you're the expert."

What the... it's not working.

"Ah ha! I think you owe someone an apology."

I have this same model at home, I swear you have to... Oh no.

"What?"

They've tampered with the internal circuitry!

"Damn, that's voided the warranty for sure."

It's worse than that, we can't turn it off!

"We're going to die!"

Now wait, there has to be some other way.

"The door!"

Not that, we've already been over that. Some other other way.

"We'll take out the batteries!"

What do you mean 'we'?

"I'll take out the batteries."

Good thinking.

"I should have thought of this earlier."

Yeah you should have.

"And..."

Are you done yet?

"Done!"

Strange... The computer is saying that there are even more electronic devices on now than there were five minutes ago!

"That's impossible! I've taken the batteries out of everything in my backpack."

There must be a second backpack.

"Oh no. What should we do?"

We'll have to find it or land manually.

"The second bomb could be anywhere! There

I was hoping it wouldn't come to this. Strap in and get ready.

"Alright."

You ready?

"Yes."

Alright, good luck.

"Wait a second, where the hell are you going?"

I've gotta take a whiz.

"This is no time for taking a whiz!"

Ugh, fine, let's do this thing. Together.

"Together."

Stop holding my hand.

"Sorry."

First thing's first. How do we tell where we're going?

"Uh... well the artificial horizon isn't working."

Right.

"And the radar is out."

Check.

"And this thing... I don't know what it is anyway."

So what are our options?

"Maybe uh... Look out the windshield?"

This thing has a windshield?

"Yes, it's right in front of us!"

Are you sure this isn't smoked glass?

"Smoked glass?"

Yeah, I can't see anything. It's all cloudy.

"That's because of the clouds we're flying through!"

Oh, that makes sense.

"And the GPS is going haywire. I have no idea where we are."

We're screwed.

"Oh wait, I see something..."

It's getting closer.

"Oh no. I think I know what that is."

Mountain!

look out below

The dragon is somewhere in this mountain.

"Where's the entrance?"

No idea.

"Maybe it's over here..."

I just looked there.

"Did you try pulling on this branch?"

How would that help?

"Might open a secret passage."

Okay, I'll try it.

"What's that sound?"

The branch snapped.

"Not that, I mean the shrieking noise."

It sounds like it's coming from up th— Hey look!

"Is that the dragon?"

I guess it could be... it's definitely big enough to lift all of our fellow unicorns off of that tower.

"Get its attention before it flies back into its lair!"

Hey! Hey! Look over here! It's not working. You wave your hooves too.

"HEY DRAGON! WE NEED YOUR HELP!"

I don't think it can see us.

"That's weird..."

What?

"Well, dragons are like birds right?"

Scaly birds of death, yeah.

"Don't birds flap their wings?"

Well yeah, but not all the time... They glide every now and then.

"They still flap every once in a while, even when they're gliding, right?"

I guess so... what's your point?

"That dragon looks stiff. I haven't seen it flap once."

Maybe dragons fly differently?

"It's spewing out smoke!"

It must be the dragon!

"The smoke is coming from its wings though..."

Shouldn't it be coming from its mouth?

"Probably just a misconception about dragons."

What's it doing?

"Flying into its lair of course."

There's no entrance for it to fly into, it's going to run right into the side
   of the—

"OH!"

DUDE.

"What... what just happened?"

I have a feeling that wasn't a dragon.

"The whole mountain is on fire!"

And the ground is shaking! I have a bad feeling about this. Duck!

"Where?"

The verb!

"Oh!"

Get behind that rock, we might be safe there.

"Stop pushing me!"

We don't have much time! Move it!

"Was the dragon in there? Is he dead?"

Stop asking so many questions, I know just as much as you do!

"Do you think this was a dragon assassination?"

Who would want to assassinate a dragon?

"Sigh. It's a lost cause. We're meant to go extinct."

Don't talk like that. There's still a chance.

"Get down! Another explosion!"

There's no way the dragon could have survived that.

prepared to fail

Hey Luke, did you see that?

"I was just about to call you, crazy huh? I'm going to get basically all
of those souls."

All you ever care about is getting more souls, don't you see what happened?

"Yeah. Plane crash. Fiery death. Incredible."

I think Bertram was in the mountain.

"Your pet lizard?"

He's not my pet lizard, he's my dinosaur son!

"So you'll see him soon, what's the big deal?"

Santa was trapped in his stomach!

"Oh, I see."

Hopefully Jesus got to him in time and they were able to escape before
the crash...

"I wouldn't bet on it."

You can at least try to be optimistic.

"Optimism never works well for me. You could say that I have little
optimism for optimism."

You do have a point. We should probably prepare for the worst.

"I don't want to get exiled with you again."

I'm packing a DVD player with noise cancelling headphones.

"Oh! Will you bring The Commish?"

No! It's for me to use! Bring your own.

"I see how it is, the Almighty God can't be bothered to share. What a
jerk."

Fine, I'll bring The Commish if you bring that one movie about the giant shark.

"Jaws?"

No, the new one.

"Jaws 2000?"

That wasn't a movie.

"What was it about?"

You know, it had that big shark... *Mega* shark even.

"Did it fight a giant octopus?"

Yes!

"That's Mega Shark Versus Giant Octopus."

Yes, Mega Shark Versus Giant Octopus! You have that on DVD don't
     you?

"Limited edition or director's cut?"

There's a director's cut?

"Yeah, it's way better than the original version."

Do you even have to ask? Director's cut! Oh... Hey, I have to go.

"What now?"

Jesus is dead.

"Again?"

Again. We're goners.

"Damn. At least we'll have plenty of entertainment."

burning rubble

Quick, we don't have much time.

"What's going on here? This place is falling apart. There's no way I
     caused all of this by bursting out of that dragon's stomach!"

This is just an extra precaution to make sure he'd be unconscious.

"You set this up?"

Maybe. That's not important. We need to find the Rock of Ages before
     this mountain collapses.

"How am I supposed to do that? Half of the treasure is buried in rubble!
     Ouch, and it's all really hot!"

Just look for something that looks like a rock.

"Everything looks like a rock! The entire mountain is crumbling!"

Look over there in that treasure chest.

"It's full of dog food."

That's... huh.

"And a couple of chew toys."

Let me see... Ho ho hold on, what's this?

"Looks fancy. Definitely not a rock though."

Damn, it's just a regular time machine.

"You're disappointed to find a time machine?"

This is a weak manmade model. It's only capable of sending one or two travelers through time and space. The Rock of Ages must still be on that damn space ship that foiled my earlier plans.

"Your plans to kill Jesus?"

No, my plans to kill Jesus were quite successful. I mean my plans to destroy the planet!

"I've been helping you try to destroy the planet this whole time?"

Yes.

"I don't approve. That's where I live, you know!"

It won't do you any good to feel bad about it, your part of the plan is complete.

"Shoot."

Don't look so glum. You're a success! Celebrate!

"I guess so."

Well... Catch ya later.

"Where are you going?"

I have some business to take care of.

"You can't just leave me here!"

I can and I will. Later ho ho homey.

"What are we looking for?"

A van. Couple of kids driving. Some damage to the front bumper.

"Like that one?"

That's them! Turn in here, I'll grab the tranq guns! This bounty is going to be so sweet.

"50/50 right?"

What? You didn't have to do any of the leg work! 70/30, that's as high as I'll go.

"I will turn this car right around."

You wouldn't.

"I would."

Prove it!

"Fine!"

Whoa watch out for that car! Damn, stop screwing around, you could have killed us!

"It wasn't that bad."

I'm about to throw up.

"So they're in a van?"

Yes.

"Down by the river?"

It's a possibility.

"Get it?"

What?

"In a van down by the river. It's a song lyric."

No it isn't.

"Sure it is!"

It's from that one television comedy program.

"All That?"

That's... No.

"Hey, what's that car doing?"

What the Hell, you maniacs!

"Go after them!"

Why?

"I've gotta give them a ticket for reckless driving."

"Mmm, D-Holes and Hot Chocobot. Could life get any better?"

Yes, with a Drippy Dippy!

"Hey, dunk that in your own Hot Chocobot!"

I don't want to ruin the pure chocolatey flavors.

"It's dripping with chocolate."

That's chocolate frosting, not... chocolate whatever they use to make the Chocobot.

"It's all basically the same."

"I'm pretty sure that's because you've been drinking."

Your driving doesn't help.

"Uh oh."

What'd I do?

"Not you, that car we almost hit back there."

Did you hit it?

"No, but I think it's…"

It's what?

"It's turning around."

Why would it be doing that?

"And now it's following us."

Quick, lose 'em!

"We don't even know who they are."

Anyone who follows someone isn't worth being followed by, especially if they're a bounty hunter or a cop. Turn into that parking lot!

"Ooh, Dippy Donuts. I didn't know

We don't have time for that!

"I have a monthly quota."

What if people are considerate drivers all month?

"I just pull over random people and hope that they aren't wearing their seat belt. But I don't like doing that. Just let me give that maniac a ticket and we can be on our way."

Fine, but make it quick.

"Do you have a siren?"

No.

"How can you not have a siren? I always keep one under my seat."

I never have need to use one.

"But now you do, and you're out of luck! Here, I have a siren app on my phone."

I don't think that's going to work

Then it shouldn't matter that I dunk it in yours.

"Then it shouldn't matter that **you** dunk it in **your own**!"

I refuse.

"Then don't dunk at all."

I won't.

"Good."

Good.

"We've been here for a while, should we get moving?"

What?

"We went through the drive through so we could avoid the cops, right?"

Yeah.

"We've been sitting here in the Drippy Donuts parking lot for like twenty minutes."

That long? We must be fine then. I'm sure if we were going to get identified we would have by now.

"We're pushing our luck." Finish your D-Holes so we can get going then.

"I was going to save the rest for later."

You can't do that. Mom would find out we went out for Dippy Donuts.

"Oh yeah, good point. Give me a minute, I have to let my stomach settle before I eat any more."

Okay.

"Do you have any soda?"

What do you need soda for?

"My stomach hurts, and the Hot Chocobot isn't really helping."

Hmm, look in the cooler. very well.

"How do I roll the window down?"

That switch over there, while pressing that button with your right shoulder.

"Like this?"

Pull on the switch.

"Ah, there we go. This should get their attention."

I still don't think that's going to work.

"It changes pitch if you wiggle it like this. Uses the built in gyroscope. Cool, huh?"

They already stopped.

"Told you it would work! Oh damn it. I dropped my phone out the window."

You can get out and pick it up.

"I know, I was just saying. Hey, this van's license plate is kind of there was one of these on this side of town. Wait, why would a bounty hunter be after you, a bounty hunter?"

I've blacked out quite a few times over the years, I can't be sure of exactly what I did or didn't do.

"Fair enough. Uh oh, the car just turned into the lot."

Act natural!

"They'll still recognize my car no matter how natural we act inside of it."

Hey, is that a van?

"Not just any van, that's the van we're looking for!"

Those grocery store robbers are going down!

"What about our tail?"

I don't have a tail.

"Not an actual... the car that was following us."

Oh. Hey, they're going up to the van. Damn it, if I get another bounty stolen...

"Let's get a move on then!"

Stop!

"This is our bounty!"

Crap, they'll know about all of my DUIs.

"Distract them and I'll get our bounty."

How am I supposed to do that?

"Give him your license and registration!"

I wasn't even driving!

"He wasn't even driving!"

I think they heard our entire conversation just now.

"I just realized that since we can hear theirs too. Did they just say familiar."

Most license plates in this state are pretty similar aside from the numbers.

"No, this van's license plate is really, really... Oh! This is them!"

Stop what?

"We're cops!"

Well, he's a cop.

"DUIs? Give me your license!"

What is this bounty they're talking about?

"The kids in the van?"

We can't let that happen. We need to know where they hit bigfoot.

"That doesn't matter!"

We're taking you in for blatant obstruction of justice!

"Is that a thing?"

Maybe not the blatant part.

"I think they can hear us."

"We have a cooler?"

Yeah, it's behind your seat.

"When were you going to tell me we had a cooler?"

Right now, I guess.

"Ooh, lime soda. Perfect!"

Tap on the top.

"Why?"

We've been in two accidents in the last 24 hours, I'm pretty sure that can is well shaken up.

"Does tapping on the top really help with that?"

Sure, why would people do it if it didn't work?

"It doesn't seem like it would actually do anything since it's a closed system."

Just to be safe, hold it out the window when you open it.

"Alright."

something about bigfoot?"

What's happening over there?

"Is that a grenade?"

It's green so it most be!

"He's pulling the pin, get down!"

Hmm. It sounds like it just kind of fizzled out.

"This is our chance."

For what?

"To capture our bounty! I wish you were sober."

Sorry.

"You go that way, and I'll go this way."

Got it.

"Ow!"

Sorry, I thought you meant I was going that way.

"No, that way."

Got it.

"Out of the car, boys!"

We said nothing about bigfoot.

"Don't fall for it, they're trying to trick us."

I think they might be serious.

"Where would they even get a grenade?"

You can get anything on the internet. Believe me.

"Really? I've been looking for this one jigsaw puzzle, it's pretty rare. You see, it's a portrait of Napoleon Bonaparte in space."

Napoleon Bonaparte in space?

"It's sort of a 'what if' kind of fantasy piece."

Obviously. So you collect that kind of thing?

"I love assembling puzzles of historical figures in fantasy settings."

Hey, what's going on outside?

"I hate it when people double park, now we'll never get out of here. Aw damn, soda all over the place."

At least it was out the window. What are these people doing?

"Uh oh, I recognize that one."

Which one?

"The cop!"

We need to get out of here!

"They have us blocked in!"

Quick, grab your gun!

"I don't have a gun."

Your water gun!

"That was yours."

I don't have it, so I figured you had it.

"They must have taken it at the police— Hey what's the big idea!"

There's a bounty on your pretty little heads, and we're here to collect.

"Struggling won't get you anywhere. Trust me, you don't want us to use our tranq guns on you."

Maybe we will. Go ahead, shoot them.

"Which one should I shoot first? The dopey one or the goofy one?"

Which one's the dopey one?

"The one with the soda."

Him first, that's what he gets for making us think he had a grenade.

"We can hear you."

Damn it! My leg!

"How dare you!"

Eat tranquilizer, jerk!

"You're not a very good shot."

That's kind of weird— Hey, they're taking the boys!

"Get back here, they're ours!"

You guys don't know what you're doing. Let them go, and we won't shoot you.

"Hey, I knew that one could talk. You little liars!"

Okay, this is getting out of hand, everybody be calm!

"Put your hands up! I aim to kill!"

Do you really have to aim to kill? Can't you just shoot them in the leg?

"I'm not actually going to shoot them."

They can hear you.

"Oh shoot, sorry!"

Back up or I'll—

"Ha, missed me!"

I'm feeling a bit woozle.

We didn't do anything! The cops let us go, that means we're innocent!

"Yeah, we're innocent!"

Go ahead and tranq us then."

"You're the liar with your... pants and stuff."

I dare you.

"Stop egging them on, I don't want to be tranquilized."

You'll like it, it's like being drunk on spiked Hot Chocolate.

"Mmm, delicious."

Right?

"Wait, is he going to shoot us?"

We can hear you.

"Holy crap!"

Quick, get in the van!

"How are we getting out?"

Through the fence, hold on!

"Look out, another fence!"

Shut up, I just got shot in the leg, okay?

"But you don't use your legs to aim."

Sure you do. A steady stance is one of the keys to accurate marksmanship. And at least I hit one of them.

"We should get you to the hospital."

No way, they would turn me in for sure.

"But at least then you wouldn't have a bullet in your leg."

Just drop me off at Johnny the Vet's place.

"Of course, good ol' Johnny the Vet."

Hand me a tranquilizer dart.

"Sure, what are you—"

Ahhh, yeah that's the stuff. If I'm not awake when we get there, just roll me onto his doorstep. He'll know what to do.

"Woozle?"

Help me get into the carzzle. You'll havtadrivel...

"I don't know how to drive that, there are way too many buttons and levers."

The drivelizing parts're sumple as niother cur.

"I think I understood that, but can you just repeat it so I can be sure?"

Snrzzle....

"Ugh."

Hold on again!

"You know, maybe we should cut it out with all this life of crime stuff."

Maybe you're right.

"Here's to a new life of upright citizenship."

To upright citizenship!

"As soon as we finish driving through all these fences."

There are a ridiculous number of fences over here.

"I think this is some kind of fence supplier."

Let's try to find the exit before they put a bounty on our heads too.

"I think the exit is this way, through this other fence."

Nope, more fences.

over yonder

Alright, then just go up this way...

"Are you sure we're in the right place?"

Of course, I've traveled these hills and valleys more times than you can
count on one hand. Paw? Do you have hands or paws?

"I have hands."

Of course, a bigfoot would have big feet and big hands, not big paws.

"I think we made a wrong turn somewhere."

We're on the right track, I can feel it.

"We're on the top of a mountain."

It's not the destination, it's the journey.

"We're stuck. This IS our destination."

But look at the beautiful view. The hills there. The mountains there.
Teufelberg right in the middle.

"I don't remember that being on fire."

Oh, you can see the flames too? I thought that was just the absinthe
kicking in.

"What absinthe?"

The absinthe in my belly, ha ha!

"Where did it come from?"

Here. There isn't any left, but you might enjoy the way the bottle feels.

"Uh..."

It's so nice and cold... like a tiled bathroom floor.

"No wonder we got lost."

What do you mean? You wanted find your friend at Teufelberg, and
there it is right in front of us!

"Wait, he's in there?"

Imagine so.

"In the mountain that's melting?"

Melting mountain? All I see are beautiful doves all around us being
chased by little men riding little rocket ships with the honorary
plaques mounted on their sides.

"What do the plaques say?"

They're flying around too fast to read.

"That's a shame... what am I talking about, I need to go help my friend.

He could be dead!"

Never stop swaying, or else the glowing peanut won't let you stuff him
in the basket!

"Uh... Okay, bye."

id the body

Oh my, Steven. Look what you've gotten yourself into now.

"Wha, who?"

It's me, Steven.

"I'm not Steven. I'm the..."

Don't try to speak, you're badly injured.

"Who are you?"

Don't you remember? I'm you, Steven.

"No, no, no. Not the voices again."

I'm disappointed in you Steven. You turned your back on who you
really are. Calling yourself Steffan was bad enough.

"I moved back to the farm like you wanted! Why can't you leave me
alone?"

You moved back to the farm for one day.

"I still did it."

And ate Bessy.

"You lied and said she was sick. She was perfectly healthy! I couldn't
pass up that succulent slab of steak... So juicy and, oh God what's
happening to me?"

You were in a plane crash, Steven. Don't worry, your friend made sure
you'll live, but it might be a very painful state of living indeed.

"Why are you doing to this me? And stop calling me Steven!"

Would you rather I call you Bucky? What a stupid name. Who would
choose to go from a perfectly respectable name like Steven to
something as ridiculous as Bucky Rimbleton?

"That's just my secret identity. I'm...

The Eradicator! Bwah ha ha oww..."

Don't you think I know that? I'm in your head. I know everything about
you. The question is, do YOU know everything about you?

"Of course I do. If you know everything about me, and you're me, then

I know everything about me too."

Enough of this bickering, Steven. You got yourself into this mess and now you have to get yourself out of it.

"Not until you stop calling me Steven. I'm a new man now, and I won't have my past coming back to screw things up!"

There are more important things than your false pride, Steven. You may have been spared in the crash, but if you don't change your ways soon you'll die anyway. Don't let that go to waste.

"MY NAME ISN'T STEVEN ANYMORE! RAAAAARRRGGGH!"

Don't give in to the anger, Steven. Be calm, peaceful, and calm.

"You said calm twice."

"Being calm is twice as important as being peaceful."

They're syno—

"Hush. Now breathe deep."

Ow!

"That's a fractured rib puncturing your lung. Relax. Calm. Peace. And breathe out."

Are you kidding me?

"And breathe in."

Whatever the point you're trying to make is, I get it! Just tell me how to make it all stop hurting.

"You have to change your ways."

I don't even know what that means.

"Stop this ridiculous super villain schtick."

Okay, I guess that's reasonable.

"Change your name back to Steven."

If it means the pain will end, I can live with that.

"Move back to the farm."

Again?

"Yes, Steven. Again."

But I hate the farm. Now all I have are the memories of sweet Bessy... and her delicious flesh...

"There will be other cows. More delicious cows. Less personable cows. Steven, the ratio of tastiness to fondness you feel towards the cattle will cause only joy from now on."

That's a strange way to put it, but alright. Then what?

"Apologize to everyone you've harmed, Steven. Only then will this unimaginable pain end."

It's not unimaginable pain anymore. It's really quite memorable pain.

"Only then will you will this quite memorable pain end, Steven."

Okay, I'll do it!

"I'll do it."

I'll do it...

space invaded

Ah, what a refreshing glass of cola. Would have been even more refreshing with a twist of lime.

"Don't glare at me."

I'll glare all I want, Lieutenant. But that's enough celebration. On to our
official mission!

"Hold on, something is happening in the cargo bay."

Pull up the surveillance camera.

"Something's got the horses spooked."

Zoom out.

"Zooming out."

Zoom out more.

"Zooming out more."

Now pan.

"Hu hu hu hu."

What are you doing?

"Panting?"

No, PAN. Pan the camera!

"Oh, sorry. Panning."

The other way.

"Panning the other way."

Okay, now zoom in.

"Zooming in."

Zoom in more.

"Zooming in mo—"

Stop! Dear God, what's that fat guy doing?

"Is he putting horns on the horses' heads?"

That doesn't even make sense. Where did this nut case come from?

"He couldn't have come through the transporter, that broke down right after the graser delivery."

We really should have that upgraded. Do we have the latest catalog?

"I put it on your desk."

I have a desk?

"Sure, it's in your den."

Den?

"You know, it's part of your living quarters."

Living quarters?! Why haven't I heard about this? I've been sleeping under the flight computer and washing my uniform in the sink!

"Really?"

Figured out how to use the hand drier as a steam iron.

"How could you not know you have your own living quarters? Even the guys who clean the ship have their own living quarters!"

Oh no.

"What?"

They weren't outside cleaning the ship when—

"They were."

Are they okay?

"I'm sure they're fine."

You haven't actually checked?

"We were only gone for a few seconds from their point of view."

You're sure?

"Yeah, I'm sure they're fine."

Okay, as long as you're sure.

"I am."

That's a relief. How embarassing would that have been, if the only casualties were the two cleaning guys and their cause of death was time travel.

"Very embarassing. We might have some very real casualties to worry about now, though."

Oh my, the fat fellow has placed a single horn on every horses' head.

"I don't know what his intentions are, but they can't be good."

Do you think he knows we're watching hi—

"Oh my God. He just looked into my soul."

That was spine chilling. We are sooo... Okay, we need to get everyone into escape pods. NOW. I'm sure he'll be coming here to the bridge next, I'll try to buy us some time.

"How are you going to—"

Let me worry about that. Go! Don't forget about George, he's taking a nap in the boiler room.

"Are you serious? He could have used on of the empty living quarters on Deck C."

I didn't know we had those, okay?

the mansion

"This place is incredible."

Yeap. S'awright if not a bit creepy.

"Must be haunted or something. Is that a blood stain over there?"

Looks like it. See the minimal blood spatter in the surrounding area? Means there wasn't much of a struggle. I'd say they bled out if this stain were bigger... Nope, this poor fellah was kept alive. Only explanation?

"Vampi—"

Aliens. Use their ray guns to sterilize ya.

"Paralyze."

That too. Then they cut ya open!

"For a second you sounded somewhat intelligent."

Love my forensics procedurals on the tiv.

"The what?"

The tiv.

"Oh, T.V."

How many times do I gotta tell ya, I know how to spell! Do you think I'm some kinda window sill?

"Imbecile."

There you go, callin' me names! I oughta shoot you right here.

"Whoa whoa whoa, I just meant that the correct word— never mind."

This must be one of them secret alien bases I've seen on tiv. Hiding in plain sight.

"I heard that's a pretty good show."

What?

"In Plain Sight."

Never seen it.

"Neither have I."

Then why'd ya bring it up?

"I've been meaning to check it out since a couple of my friends on Tumblr seem to like it."

Your friends on Tumblr?

"Yeah, Tumblr is a blogging websi—"

No, I know what Tumblr is. I'm sayin' nobody who uses Tumblr's got any friends. Buncha whiny introverts with photoshop.

"That's quite the generalization, I'm offended!"

You know it's true.

"Yeah, it is pretty accurate."

Stop brooding and help me find a hidden lever, switch, button...

"Maybe one of these DVDs will activate the secret passage? I've seen that done before."

Let's see... Try season one of Leverage.

"That did it!"

I'm going in.

"Right behind you."

No you don't! You hafta stay here and keep an eye out for the aliens. This might be a set up! Shoot anyone who comes in that ain't me! No hesistation!

dead again

"Just great, killed by a freakin... I don't even know what happened."

An airplane crashed into the mountain you were in which caused the entire place to explode and catch on fire.

"I've had it! I'm never going back to Earth again. I always end up dying a terrible death."

At least it didn't hurt this time, right?

"No! It hurt a lot! More than any of the other times!"

Oops, I must have resurrected you wrong.

"It didn't help that you gave me a decomposing body. Every little gust of wind felt like rubbing alcohol on a scraped knee."

I said I'm sorry. You won't ever have to live as a mortal again, okay?

"I'm sure I'll miss it and want to go back... but next time I get to be immortal like Bertram."

He didn't die? Wasn't he with you in the explosion?

"He's not here in Heaven, is he? I assume that means he survived. Why didn't you mention he was a dragon, anyway?"

Humans. Dragons. Whatever, they're all the same to me. I didn't think I needed to specify.

"How are they all the same to you? Humans look just like you and me, and dragons don't!"

No, no, no. Humans look just like you. I only look this way because you're the one looking at me.

"What do you mean?"

You think humans are the most important species?

"Sure, you created them in your image, right?"

Ha! How self centered... no, humans see me in their image, because that's the only way they can understand how I look.

"So all the books and paintings are wrong? What my eyes are telling me right now is wrong?"

There's no right or wrong to it. Whatever someone believes in, that's how it is. Whether they believe in a guy with a white beard, or a guy with a brown beard, that's what they see when they look upon me.

"So... if someone truly believes they're doing good, then they aren't sinning?"

I'm only talking about how I appear to them when they die. Everyone
is still held up to the same incredibly strict criteria for entry into
Heaven.

"You mean the ninety commandments?"

Yes, of course.

"Maybe more people would make it into Heaven if they actually knew
all of the criteria?"

I tried that, remember? The schmuck only got ten of them written
down!

"But nowadays people have these slick portable tablets that—"

Yeah, he had tablets too!

"You know, this place is actually kind of nice without anyone around."

Isn't it? I think I might add a few more sins to the commandments and
not tell anyone.

first meal

That didn't take as long as I expected.

"Some vampires luck out with that whole super speed thing. Makes
repetitive tasks really easy."

Pretty damn cool. So you can't do that?

"No."

Ha! In your face!

"Shut up!"

Come on, I'm just kidding around.

"No, I mean be quiet. I think someone is coming down the corridor."

Oh no, is he back?

"No, just some old man from the smell of it."

I'm hungry. All that filing really took it out of me.

"Perfect, this can be your first meal."

Ew, an old guy?

"The average lifespan of a blood cell is 120 days, so regardless of the
victims age you may as well be drinking from an infant."

He might have some kind of old man disease.

"Old timer's disease?"

Alzheimer's disease.

"Really? I thought it was called old timer's."

Either way, I don't want any of that.

"Don't worry, we're immunse to all human diseases."

I'd still have to put my mouth on his leathery skin.

"You're hungry, right?"

Yeah.

"Then get over it. Hold on, you haven't sharpened your teeth yet. You'll
     have to use one of these QuickSip™ straws."

How does that work?

"Just stab him with the straw, and sip away."

Oh, kind of like Capri Sun.

"Exactly."

Sounds easy enough. Wait, I can file really fast, why don't I just sharpen
     my teeth real quick?

"Oh yeah, sure."

Done.

"Lucky bastard... Okay, you're going to sneak out into the corridor and
     press yourself up against the wall. Press up against the wall until
     he passes, then pou—"

That was easy.

"How did you—"

Super spccd, rcmcmbcr?

"Ugh, that's so annoying. How much did you drink?"

A few sips maybe. And a gulp. A few sips and a gulp.

"Did he stop bleeding when you were done?"

What do you mean?

"Crap, he's still bleeding. Don't let it go to waste!"

Where's a jar? A bottle? Bucket?

"No, just drink it!"

Oh, okay.

"Damn it, I should have known this would happen. You can't bite too
     hard, especially the old people. Their skin is like tissue paper."

Am I going to have to make him into a vampire?

"Stop talking and keep sucking!"

Because I don't think I can train my own vampire.

"No kidding."

We can't just let him die though, can we?

"Well, he is pretty old... No, we won't let him perish. Move over, I'll turn him. Might as well train you together. You can be study buddies."

More like study bloodies.

santa's sleight

Ho ho ho! Are you the Commander of this ship?

"Yes, and who might you be? Let me guess, you must be Raving Lunatic McGee!"

What a shame my legend hasn't persisted into this time. I'm Santa Claus, of course!

"Santa Claus isn't real."

Yes he is. Yes I am! I am real, and I am Santa Clause, so Santa Clause is real!

"I don't care who you are, or who you think you are, you need to get the Hell off of my ship!"

I will... As soon as you give me the Rock of Ages.

"The what?"

You know damn well what!

"Oh, the time travel thingy."

Ugh... Yes, the time travel thingy. Hand it over!

"Never! If there were any rules for who can possess and operate time machines, I'm pretty sure that you wouldn't qualify."

But I already have a time machine of my own.

"Hey, that's the time machine George was using. If you already have a time machine, why do you need another one?"

You know very well this time machine is merely a toy compared to that one. Hand it over!

"No!"

I didn't want to have to do this, but...

"Ow! What did you— Did you just throw a lump of coal at me?"

I did, and there's plenty where that came from.

"It hit me right in the ear. Ugh, that really stings. Fine, you win. Time travel gives me a headache anyway. Here."

Fantastic! I've waited millions of years for this...

"But you have a time machine, couldn't you have—"

Silence! Now go to your crew and their escape pods.

"You said you would leave!"

I lied. I do that a lot. Leave before I change my mind about sparing your
     life!

"This is my ship, there's no way I'm going to let some nutcase with a
     time machine take if from me!"

Oh really? I have an army of unicorns that say you will let me take it.

"Unicorns?"

Ho ho ho, yes. You could say I gave all your horses a little present.

"You monster!"

Alright boys, ready to impale?

"Fine, fine, fine, I'll go! But you haven't heard the last of me!"

I think I have. Ta ta. What's that squeaking sound? Is that... Oh, hello
     there little mice. What are you doing here? Oh, you hitched a
     ride on some guy's leg? I see. Dinosaurs, you say? Douchebags?
     That's not a very nice word, but I am pretty sick of them too.
     How would you like to show those dinosaurs who's boss? I'll
     give you everything you need to kill them off, but first you have
     to do a little something for me...

whatever happened

Arooo!

"Is that you?"

Yes, it's me!

"But you're gigantic! How did that happen?"

You know that stone we found in the bag? Turns out it can make you
     grow and shrink!

"Neat. I see you got some pretty nice pants, too!"

Leg coverings. Not supposed to all them pants.

"That's kind of... anyway, very stylish. Hey, would you mind shrinking
     back down to normal size? You're freaking me out a bit."

Sure. I had to get really big to escape that cavern.

"So you were inside that mountain after all?"

Not only that, I was inside a dragon's stomach!

"Wow, you've had quite the adventure. All I've done today is have drinks with a leprechaun."

Did you get any gold from him?

"I didn't even think of that..."

Don't worry, once this fire burns out we can go back in and get all the gold we want.

"Won't it all be melted together?"

I can become huge and pick up the entire lump!

"I guess you could say it all worked out for the best."

There is just one other thing... Santa Claus was in the dragon's stomach with me.

"Oh, so he was fine after we bailed on him?"

Other than being in a dragon's stomach, yeah.

"I felt kind of bad about ditching him, but we were totally going to lose."

Forget that, he's evil. He has a time machine and is going to destroy the planet!

"Oh, I see... Well we don't really have to worry about that, do we?"

What do you mean?

"If he's using the time machine to destroy the planet, then he's probably going back in time to do it."

And?

"If he's already tried to destroy the planet in the past, he must have failed since we're still here."

I see, so you're saying that whatever he does while time traveling has always happened, and we can't do anything about it. Unless we've always done something about it, in which case we'll end up doing what we're supposed to do anyway.

"Something like that."

Works for me.

"Looks like the flames are starting to die down."

Time to loot!

kablam!

Ow, my arm! Why is everyone getting shot today?!

"Are you an alien?"

What? No! Why would you think I'm an alien?

"How can I be sure?"

Because I said I'm not!

"That's exactly the sort of thing an alien would say."

I'm not an alien! Why would you even think that... I'm a vampire hunter. I've come here to kill a couple of vampires.

"Vampires? That's abs— actually that makes a lot more sense than aliens.
Why would aliens use an old mansion as their secret base? That
old guy is out of his mind..."

What old guy?

"Some hillbilly I've been traveling with."

Where is he?

"Went down into that secret passage over there."

We have to get out of here.

"We can't just ditch him!"

There are two vampires down there. Hungry, angry, and cornered.

"So he's dead."

Probably. And thanks to you, I'm bleeding like a son of a bitch here.
It won't be long before they catch the scent and come after us.
They're like sharks.

"They'll only come after you. I don't have any blood on me."

Now you do.

"Come on man, what the Hell?"

Now we're in this together.

"This was my nicest shirt! I wore it especially for my job interview
and— ugh!"

Would you rather I have shot you in the arm?

"No."

Then you're welcome. Let's get out of here.

"We better be going to E.J. Waxx for a new shirt."

You got the nicest shirt you own at E.J. Waxx?

"Yeah, they have great products for great prices."

Ugh. I know a place where we can get you something that isn't so embarassing.

"Hey, this shirt isn't that bad..."

Yes, it's that bad. Come on, it's where I get all my clothes. It's one of those high end boutiques. But whatever you do, don't call them shirts. Call them torso coverings.

"You're being really nice considering I shot you."

Happens all the time, don't worry about it. Plus, if they do come after us I'll have a better chance of killing them when they're busy feeding on you.

"What?"

found

Eradicator! Where are you?

"The... Eradicator, bwah ha cough."

You made it! Told you I'd make sure you would live.

"I'm horribly injured."

But alive! We'll get you fixed right up. You know, I wasn't really sure I would be able to keep you alive. I'm new to this whole powers of Hell at the tips of my fingers thing. Not quite sure how it all works yet.

"I can't move my legs."

I can probably fix that. Oh, a tree fell on you.

"Where's the airplane? I don't see any wreckage."

I teleported us into this little grove right after impact.

"Why didn't you do it right before?"

Something to do with the adrenaline rush.

"So everyone else on the flight..."

Vaporized. Or burnt to the crisp. Depends on what section of the plane they were on.

"That's horrible."

It happens. The great news, all but one of them are on their way to Hell.

"Who was the one going to Heaven?"

Some old lady. Never left her house in seventy years. Finally decided to take a vacation to Guam and BAM! Vaporized.

"How sad."

At least she's going to Heaven.

"True."

So what now, Eradicator?

"Oh, actually... uh, just call me Steven from now on."

Steven?

"That's my real name."

Oh Steven, I'm touched! You think we're good enough friends for me to call you Steven.

"Stop calling me Steven so much, it's annoying."

Sorry Steven. Er... Sorry.

"I need to get back to the farm."

Whoa whoa whoa, what farm?

"Where I used to live. I have to return to a simple life as a farm hand."

Oh no you don't. I kept you alive so you can be The Eradicator. Killing, punishing, and most importantly striking fear in the hearts of all those who hear your name.

"But he said I'd stop hurting if I go back to my life as a farm hand..."

Who said that?

"The... me. I said it to myself, I guess. I don't know. There's a voice in my head sometimes."

Forget the voice. As long as you eradicate the sinful you will never die. I'll make sure of it. That's pretty much the perfect power for a super villain to have, isn't it?

"That's true... so I'll be kind of like the grim reaper?"

Yeah, exactly. But instead of being stuck with a scythe you can use whatever weapons you want.

"How about a shotgun?"

Sure.

"Sawed off shotgun?"

Absolutely.

"Two barreled sh—"

Any kind of shotgun.

"Okay, I'll do it but I want a really cool theme song."

You got it.

Wow, what a great concert!

"Unbelievable, right?"

I'm so sorry I didn't believe you when you said they were the greatest
superhero folk-punk-rock band in all of Gilpin County!

"I knew you would come around."

You know what part I absolutely loved?

"When he threw his bass like a boomerang?"

I absolutely **loved** the part when he threw his bass like a boomerang!

"He calls that the Whamarang. Kind of his signature move. It wows me
every single time."

And who thought anyone could beat box like that?

"I sure didn't. They used to have an actual drummer."

And he was doing it while playing lead guitar!

"Rapido is the fastest man alive, after all."

Then there was Lady Love Lumps, best keyboardist I've ever heard.

"Wow, I know you're quite the keyboard aficionado."

Well, it's just a hobby, but I'd say my ear is trained to recognize skillful
moog handling.

"She can handle my moog any day..."

Damn, I can't wait to see them play again!

"I have some bad news."

Oh no.

"They told me this is their last show. They came out of retirement to go
out with a wham."

Bummer.

bedside manner

"Hrmph. Whrr m ee?"

You just finished the implant surgery.

"Hwdt gll?"

It went well. The doctor said you're already almost fully recovered.

"Wh cnt ee mvv mmtth?"

Oh, let me help you with that.

"Ahhh, much better."

They had to wire your jaw shut while you healed.

"Ooh, yeah this jaw already feels at least twice as powerful as before!"

Here, try biting this plate.

"And..."

Nice!

"Wow, like a hot knife through butter!"

Uh oh.

"What?"

That little sign on the table says we're responsible for any damaged
        eating implements.

"Oops."

Let's just slide that under the mattress...

"We'll be long gone by the time they notice."

Alright, so let's see the CD tray and laser paws.

"Do you have a CD?"

No.

"DVD?"

Wait, can you read DVDs with it?

"I didn't specify when I asked..."

And what about Blu-rays?

"Crap, if all I can use this for are CDs..."

We'll find out later. Let's get out of here before they find out we don't
        have any money.

"Where to?"

The question is **when** to. Back to dinosaur times we go! We can stop
        whatever caused them to go extinct. Grab on and hold tight!

"Oof, I will not get used to that."

Damn, we're too late.

"That is a huge comet."

Look over there, that space ship! It must have used a tractor beam to alter the comet's path.

"Isn't that the same ship from when—"

It is. Hurry, head over to that cave. I think we'll be safe there!

"Why don't we use the time machine again and go back a bit further?"

I think if we time travel one more time, I'm going to puke... and that defeats the purpose of having Santa trapped in my stomach. For now, I guess we'll just hang out in this cave.

"I wish I had brought some CDs to listen to."

call backpack

Hello?

"It's done."

What's fun?

"Done. DONE. It's done."

Sorry, cell reception isn't the best up here on the space station. Van Allen belt and all.

"Well, I did everything you asked."

I told you, everything you need to know is in the instruction booklet I gave you.

"I know. The instructions said to call you for further instructions."

Damn, that's exactly the kind of thing I would do. So you say Operation Backpack was a success?

"As far as I can tell. I switched both backp—"

Ah ah ah, codenames. You never know who might be listening in.

"I switched both reams of paper. I was very careful, and nobody in my vicinity suspected anything."

Great work. I'm placing you on my nice list.

"Your what list?"

Never mind. So that is that, then.

"Hold on, how am I supposed to get back home?"

Consult your instructions.

"I did, the last instruction is to call you and ask for more instructions!"

I'm sure you can find your way, bye!

"Come on, I risked being groped by security for your stupid task! The
      least you can do is get me a flight back."

Fine, I'll send Rudolph to pick you up.

"The reindeer?"

Er, yes...

"Are you...?"

Ho ho— ahem. Mere coincidence. Thank you for your service, you
      have helped more than you'll ever know. Your ride will be there
      shortly.

"My sleigh ride."

I'm not sending the entire sleigh! You don't have a sack of presents to
      deliver!

"Ah ha, you ARE Santa!"

Please, call me Nick.

brb

Oh man, I think I drank too much lime soda.

"This stuff's addictive."

My bladder is about to burst, I'll be right back.

"Don't fall in."

Hey, the light's burnt out.

Erik J Skinner wrote this.

Visit his website
erikjskinner.com